GOOD MORNING, BELLINGHAM

MARINA RAYDUN

Copyright © 2019 Marina Raydun

Cover art created by Rahul Philip. For more information visit: www.rahulphilip.com

First Paperback Edition: September 2019

For more information please visit:
www.facebook.com/AuthorMarinaRaydun
www.marinaraydun.com

Follow the author on Twitter and Instagram:
@Author_MRaydun

Books by Marina Raydun:
-One Year in Berlin/Foreign Bride
-Joe After Maya
-Effortless (Book 1)
-Inevitable (Book 2)

ISBN-10: 0-578-55986-2
ISBN-13: 978-0-578-55986-5

Dedication

"A writer should be writing."
My father, Yakov Raydun
1949-2018

CONTENTS

Acknowledgements

This book was conceived in the spring of 2015. A few things have happened in the interim that have caused a few delays along the way, but it's finally here. Thank you to my small but mighty village for seeing this special puppy through to fruition. Vadim—you are my one-man support system, my one-man entourage. Without you, little is possible. I love you. My editor, Nili Yammer, thank you for your tireless edits from across the globe. Working in two different time zones is not the easiest but we made it work. Thank you! A huge thank you to you, Rahul Philip, for designing yet another fantastic cover. Your talent is bottomless. It's an honor to be working with you. To all you awesome beta readers, thank you so much for your input and encouragement. I appreciate your time. A heartfelt thank you to my sister for actually believing I am a writer, and to my mom for always asking when my book will be out. Now, mom! NOW!

Monday, October 1st

Sioux

She does not get off the 4:05 train. I wait. And I wait. A long time I wait. My teeth chatter from the harsh autumn breeze. My eyes burn from the fine dust it picks up, but I wait. My knees are locked, my feet are cemented to the platform, my throat is getting uncomfortably tight. I blink and I swallow. I check my phone and reread her messages. And I wait.

I wait for the next one—the 5:05. And then the 6:05. I crane my neck and look up and down the tracks more often than logically necessary, intensifying the headache that had taken root in my temples when my sister hadn't gotten off at 4:05. But nothing. She's not there. She's not *here*. And so, committed to my spot, I vow to wait for hours. To stand there like a school girl waiting for her pick-up when everyone but the teacher had already gone home for the day. I should know what that feels like from experience—mostly you feel silly to have ever expected any better.

I watch as the sun begins to set now. It's growing colder and emptier by the minute, but I keep waiting. My clothes, still mostly hand-me-downs from my sister's high school days, aren't doing the job. I eventually must button up my denim jacket and stuff my fisted palms into its wasteful pockets. I continue to wait in remote comfort. I'm patient. Or stubborn. This doesn't feel like a choice.

Fewer people disembark off the 7:05. Fewer still at 8:05. That's when I fold and call Peter.

"She definitely left," he tells me between carefully spaced breaths. "She's not here at any rate. She texted me on her way out, that's all I know. Maybe she missed the train? Was— I thought she— she was supposed to arrive hours ago?" He sounds vaguely irritated. Busy. I hear Gwenny cooing in the background. She is yet to say her first words, but she sure is babbling up a storm from what I understand. Or is it called jargoning? I call Peta every day and so I hear Gwenny in the background every day. So I know. I imagine Peter now, phone wedged between his ear and his shoulder, swaying over his daughter seated in her playpen surrounded by a plush family of Winnie the Pooh characters—her favorite. He must've just gotten home, I remind myself. He'd have to go to bed within minutes in order to be up in only seven hours for work. I should not have worried him. I want to kick myself.

It's 8:30 and I haven't eaten since noon when I'd grabbed a yogurt after psych with Gael. Well, I also had a cup of coffee before I got here, but that's it. This is against protocol. I'm getting lightheaded and turning my head to look up and down the platform every few minutes sure doesn't help. I call Gael. He's in organic bio lab, I think. But I need a juice, a *Snickers*, something. I can't afford to step away in search of a vending machine for fear of missing seeing Peta finally disembark one of these trains. The film forming before my eyes is obstructing my vision as it is.

"Something must've happened," I tell Gael. I'm not sure why I say this, but now that the words are out my voice box has tightened and become strained when I wasn't paying attention. This feeling is all too familiar. This is exactly what my throat did that dreadful morning when Peta called to tell me that Harry died. Obviously, it naturally follows, something dreadful must've happened to her now. Otherwise I wouldn't feel what I'm feeling. I wouldn't have said what I said. It may not be rational but there it is. She wouldn't leave me standing here in the cold, darkening night. She was so excited when she called to tell me she's coming. Just yesterday! She wouldn't just leave me hanging now and not pick up the phone or answer my myriad text messages. No, that would never happen.

Great, now I'm thinking about Harry, which isn't helpful. The day Harry died, to be more specific. I don't remember much else about him, to be honest. It seems so long ago now, though it wasn't really. Not objectively. I was just about to take my SATs when my phone rang with the news. Of course, once I was brought up to speed, I had to reschedule. While my mind was at once crystal clear with the adrenaline of the information shocking my system, my entire body went numb and began to pulse, lightly, within seconds. I simply couldn't hold my number 2 pencil, it was that simple. I had to reschedule. It was a no brainer to leave. Perhaps it was a blessing in disguise—the timing of it all, not the fact of the matter of his untimely passing, obviously. As a result, I got to retake the test and wound up scoring in the 97th percentile. Though Harry unlikely knew what the SATs were, I imagined him smiling down at me when I finally received my score, clicking open the e-mail with my heart heavy and my stomach soft. He did have the goofiest smile, all four teeth visible, from what I remember. There are no pictures.

Well, there are no SATs now, but I do have midterms next week. I'd have to get extensions from my professors, I catch myself thinking. If she never disembarks, that is. I hate myself for thinking any of this and screw my eyes shut against the sun descending further, practically invisible on the horizon. I want to smack my forehead to stop. I almost do, but it wouldn't help. The logistics aren't important, I lament, pointlessly, already having buried her. This would be considered eerily prophetic if I weren't so prone to overdramatizing uncertainties on a daily basis. Mommy can tell you. Or Gael. Or Peta.

The clock tower ticks mutely, as if mocking me with its pronouncement of time—9:05. My throat begins to hurt now.

"Is Peter sure she left?" Gael ventures, finally at my side with a mason jar of cooling mate.

And then I finally cry.

Peter

Peter looked up to the pale, darkening sky above. The moon and its milky, soft edges. You could actually make out the stars out here, not like in Seattle, where it was too bright to see much of anything. There are too many buildings, too much electricity in the way there. He'd tried—telescopes and all. He was twelve when he first did, having just been placed with a family that lived arguably too close to downtown. He couldn't remember the name now. It didn't work out. The family moved and taking a foster kid out of county was tricky. But, when he first arrived, the dad there had a Tasco telescope in his den and Peter was encouraged to use it his first night there. It was a demonstrative effort to help him feel comfortable in his new home. The offer did little to quell the nausea he was nursing in the pit of his stomach that evening, but the social worker gave him a gentle nudge forward and he complied. Eventually he'd grown fond of the activity despite often seeing not much more than the vacuous sky itself, unable to make out any details. It was just that standing next to this powerful rod, looking up at something so expansive, it filled him with unjustified, dumb hope. Long after he left that cold loft, he continued with the tradition when he got to college and used his scholarship refund money to get a telescope of his own. There, on campus, he'd trudge it out to the quad and squint tirelessly to make out as much as possible through all the unfortunate byproducts of human progress. But here in Bellingham less civilization stood in the way of stargazing. He could finally see the stars. He was going to show Harry the telescope when he was old enough. It was in his half-basement office now.

The water in the hot tub was scalding but the air above it was frigid. October was always a cool month up here. The combination made for a refreshing, exhilarating effect—sweat and goosebumps. Peter loved the sensation. He could spend hours fighting the chills of the breeze hitting his face while watching the steam rise around him. The contrast both soothed him and made him alert. This was what he imagined meditation to be like.

Gwenny was now supposed to be actively rocked to sleep by Marsha. He finally had a few minutes to gather his thoughts, but they refused to gather. Without getting his story straight, there was no point to this ill-timed soak. But he was too tired to think and the adrenaline he was

5

expecting to be pulsing through his veins by now was slow to start. It was late in his personal time zone. On a regular day, he would've had to be up at 3:30 A.M. tomorrow and 8:30 P.M. was his usual bedtime. Now, it was 9:30 and sleep was no longer in the cards. One of the many town's busybodies had already called to inform him that he'd spotted his wife's car in the Organic Produce parking lot and that she wasn't to be found anywhere near it. The same good Samaritan wanted to know if Peta was all right. Was she okay? Peter had placated the man by assuring the geriatric groupie that he was sure she was just fine and that her truck had simply broken down. For all he knew, maybe it had. Soon enough, everyone would know and everyone would inquire. And then there would definitely be no sleep.

Clearly, there was no sense in going through with the pretense of driving to the train station to look for Peta now. Undoubtedly, the cops already knew that he'd been dutifully informed by that same concerned citizen of the city of Bellingham as to the location of his wife's car hours ago so he may as well just go directly to the police station now, he reasoned. But this soak was just so tempting. It'd been a long time since he'd had time for something so frivolous and solitary, and he didn't know when the next opportunity would avail itself. When he'd first lowered himself into the bubbling water, it seemed like a "now or never" situation, but now that he was in, he wasn't so sure it had been. The neighbors weren't that great a distance away and steam was known to travel. He exhaled forcefully, savoring the sight of vapor rolling out of his likely blue lips. He'd have to get out soon. He had dry clothes waiting in his office—a carefully chosen khakis and a pale blue button-down shirt made up of fine white stripes. He'd kiss Gwenny through the monitor screen and then head to the police station. He would have to consider all these optics a lot more carefully from now on.

Peter rubbed his face awake. He didn't want to start the car. His hair was still wet and that wouldn't look good. This much he knew even back in the tub but styling his hair too seemed in poor taste. He'd just have to explain the hair somehow. And the soak itself in case any neighbor decided to be helpful and report the steam in the effort to bring Peta back. It was better to be proactive, upfront. Be in control of the narrative, so to speak. Put his professional skills to some use. The thought of it seemed to sober him up, if only momentarily. He floored the break and let his index finger hover over the "start" button.

The dashboard clock read 10:30, which meant he'd been awake roughly eighteen hours straight now, he calculated as he sipped the now lukewarm coffee in his thermos, his headlights on. He drank this bitter Ethiopian blend by the gallon. So did Peta. Given that there'd be no sleep that night, Peter knew it was wise to ingest his caffeine early. He didn't know when he'd be back. Reclined in his seat, he was reluctant to get moving but took the manual break off anyway. He moved half way out of his driveway before he called Lucia. Someone would have to fill in tomorrow.

"Is Peta okay? I heard her car was found without her in it? Did it break down or something? Is she all right?" It was nice of Lucia to pretend to care this much, if only she didn't sound so damn eager.

"I hope so," Peter muttered, feeling his car roll down his driveway.

"Where was she going? To visit her sister tonight, no?"

"Right," Peter nodded to himself in his rearview mirror. There'd be no cars on their street this time a night, so it didn't matter that half his truck now created a hazard. It wasn't strenuous mathematics but would everybody know about this trip now? All the notice he got was a text after her therapy appointment. *Going to see Sioux. Marsha is here early. I'm out.* "She was. She— she is staying the night so I need to be there for Gwenny. It's Ma— Marsha's day off," he lied, easily. No sense of giving the woman too much giddy excitement over the prospect of taking over fully just yet.

"Super! See you tomorrow," Lucia beamed through the phone as Peter backed a few more feet further away from the house and unto the bare street.

"That's what I'm saying, Lucia—you won't." Who knew when he'd be back at the station now, although his headshot would sure appear on his viewers' TV sets as early as 6am tomorrow. Before Lucia could ask any more questions he hung up and backed all the way out onto the dark street, his headlights the only source of light.

"So is she there yet?" he yawned when he called Sioux back.

"No," the girl sniffled, her raspy voice distant by way of his patchy Bluetooth connection. "I'm still here, waiting."

"At the train station?"

"At the train station."

8

She could abandon post, Peter knew; clearly Peta wasn't coming. Even Sioux had to realize that. Her loyalty often came across as dimwitted.

He scratched his stubble, navigating with his left hand on the wheel. He squinted in the rearview mirror to see if he could still see his house behind him. No, he couldn't admire it tonight. Definitely not tonight. There was too much talking ahead of him. Taking pride in his accomplishments may be deemed misplaced, untimely. The soak was bad enough. Now he had to go answer all the textbook questions. He already knew what was coming: Did they fight? Did she have reason to leave? Would anyone want to hurt her? What was he doing all day today? Could anyone account for his whereabouts? He would be asking similar questions were he still employed in his original capacity.

Peter sighed.

"Did you eat?"

"Yes. Gael is with me."

And then she cried.

Andrew

Andrew never meant to make falling asleep in his clothes a habit. It happened of its own accord. Somehow, without paying enough attention to routine, he woke up every so often still wearing his jeans. His shirt, he'd routinely note with amusement, he'd manage to somehow wrestle off without waking; he'd find it curled under his head, used as a makeshift pillow any particular night. If this was how much he was capable of accomplishing without a shred of consciousness, he feared to think what else he was capable of that he was yet to discover about himself. On the plus side, he mused, mid-40s was as good an age as any to continue learning about yourself. To be fair, general worldliness and pedestrian Buddhism was also something he never meant to intentionally adhere to but, surrounded by youth day in and day out, this too became unavoidable once Andrew found himself alone in the house once John left.

His phone ringer, being standard iPhone issue, worked its way seamlessly into his dream. It usually did. Every student had that phone, every student had that ringer. It wasn't a stretch of imagination for his brain to manufacture a dream where it was his student's phone going off during his lecture on contractual offer and acceptance. First one, then another. Then another. In his dream, he was about to hurl his own phone off the desk and in the direction of the careless, sleepy-eyed teenagers in front of him. The fat kid with glasses, the one always interrupting his train of thought with irrelevant comment on the utility of architects had been getting on his last nerve for months. He had it coming. When he raised it above his head, he caught the sight of the screen. *Lena.*

"What?"

His voice was hallow. When he threw his elbow off of his eyes, he was rudely reminded that the light was on, as was the TV. He was, of course, in the living room. The television blaring Don Lemon was suddenly much louder than it must've been when he fell asleep.

"What?" he tried again, croaking through what he could only visualize as cobwebs in his throat.

"John still isn't home. His shift was over hours ago. The store is not even open anymore, but he still isn't home."

She was drunk. There was enough familiarity there for it to make it almost endearing. Slowly Andrew curled into a position that resembled sitting. He muted Don Lemon and rubbed his eyes. They protested but he willed them open. The unkempt room greeted him and he wanted to shut them again. An overstuffed sectional, a coffee table the glass of which was not visible under the many piles of papers. Why hadn't he moved?

He rarely made it to the bedroom. He couldn't remember the last time he slept there. It couldn't quite be chucked off to mourning his failed marriage—he didn't remember sleeping there even before they separated and Lena moved. That brown leather sectional with popped leather was hardly made for routine slumber but Andrew never quite made it to bed, whose mattress was designed for just that. What would start as five minutes of TV and grading papers would morph into an hour of TV and a nap.

"What are you talking about?"

Sobs. That's what happened when Lena drank more than one bottle in one sitting. It didn't happen often but when it did, sobbing was usually involved.

"He is not answering my calls… It's all because of her! You knew! You fucking knew!"

Andrew didn't take bait. This was part of their game.

11

"You knew," she hiccupped again.

Andrew rubbed his face, scratching his stubble.

"What exactly did I know?" he tried against his better judgment.

"Well, she told him! Hope you're happy!" Lena shrieked with renewed vigor.

"Who? What are you talking about?"

He was up now, naked toes in the shaggy, gray carpet. If he wasn't careful and turned on his heels without mentally preparing for it, it would slice into his dry skin.

"He is mine, do you understand this?" Choking on her own tears as she may have been, her volume was impressive, Andrew noted. "He doesn't pick up the phone!" his ex-wife wailed.

Andrew considered this unexpected flow of information rushing at him, balancing tomorrow's schedule against it.

"I'll be there soon."

Evelyn

When she was a little girl, she dreamed of a bed nestled underneath a slanted roof. A far cry from her reality that dream of hers was. The ceiling of her childhood was tall and stained. It was mold but, at twelve, she imagined it to be urine. She'd be afraid to give in to sleep many a night for fear of it dripping, as if keeping her eyes open was acting as a deterrent. Now that her ceiling sloped inches from her nose, she wanted distance.

"Yes?"

Her son-in-law's name on her screen was never a good thing.

"Is Peta with you?"

Heavy with sleep, Evelyn allowed herself a chuckle. Her daughter hadn't voluntarily kept her mother company since the age of eighteen.

"No, Peter, she is not."

Doing her best to ignore the nauseating sensation of her stomach plummeting to her heels, Evelyn probed her mattress for her glasses.

12:15 read the projection from her side table clock on her sloped ceiling.

She swung her feet off the bed and groaned. Every single morning for two years now the sight of those stairs leading from her little penthouse down into the kitchen she regretted the choice of this move. It was the first time in her life that she lived alone, not counting the however many suffocating months in the Greenwald's stuffy attic in Topeka. Sharing a bathroom with four other families at the age of ten, she swore she'd spend the rest of her life living as solitary as possible. She instinctively knew she would not miss warm toilet seats. But once she found Peta growing inside her and then next to her in a borrowed bassinette, it was like her decisions were no long her own, much like her body. As if a force stronger than her was suddenly in control of her fingers. One morning she answered a classified ad by calling the advertised phone number (people had phone lines of their own! Her own landlord did! It had blown her immigrant mind!), hoisted her pale baby on her hip and joined three other writers in search of communal housing. It's like she knew she'd need the proverbial village before she even learned that expression. With Sioux it was different—then she ventured out on her own with the first positive pregnancy test. For Evelyn, moving felt like the first long-overdue decision she made of and for herself. Technically, it was her second. And eighteen years later, when her second-born attempted independence on the good word of the first-born, Evelyn moved out of the country on a whim she hadn't been permitted in ages. The impulse for solitude was long overdue. Still, though, there were no queues for the laundry now, she missed having more than a glorified studio apartment to call her own. The temperate climate of Victoria and the exclusive roof-rights made up for it most days, but right now, she wished she had someone's wall to knock on. No good news was coming.

"Did you have a fight? I imagine you'll have to answer these questions with the police, might as well practice."

She started the Keurig, hoping the sound of the coffee brewing would mute that of her heart thumping.

This was smart, Evelyn thought. Establish a record of yourself calling with concern, why don't you. And not a single incident of stuttering, which didn't speak to concern. Before she could verbalize any of this, the line went dead.

"Where was she going?" Evelyn asked, having stepped out on her rooftop terrace and replaced the phone to her ear. Reception was better out here.

"Sioux."

"Sioux? What did she want with my Sioux?" She was about to argue, insist that Peta was going to visit her, but it didn't seem immediately necessary. She'd never visited her up here, after all; maybe it was just a figure of speech she used when she last texted.

Straining to hear Peter's every breath Evelyn squinted instinctively, though there were no lights in the immediate vicinity. This place was dark at night.

"I have no idea. I just got a text informing me she was going down for the day. Sioux says Peta said she had a surprise for her."

Evelyn rolled her eyes. Peta had never ever been good with surprises—she'd always spoil them. She wrapped her arms around herself, keenly aware of her hair in a heap on top of her head.

"Goodbye, Peter," she said when she felt her pulse quicken. "I have to call my daughter now." But she didn't pick up. Neither one of them.

Tuesday, October 2nd

Gael

Gael feared it would be considered in poor taste to sleep while his girlfriend lay next to him weeping. He didn't quite get the tragedy of it all: an adult changes her mind and their home turns into a downright Shiva house. His best friend's great-grandmother died in high school and he had to go visit him as his family sat one of those. A whole week they sat! In fact, the family sat on low, hard sitting surfaces, and all the mirrors were draped with sheets. As the mourners cried, all Gael remembered was feeling uncomfortable, sitting on a low, hard, round stool next to Josh, shifting his weight from one buttock to the other, crossing and uncrossing his legs. The deceased was deep into her eighties, what exactly was the expectation here? The whole thing seemed a little overblown. He got it—it was sad, but how sad, exactly? It just made no sense—there was no proportionality to that response. This is what this Peta missing the train situation reminded him of, but just like that day at Josh's house, Gael reminded himself that it was not up to him to decide any of that. He was not a relation to Sioux or some such, just like he wasn't to Josh or his red-nosed father. He knew his place and that was not it. Only when Sioux's chest stopped heaving, her braided hair splayed artfully across his chest, did Gael let his eyes draw closed. If he stopped thinking right now, maybe he could sleep through Sioux's next panic attack. It was hard not to say the wrong thing, and it was hard to say nothing. Sleep was arguably safer. Gael did not like to argue. Not out loud, anyway. Judging by the light outside his dorm room window it was already roughly half past seven. It was a bright room and its window stretched wall to wall, an accurate teller of time. He'd better get up and get Sioux some breakfast, which she likely wasn't going to eat.

Dr. Burgos

Doctor Burgos was a woman of deceptive appearance. Doctor Burgos knew that's what Detective Clark had decided so when she first stepped foot into her office. She even saw the woman note so in her little notebook. The doctor was fully aware that she had a face of a thirty-five-year-old but it was attached to a neck of a forty-eight- year-old, give or take, she estimated. She was of impressive presence and stature, with shoulders small but breasts significant. Her hair was dyed a privileged shade of blonde but there was not one styling effort of note. Detective Clark wouldn't be the first one to take all of this in.

"Was she depressed?" the doctor was asked.

"Did she fear her husband?"

"Did she have stalkers, being on TV?"

She didn't get any preliminary phone calls prior to this visit. No warning. She should've, of course, on the other hand, had anticipated it—Peta Knudsen being Peta

Knudsen and all. Her car turns up abandoned, she doesn't come home the night before, doesn't turn up in Seattle as planned and *BAM*, there are cops at her door and every structure that could pass for a pole along Bellwether Way is graced with a *Missing* poster.

This wasn't innovative police work—the entire town knew Peta was a patient since she got pregnant. The second time, that is. She was one of her first patients in town, imagine that. It was great for business. Given the circumstances, it was only logical that the police would come to her right after talking to Peter. Checking him and his alibi no doubt. Wasn't it something like "three women are killed by their intimate partners every day" according to some statistic? No, she should've planned better. She hadn't slept all night and she actually had a patient sitting in that ridiculously overpriced chair from *West Elm* (paid for by all those sessions with Peta, as the inappropriate use of the word "irony" would have it), when they knocked on the door.

"Had she ever expressed suicidal thoughts?"

These detectives likely fancied themselves perceptive, but Dr. Burgos was pretty sure she could outwit them even given her frenzied state. Not that she needed to outwit them, per se, but she did need them out of her hair, which she brushed with her fingers like it was a tick. They were long, veiny, like a dragon's or a gargoyle's, as the lovely Peta had once noted. She wasn't known for her subtlety in this two-room office. Peta, as you knew from your morning news, was not the everyday Peta. *Peta*—she'd be everywhere now.

"Of course she had! But she's entitled to express them. You know their history, I'm sure," the doctor scoffed, rubbing her eyes as discreetly as possible. Maybe if she'd rub them harder, they'd believe they were inflamed from the physical contact just imparted on them and from nothing else. "But they never sounded genuine enough, or else I'd do something about it, as my professional duties mandate. So yes and no. These were more of the rehearsed, dramatic variety."

"Was she on any medication?"

"I'm not entirely sure these questions are one hundred percent kosher, if you know what I mean. But no, not anymore. She got off those quickly enough on my watch," the doctor rattled off without a second's hesitation. On second thought, she regretted not taking a moment for fear of looking defensive or prideful, or both. It was her hook, after all—holistic treatment over medicating into stupor. Her ad said so, if not in so many words. She had a website full of testimonials.

"In your professional opinion, would you say there is fair basis for presuming that Mrs. Knudsen could've just left on her own? Voluntarily?"

It was Detective Clark doing all the asking. That's how she introduced herself, blinking those emerald eyes as she shook the doctor's hand earlier. She was so slender and petite that Dr. Burgos expected her protruding hipbones to be as sharp as paper.

Dr. Burgos shrugged, assessing the form dressed in a suit that she could only assume itched. Real-life cops never looked like Olivia Benson.

"Well, she is old enough…"

"In your sessions, was she happy? With her husband, her daughter?"

That was Detective Foster. A little too blunt, that one. A small-town cop keen a little too obviously on having you think that he was growing too old for this bullshit, the Doctor guessed. His graying hair looked like it did not belong on the same head, same face, as his bright blue eyes. He had a scar on his chin, she noticed. She was surprised at her own alertness. She was electricity.

"How familiar are you with the concept of doctor-patient confidentiality? It's something similar to that infamous attorney-client arrangement you may have heard of in your line of work. You guys may not like it, but it's one of those pesky little things the law makes you respect, anyway."

She was downright astounded by her reflexes, but she didn't want to push her luck.

"Ms. Bur—"

"*Doctor!*"

"Forgive me," Clark pleaded, almost convincingly. "*Doctor* Burgos, we're not trying to trespass on anyone's rights, but little Gwenny's mother is missing. We're not trying to delve into anything too private here, but we have to cover all of our bases. Now, the search is on as it is, of course, so no one's wasting any time here—" *Of course,* Doctor Burgos thought. Of course, little Gwenny had to be mentioned, for fear of this conversation not slanting sexist!

Dr. Burgos could feel her jaws tighten. "—it's only logical to at least humor the possibility that she may have left on her own. She's an adult, she's entitled—"

In a move less strategic as much as it was involuntary, she picked up a framed photo of off her desk and stroked it. His father's son, John really was a beautiful boy. Just remembering the hungry eyes with which Peta looked at her baby made her stomach burn. Dr. Burgos slid the frame into her desk's top drawer, where more photos used to live, tucked away from prying eyes.

She sighed and felt her knees begin to vibrate. The adrenaline she was just about ready to praise for her alarming vigilance was slowly evaporating with the stuffy air around her. She thought about opening a window but that would let in street noise. Peta Knudsen's disappearance was giving everyone in this town something to talk about. According to her calculations, this would fare well with her practice—only three hours into her business day and already she had new patient enquiries. Sure, for now they all just wanted to know about the pretty doll who was missing. It wouldn't be difficult to find issues requiring infinite appointments to untangle with each one of those curious little souls. The fact that they were intrigued by a disappearance of a person they felt they each knew intimately simply because she used to appear daily on their television screens was issue enough. This part was easy. One needy pretty girl out, twenty needy (albeit potentially less pretty) patients in.

"Look," she called to the Detectives when she saw them inch their way toward the exit, losing interest. "I refuse to talk to you about their personal life, but I will tell you that she kept a journal."

Peta's Journal Entry

Peter never cries. His eyes are always glossy—watery, even—but he never actually cries. It's like he is still trying to be that perfect foster kid, up for adoption: see, potential mommy, I'm a good boy, I don't cry. Not that I want to see him cry. Or any man, for that matter. I saw one of mommy's boyfriends cry once and that was enough for me. The way his voice cracked, the way his chin shook. And all because mommy kicked him out of whatever old and haunted colonial her wannabe-commune was calling home at the time. I don't know what he did to deserve the privilege. But no. Nah-uh. Unbecoming. Add on top of that my plentiful access to the plethora of human emotion by way of spending a solid fifteen years inside a TV studio and you can say my tolerance for men crying has pretty much been tapped out. And were his eyes not perpetually threatening to spill over, I wouldn't expect him to cry, at all, wouldn't even bring it up here, in my very first journal entry. But this incessant taunt has been wearing me a little thin for some time now. Either cry or don't, but you have to pick one—you can't have the world think what a gentle, sensitive soul you are and then not actually shed the promised tears. Shit or get off the pot, man.

Not even when Harry died did he cry. It's all locked up in there, that moisture. Dr. Burgos, you tried to spell this all out for me, once: "Given his traumatic childhood, challenging adolescence, you have to adjust your expectations," you've told me time and time again. But when your son dies, it's okay to hit the eject button on those perennially preloaded tears of yours, don't you think? Wouldn't you? It's maddening—frightening, even! —that you don't. Or fine! Do as you like—don't cry! But then just reabsorb that moisture that's always there inside your lightly reddened rims. One or the other. You can't have it both ways. You can't just straddle the fence. This has always bothered me, I think, but, needless to say, it's gotten worse P.H.— post Harry. I don't care how many families you tried to impress with your group home performance in order to be picked out of the rest of the litter and be taken home, Peter. I don't, not anymore. We'd sworn we wouldn't become statistic, but who doesn't?

This journal was your idea, Dr. Burgos. I told you I don't believe in journals, but that made you laugh. Not everything needs my faith in order to be real and effective, apparently. You're not wrong, for all I know. But don't be upset if I don't exactly pour my heart out here.

I just write. Twenty minutes a day. Stream of consciousness. Very Hemingway of me, I suppose. Though it's unlikely that he did his writing under shrink's orders. I will try to give my entries some sort of order, keep it all topical, as per your assignments, but I won't date them. And I can't guarantee you that I'm doing this exercise wholeheartedly. This exercise is mainly to frustrate my reader. I imagine some anthropologist digging it up and studying it one day. I suppose an archeologist would have to find it first and then some bored college freshmen would be assigned it on a rainy Friday, sitting there highlighting it to try to make sense of an American woman in 2015. So at least I need to make this material somewhat interesting. Children are our future, after all.

It'd be fun to know a little bit more about you, Doctor. You are always so smug there with your ombré blonde mane resting on your shoulders, your steel eyes behind those inoffensive wire frames. What is with those glasses, anyway—it's not like because the frames are so thin we don't know you're wearing them, so what's the esthetic appeal? And those highlights—is that a preemptive fashion choice for when you actually have to start covering up grays? Everyone knows you aren't a real blonde. In this town everyone knows everything. There are no real secrets. Soon, I'll know all of yours. And you'll likely know some of mine. It's what I'm paying you to do, in a way, no? You see, there's no escaping anything or anyone here.

Peter says I am free to change my therapist since I sound so bitter about you and your fancy office. He says that this is all for me, but I'm not and it's not. And anyway, you are sort of "it" in this town, Doc. You know that whole Connelly's Best Doctors guide? Well, if Bellingham had one, you'd be it. It doesn't, I don't think, but you get the point. Besides, we've been together since before Gwenny was born, you and me—you know all about Peter's stutter and all that jazz. So where else could I go, anyway?

But I digress. Clearly, this entry is about Peter and his watery eyes, not about my feeling of being sour about this compulsory journal-keeping exercise. This is my first entry.

Hold on, what was the assignment, again? Crap, am I failing at this already?

End of Entry.

<u>Andrew</u>

A canary yellow Honda FIT was not Andrew's first choice of a car, but he wasn't expecting much of a selection to begin with. It took three flights and a total of nine hours to finally land here and he wasn't about to waste many more of them looking for an ideal rental. He wasn't sure how many days he would be needing to take off work. With Lena's obvious breakdown, he wasn't about to waste energy on picking a vehicle. He signed the paperwork and scanned the posters of the all the Wanted and the Missing on the wall with cracking avocado-green paint while, he tried to wait patiently for his ID to be returned to him having been photocopied. He squinted to make out the faces, but the features blended in the thirty spare seconds he had to study them.

Punching in the address of Lena's rented house, Andrew stopped typing mid "Magrath." It wasn't too late to turn back. It would mean spending the remainder of his miles and countless more hours, but he could, theoretically, return the car and walk back inside the airport. This wasn't the first time Lena called with some nonsensical crisis and never did he ever feel the need to cancel classes and hop on a plane. She was likely sober now and may not even remember their conversation. What was he doing here? He couldn't quite pinpoint what it was about this particular call that made it different. It wasn't even the first time she involved John in her drunken tirade. Maybe it was simply that he was done with Lena's phone calls. He decided that's what it was as he pulled out of the spot.

He'd visited before, when John first decided to move. Growing up, the boy hated Juneau—he hated the way he stood out and he hated the cold. Their friendship was no match for societal and meteorological advantages of the State of Washington. Not like when he was five. The house Lena had rented was nice, he couldn't argue with that. The furniture she was renting too was nice enough. But none of it masked the smell of liquor on his ex-wife's breath as he hugged her hello with his son by his side. It was sold to him as a celebratory drink or two ahead of schedule, but deep down inside, he knew better. It wasn't even that deep. He could've turned right back then too but didn't. He tried imagining dragging poor John all the way back to the airport and further—a twenty-one year old man of his own height. Not only would it be not physically possible, it would be comical. The boy was grown and likely would have handled the disappointment. But by the same token, given that the boy was an adult, he too should've known better. He didn't, and that was disappointing in itself. A part of Andrew wanted to let him test-drive this move, get to know his mom one-on-one, without his own adlibs and interpretations. That part won—it was a teaching moment of sorts. As a teacher, he knew now it was to be a shitty one, too. You don't entrust your child, no matter the age, to a drunk. It may have taken a little bit of time, but the deterioration was obvious and there was no way it wasn't going to leave permanent damage. He could've left that night but instead, he huffily helped his son bring in the suitcases and stayed for a dinner of Thai takeout. He spent the night on the pullout couch in an otherwise empty room in his ex's house and left as soon as the sun hit the horizon. He locked up behind him with the key entrusted to him in case of "emergencies." He hadn't been back since. It had been over a year.

It seemed more rural to him now than a year ago. Houses stood sparser than in the twilight that he drove through last time. Not that he's ever really been to a raging metropolis, but this looked downright sleepy. Certainly not any less sleepy than Juneau. Lena claimed boredom led her to liquor but Lena also apparently grew up in Bellingham. Andrew didn't know this until she announced where she would be moving after their separation. They met in Portland, when both were in school- Different schools. Home towns were never really important topics in their conversations—their careless, flirty courtship morphed into somber responsibility too quickly, editing out any opportunity for small talks of childhoods. She claimed her folks didn't want her marrying outside of race and he never questioned this one way or another. He wasn't sure if he was expected to hate them or be grateful to her for choosing him. He knew nothing about his in-laws and he was fine

26

with it forever remaining so. He never met them and was now genuinely unsure if his ex-wife had ever traveled to see them during their marriage. Had they ever met their grandson? Did John think his mom was born an adult? Somehow he never seemed bothered by the fact that he only ever knew one set of grandparents. Was this testament to John's stupidity or his resilience? He didn't know, but he was pretty sure the boy's maternal grandparents were dead now, though he wasn't sure how he came to know this. Andrew and Lena moved to Juneau following job offers and Andrew, for one, never looked back. Home was where John was but it wasn't clear where he was now.

John

It would've been better if they asked me to come to the precinct; being interrogated by two cops right outside your work cannot possibly look good. Dad certainly wouldn't approve. My manager saw me as she was coming in.

"Everything okay, officers?" she asked in her most professional voice, as if she weren't actually a twenty-one-year- old college student in media studies.

"Yes," the detective told her. "We just need to confirm something with John over here." He kept this smile on his face that stayed put for so long, I had to practically pinch myself to be sure this wasn't a dream. If only for a few seconds, the scene looked like a still from a movie. I was observing the exchange as if I weren't its central character. "You can go on in," the cop added when Julie didn't move, probably just as mesmerized by the stoic smile. As much as I didn't want Julie making my time with Bellingham's finest a proverbial water cooler talk, I was glad for the distraction. Eventually, the automatic doors closed behind her. I'm pretty sure I saw her snap a photo over her shoulder though. With Julie gone, my only distractions are the occasional senior citizens pausing on their slow way from their vehicles and into the store. "You were saying?" the cop now turns his attention back to me, the smile so far gone, it didn't seem possible that the man even knew how to smile.

"Right," I swallow, trying to wake myself without being grotesque about it. I didn't sleep well. Between it being Julie's couch and mulling over the previous day, it didn't seem wise to truly rest. "She asked me to go to Seattle with her."

The lady cop looks suspicious. Either that or she lacks basic control of facial muscles. Her lip, her brow! I wouldn't recommend she play poker. It's like this is funny to her. I consider asking her what she finds so amusing, but dad would probably advise me to drop it before starting anything. Laying low is sort of his life's mission. I didn't inherit that from him.

"What do you mean, she wanted you to come with her to Seattle?" she eventually asks, her smile lingering on the corners of her mouth.

"What I said—she walked straight up to my register, landed a bottle of water or something on my belt, and asked if I wanted to go to Seattle with her." I ache to light up a cigarette but I'm not sure about how that would look.

"You mean to tell me that a successful, married woman, who is also well into her forties, suddenly developed the hots for a twenty-something cashier boy?" the tall man interjects. I can only assume this is where I'm supposed to get defensive and confess to something.

"Don't know what to tell ya'," I shrug, instead. I'm not sure what my objective is but it works—they are silent, if only for a moment. The cop lights a cigarette of his own and I take a gamble and bum one.

"Has she ever spoken to you before? You know, besides what sales were on any particular week?"

I exhale improbable amounts of smoke. Mistake upon mistake upon mistake. But it's a tough question. We've talked, sure. Small talk, mostly. She spoke animatedly and fast. Much faster than on TV. We have TVs at the store and they are always tuned to the local channel. I guess that's better than watching day time soaps while you're restocking the almond beverages we are no longer permitted to call "milk" for the obvious reason of it having nothing in common with a dairy product, but they loop stories a lot, because, let's face it—this isn't the most booming town. She talked a mile a minute but I was usually too mesmerized by her sad face to listen. And when she wasn't rattling at a rate much too fast for a real human, she just stared. I'm not sure if it's the right thing to say out loud, but I always had my doubts about the lady's sanity. With that aside, she was dizzying.

"We spoke, I guess," I answer as truthfully as I can.

I can see them calculating if they should press me on this or step back and watch. They don't confer and I don't think they agree, either.

"Did she say anything about her upcoming trip—why did she suddenly want to take you?" the lady asks.

I feel my teeth clench the cigarette. It can't possibly be of any consequence. If I hadn't seen mom's car parked right outside the goddamn window, as well as mom herself in all her less than sober glory doing her best impression of a cartoon spy by the stack of bagels, none of this would be.

"She said she wanted me to meet her sister."

Sioux

On a good day, you can drive to Bellingham in about an hour and a half. But that's on a good day and this isn't one. Plus, I don't feel comfortable letting Gael go a mile over sixty so there's that, too. He is a good graphic artist, but his driving makes me nauseous even on that fictional good day, which today isn't, as we've already established. My seat is reclined all the way back, and I've been instructed to keep my eyes closed to at least rest them if not actually sleep. *Fine, Gael.* He's one of the good ones. Mommy says so, and mommy doesn't like many men.

When my ringer blasts some scream rock I'd downloaded on a dare in high school, I jerk upright to be rewarded with a hefty head rush. *Peta?* I mouth, breathless.

"Honey, have you eaten?"

My heart throws itself against my ribcage only to bounce back and tumble around awkwardly within its hallow cavity. It's not Peta.

"Yes, mommy."

"Gael driving?"

I'd barely slept the night before (barely ate too), so Gael won—I am not allowed behind the wheel until I'd slept a consecutive six hours and my blood sugar is a stable 78. All around an unrealistic goal, really.

"Yes, mommy."

Gael's brown eyes are off the road and on me, momentarily, and I have no choice but to lie back down and throw my free hand over my eyes.

"I'll try to be there tomorrow. I want to try to stay put for a bit, in case she's coming to me."

"Oh no, should I have stayed put?" A boulder of ice settles atop my chest. I feel Gael begin to slow down. He'd mentioned this idea too—he wanted us to stay in Seattle, not "add to the unknowns," as he put it.

"No, honey, don't be ridiculous. She would've come yesterday if she were coming to see you, like she said. Everything is fine, love. I'm sure of it. Go to Bellingham, if you want to go. You can entertain Gwenny. But it's fine one way or the other. It's fine," she repeats, again, each time with slightly more forced conviction. I think I even hear a rare appearance of her accent. I want to argue, to protest. To say that Peta had something to tell me so no way she'd just leave me hanging. But I don't say anything at all. I just try to keep breathing. Smell the flowers, blow out the candles, the way I was taught by that sweet school nurse Ana the first time I had a panic attack in seventh grade.

31

My arm flings off my face and I watch us pass the exit for Everett. We have a ways to go; maybe we could still turn around.

"But what if Peta turns up in Seattle, after all?"

I see Gael's mouth twitch and part in preparation for an answer, but mommy's voice reaches me first.

"Honey, don't worry so much! I'm sure she's fine, but you're the one who'll need help with all these nerves! Maybe she and Peter had a fight and she's cooling off at a girlfriend's or something. You know she's been stubborn since she was sperm."

Peta doesn't have girlfriends. I wonder if mommy knows how ridiculous she sounds.

I hear her readying to hang up and feign growing distance from the receiver before I hang up first. I call Peter.

"Did you get any sleep last night?" When I see Gael shake his head, his lip bitten, it almost breaks my heart to realize that, again, he thinks I'm talking to him. His knuckles are pale from the grip on the wheel. He releases one hand and maneuvers only with his left, reaching for me with the right. I have to close my eyes again.

"A little. I came back from the station at four in the morning and Gwenny takes her bottle at six. I mean, Marsha's here to do that, but still."

With my eyes shut, I switch hands and reach for Gael with my free one, squeezing his fingers. He squeezes back. He always squeezes back.

32

"We're on our way. Do you think we should turn back and wait in Seattle? What if she turns up?"

I hear Peter sigh. He still sounds tired. Even more tired than usual. His words are carefully chosen, his pauses are longer than ever.

"Either way. Gwenny will be happy to see you. And I'm sure Peta's fine. The cops are looking into it, but I'm sure she's fine, really. Her car is nowhere near the train station, so maybe she never got on the train to begin with—maybe she changed her mind and sleeping at some friend's house. But you can come."

"You think?" I squeeze Gael harder. Mommy may not know better, but Peter does; he knows Peta has no friends. Now he's just lying. Probably for my benefit. What else can suddenly make everyone believe that Peta has friends?

"I'm sure! Who would want to hurt her?" Peter adds "She is the sweet— sweetheart of the Pacific Northwest, after all, haven't you heard? And she's very recognizable around here, so some— someone must've seen her. She probably needed some time away. I don't blame her...the timing being symbolic and such. You know, with Gwenny turning one and Harry... Look, I get it. We just need to make sure..." He sounds almost certain. Those years of Standard American English weren't for nothing. Even that stutter seems to add a little certitude to his words—a purpose, at least. "Look, you are welcome here, okay? You always are. But I don't want you to worry. Have you eaten?"

My eyes closed, I smile, something akin to warm hope pushing out that ice brick from its twelve-hour home in my

33

chest, forcing it down into my abdomen, where I pray it will eventually melt.

"Yes, Gael fed me," I sing, giving my boyfriend's hand yet another squeeze. When I open my eyes, he is smiling. It's worth it. It is an endearing smile he has. Broad and open. That's what won me over at that freshman orientation event where we met—super pink long lips, two rows of slightly crooked teeth, and that jaw-length hair that frizzes up frustratingly in the Pacific Northwest humidity, leaving him with some cross of an Afro and a Jewfro. It's funny because he's neither. He did a 23andMe test to confirm.

"Good," Peter approves. "Then we'll see you soon. I may still be at the station when you arrive—I have to sto— stop by again for more questions, apparently, but Marsha will let you in."

I let the phone drop on my belly. It just grazes the insulin pump. I feel it with my fingertips just to be sure it hadn't been dislodged, which, of course, I already know it hadn't been. When it was first installed, the toddler that I was, I scratched at it with a rodent's abandon. Mommy could barely swat my hands away in time before I had enough time to do any damage. I really was a handful for mommy to deal with at her age, now that I think about it. She had Peta at twenty-five; me—forty-five. I cringe at the realization that Peta was more or less my age when I was born. I cringe not at the age difference but at the fact that such basic math occurs to me only now as I lie flat in the passenger seat of Gael's old Toyota Echo, screwing my eyes shut to miss as many signs as possible.

Evelyn

Evelyn didn't know why she lied to her daughter. She did and she didn't. It should've been easy enough to tell the truth, but she hadn't all those years and now it just felt like duress. Or was it coercion? She never did learn the difference in those church-organized English lessons for the pregnant soviet refugee. Whatever the proper term was, that's how Peta had made her feel.

I'm seeing Sioux later today. I'm telling her everything. Once I'm done, we'll come up to you. Together. See how you can fill in the gaps— both, in terms of my pieced-together narrative and some fucking justification.

That was the last text message she received from her daughter. They'd been others, each one progressively less abstract but more aggressive. Each one flooded her with hot terror and cold sweat, leaving her lightheaded with confusion. It was as if with each new text, the cracks in her daughter's sanity threatened to widen irrevocably, swallowing whole the neat little life she'd made up for Sioux.

Evelyn's thumb danced over the text. Deleting it felt all sorts of wrong. She scrolled up and down considering her options. This may have been the last communication from her daughter. And she never replied. In fact, she hadn't acknowledged any of her texts in this series. This, of course, wouldn't look good if anyone chose to check her phone now. And, not that it would balance anything out, but it didn't feel good either. Not then, not now.

Evelyn's heart hadn't stopped thudding since last night. Peter must've known she would not sleep a wink knowing

35

her daughter was not accounted for. He could've waited until the morning to let her know, she thought. There was nothing practical she could do at the time, or now even, so what was the practical purpose for calling her and rousing her out of bed? Sure, officially he called to check if Peta was with her but surely he knew better. She may not have liked Peter but the man was not stupid—he knew better than to genuinely believe Peta was with her. No, he was simultaneously looking busy and intentionally hurting her. Of course Peta wasn't with her. When was Peta voluntarily with her anymore? Of course she wasn't. Sure, she threatened to ambush her with some half-baked theories and discovery but that was an outlier. There was no precedent for this but there *was* a small chance her daughter was on her way to her. Maybe she bypassed Seattle all together. On purpose! Maybe, for once in her life, she was giving her mother a chance to explain first. There was no reason for Peter to know this.

Dr. Burgos

Dr. Burgos gathered her voluminous hair before climbing out of her shiny red Jeep inside her musty garage. She'd been meaning to get the landlord to investigate the source of the smell and cure it but somehow something always got in the way. Maybe she didn't want it fixed after all, she mused whenever she'd park and remember again. Maybe it was good to have her lungs acclimate to some likely fungus. Build up some immunity.

She was stalling. She knew that. Were she her own patient, she'd ask herself what she was so afraid of. What was the worst that could happen? Andrew was only being a good father. Wasn't that why she called him? She couldn't actually remember: why *did* she call him?

"Lena?" His voice hit her the moment she slowly yawned the door to the kitchen open. It was just as deep, low, and penetrating as it was twenty-three years ago. She felt it on contact.

"Yes, Andrew, it's me. Is John home?" she croaked, her voice breaking and struggling to regroup before being found out. She'd forgotten that she gave him a key when he first brought John down.

"It's funny you should ask me that question. The only reason I let him come live with you is because you promised your eyes were no longer lined crimson on a daily basis, and here you are—lids red as a rabbit's." He was calm, academic in his observation, even, always more comfortable in his profession rather than his person. He stood firmly rooted in his spot at her kitchen counter, waiting for her to explain. He was still striking. She remembered once describing him as "sex" to her roommate when they first met. The girl blushed and giggled but the moniker still fit. His lips full, spikes of gray in his beard, he still left her breathless. When he saw that words were hard for Lena, he threw his scarf around his neck one extra, unnecessary loop in exasperation. He always did dress like a high fashion fisherman.

"What does the color of my eyelids have to do with any of this?" she finally muttered, half under her breath.

This was an immature response by any measure, she knew. She was certainly better than this, she was positive, but her head was still dizzy with the abundance of wine, the

37

lack of sleep, and the conversation with the police. They wouldn't stop, not for their local fucking Katie Couric. Or would Al Rocker make for a better comparison?

"Lena, you can't have it both ways. You call me in the middle of the night, slurring your words, talking about some woman and how you can't reach John. It's like you're speaking code when you're drunk, I swear to God." Andrew was likely growing hot in his oversized chunky sweater and began to wrestle his way out of it. There was a reason this man's office hours never seemed long enough—college girls were ready to kill just to watch him reveal his toned arms out of the confines of his jacket after lectures.

Lena struggled to answer through a lump in her throat. She couldn't remember how many times she'd wanted him to hop on a plane and check on her after another one of her drunken midnight phone calls, but now that he was here, she wasn't sure if she could keep her legs rigid enough.

"He's an adult, it's okay if he spends an occasional night at a friend's house."

Lena was sweating now. She stepped out of her shoes to buy time. He wasn't here for her, she shook her head, remembering—it was all about John. It stopped being about her the moment that drugstore pregnancy test came back positive.

"Why are my juniors missing their workshop right now? There are no direct flights here, Lena. You remember that, right? I spent almost more hours in the air than I would ideally prefer for this. Whatever *this* is. You were hysterical on the phone! What happened?"

38

Lena watched as Andrew scratched the stubble on his right cheek.

"Honestly, what the fuck, Lena?"

The stubble on his face was artful, the glasses on his nose were sleek. Lena rubbed her eyes. She wasn't sure if this was worth it.

"Why am I here, Lena?" His voice was fuller now, louder. Her knees buckled. She considered taking the few strides toward him, lowering her fingers into his jeans. She had to shake herself awake for fear of muscle memory taking over. It was an act of drunken desperation to call Andrew, especially that she did this with alarming frequency as it was. She did this all the time, in fact. At least twice a week. She was the proverbial boy who cried wolf. How could he possibly take her seriously now?

"She's a local meteorologist. And she's missing—"

"She's missing?"

"Yes."

"Okay—"

"They know each other—?"

"Who?"

"This meteorologist and John?"

"That's why I'm missing work right now? Because John has a friend?"

Andrew lowered himself onto one of Lena's rented stools. Two years in Bellingham and she was still renting everything. Again, were she a patient in her own practice, she'd like to delve into possible commitment issues at fault.

"You don't understand!" Lena cried. "She was obsessed with him! Asked about him all the time! She saw him before going missing and then he didn't come home last night. He won't take my calls so I have absolutely no idea if he's with her or face down in a ditch somewhere. And the cops are all over this—they were in my office already!"

"Why were they at your office?"

"Because she's my patient. She's been suffering from depression for years. That's how I know she was obsessed with your son! Everyone thinks she's so darling but she's practically a pedophile! All she wanted to do her last few sessions was talk about John!"

"Only John is an adult..." Andrew swallowed and massaged his beard. "They are speaking to everyone with any kind of relationship to the missing, that's normal. Lena, you're fine. And did you talk to John about this? You know, before you began writing some sordid affair involving your son in your mind? He works at that store, that's probably how they know each other. And if you're worried they have John in mind for anything, just remember—you're drunk!" He was defensive. For a lawyer, he'd always shown his flusters too quickly. This was why he chose to teach, instead. At least in part. "Do you hate all your patients with this amount of passion or is this woman special?"

Dr. Burgos pretended not to hear this question. She needed more time before she could.

"Well, she did go see him before she vanished! Are you listening to anything I'm saying? And, before you ask, I know she did because I followed her after our session, okay? And when they'll check the surveillance tapes at the store, they'll see them together and all the questions will begin." Andrew removed his glasses wiped them on his t-shirt, revealing a set of painfully sculpted abdominal muscles. She couldn't believe he was officially in his late 40s now. Lena swallowed the excess saliva flooding her mouth at the sight of his skin before she could continue. "The three of us need to talk."

Gael

She wasn't kidding. Her sister's house was beyond anything he had ever seen outside aimless browsing on Zillow.com. He'd always get sucked in too quickly and come to hours later. It was like falling down a black hole—click after click after click. House after house after house. He'd adjust the presets just so—his minimum price point unrealistically high, just be to be sure it never became a realistic search, and go to town. It was like writing his own fairy tale each and every time. And this house was straight off his screen. He knew his girlfriend's sister was rich but no way was this in the budget of super local TV people. He'd only met her two or three times (and met *him* the one time), but seeing the house up close, he had to question that there was no side income involved.

To park in the spacious driveway to the left of the massive double doors of the house's main entrance Gael had to use his horn. He understood why this trip was necessary, but it was all so in key with the rest of Peta

41

Knudsen, formerly Morozova. The last name meant "cold"; it would be a marketable one, given her career of choice. But Gael guessed Peta couldn't wait to shed as much of her mother as possible, leaving Sioux doing the work for two. It was hard but not impossible to blame her.

My God, Gael groaned as inaudibly as he could so as not to wake up Sioux. It was like parting the red sea getting through the fresh-faced members of the press without knocking over anyone or their high-tech accessories. He couldn't believe they beat them here.

"Oh fuck, they are here already."

Effort wasted—Sioux was awake. She could not have slept more than twenty minutes. It was better than nothing.

"Yeah," Gael sighed, calibrating the tone of his own voice.

"I can't believe them! They are his friends! They are going to destroy Peter."

For someone so stressed and under slept, Sioux sure was animated. She liked Peter. Gael wasn't big on pedestrian psychology, but he presumed it was because she never knew her dad and, biologically, Peter was close enough in age to play the part. It had to be either that or she just had a thing for bug-eyed men in their forties.

"This is their job. It's what they do," he announced as if it needed announcing. "Ready?" She was. Sioux was ready as early as ten last night. "Wait! I'll get the door."

Shoulders proud but gaze lowered, Gael took three large strides around his car to get Sioux. The girl unfolded her limbs with an enviable amount of determination. Though her gaze was down, her faux jog to the doorstep was dignified. She must've gotten this from her mother, Gael caught himself thinking. The lady, albeit a physical pain to talk to, did possess a level of elegance not often matched out there in the wild. Three bangs on the door and they were in. The reporters barely had the time to open their mouths, let alone utter a syllable to the girl they unlikely even realized was Peta Knudsen's baby sister. Marsha, a woman very obviously of few words, let them in and receded into the background, somehow managing to leave plump little Gwenny behind in Sioux's arms. The action was so smooth, so seamless, Gael barely had the time to register any of it. Five minutes prior he was in a car silent as a tomb, his exhausted girlfriend peacefully asleep at his side, and now he was inside a house bigger than he'd previously dared to Zillow, and his frail girlfriend was laden with a baby.

Peter

The footage was grainy. To think, in 2015, security cameras still could not produce anything even remotely resembling something out of CSI, Peter mused to himself as he watched the detectives lean their heads this way and that, fast-forwarding and rewinding over and over again. They did a good enough job pretending it was their first run-through. Zooming in only created more interference so they mercifully gave that up quickly enough.

This is nothing like TV. Peter was surprised to be surprised by this.

There was no doubt in his mind. The woman in the video was wearing a cropped jacket. It was red, Peter knew, but that wasn't reflected in the black and white video. Massive frames could be seen concealing an arguably critical portion of her face, but it was her, all right. He saw it in the posture with which he'd become so familiar over the years. *Peta.* That vaguely apologetic curve of the shoulders, that forward driving force of her torso. She seemed to storm into that store with such urgency, the automatic doors barely had the time to open. It didn't necessarily mean she'd been in a hurry that day. The realization that "that day" was literally yesterday felt like fist to his sternum, but the point remained—that walk did not necessarily mean to express something about her mental state or mood then or any other time. That was just her walk. This was his no-nonsense, no-time-to-waste Peta—the one he fell in love with back in 1993. He watched as she appeared to stall for a second in order to not make impact with the glass door. Comical, really. Peter considered chuckling, his lips were on the verge of twitching, but, with the detectives' eyes on him, he stabilized them in time. He squinted at the screen instead—serious, contemplative.

She must've been inside a total of seven minutes. So indicated the little time stamp in the lower right hand corner of the screen. She then stormed out in her customary fashion, and headed for her truck, presumably. She paused and turned over her shoulder, as if doing a double take, and then resumed her stomping outside of the camera's view. That was the last time anyone ever saw her. At least on the record.

He couldn't get it straight—has it been *only* a day or a *whole* day.

44

There was also footage from inside the store, a separate file, but what it captured seemed even more meaningless than the footage from the parking lot and the entrance, if anything. All Peter saw was Peta snatching a bottle of water from a fridge with some noticeably charged energy and then grab a candy bar from the display next to one of the cash registers with the same hunger. If she were about to board the train, her purchases, and the haste, seemed entirely fitting. The guy at the register took her money in the manner that was not outstanding in any way, either: he tossed his dreadlocks aside, scanned the items, likely offered her a plastic bag for her modest purchases, as evidenced by a brief verbal exchange, and called it a day. That was it. End scene. Peter yawned. He glanced at the wall clock. *8:30 P.M.* He'd been awake too long now, and he likely wouldn't be making his routine bedtime from now on. It remained to be seen how much longer this useless exercise was going to take.

"Does she ever come back?" Peter heard himself ask.

"No."

"Look, I was not in the parking lot that day," he sighed preemptively, itching to rub his eyes. He's been staring at the screen too hard and he was obviously falling out of habit. "You already have my alibi. Janet Kallarny can attest to the fact that I was in her office for therapy between noon and two in the afternoon. I was at the TV station by 2:20. I was nowhere near Organic Produce."

He did protest too much, he knew. No one's asked, no one accused him of anything. Not yet, anyway. He was just so excited to get it all out without stuttering, he couldn't help himself.

45

The detectives nodded in careful unison.

"Nothing stands out to you?"

Peter shook his head, carefully.

"Peta appears to look back at something. Any guess at to what that can be about?" Detective Clark asked, just as delicately, as if Peter could shatter and break at the sound of her voice. He didn't believe he looked that tired. He shrugged.

"Could literally be anything. Anybody. She was on TV, maybe somebody recognized her, called her. She looked at something and moved on. So what?"

They nodded again. As if this were all some precise, choreographed dance that Peter was meant to rehearse at home but forgot.

"And the young man at the cash register?"

"What about him?"

"Do you know him?"

"I've seen him, sure. He stands out a bit, with the dreadlocks and all. But that's about it."

More nodding. It was making Peter dizzy.

"Did you notice—they appear to be talking."

Careful not to squint while looking for the intended implication, Peter suddenly felt his face begin to flush.

"Really? For what—10-20 seconds? She's a local TV personality! Maybe he asked her about the weather. It would be appropriate. Or maybe he was expressing condolences. Wouldn't be uncommon, either."

Tempted to close his eyes in order not to register the disappointment on the cops' faces, Peter settled for a lengthy blink. It had to be about 8pm. There were no windows here to gauge.

"Well, if you think of anything…" he eventually heard one of them say. The whoosh of blood in his ears made it difficult for him to register if it was the man or the woman.

None of this was rocket science, of course—the husband is always a suspect in his wife's disappearance. As a journalist, he would've been hard on the police department were they not questioning the husband. Still, he wished they'd summoned him here under a slightly better veil. Nobody needed his opinion on this security tape. He was here to be observed some more. Next, he knew, they'd want to observe him in his natural environment. If he had anyone to bet on this with, he would've. It was a winner. Especially now that his co-workers were setting up shop in front of his house.

Peter's fingers dug into the styrofoam of his cup before he could do anything about it. They tore white strips into small bits before flicking them all into the trash bin at the foot of the table. The promise of Peta was once something iridescent—every image of her in his mind eye shimmered at one point in time. That elastic smile, those teeth perfect but for that one slightly crooked canine, her hair often braided like that of a German milkmaid. She was fun once.

47

Fun and maternal. And even he wasn't above the stereotype.

"Detectives, why am I here?" His therapist would be proud of this flawless delivery. Now, with Peta gone, he was sure to have a full-blown, not episodic, relapse. Long gone were the days when she made things better. Six words in succession was a win for Peter now—that's what it had come down to. "Is all this just to gauge my reaction? I've spent my life in front of the camera—most of my training is in not visibly flustering as a producer is screaming—screaming in my ear."

He was so close.

Peta's Journal Entry

I want to fall asleep. Rather, to fall asleep and not wake up. Ever. I just want the wheel to stop turning. Correction— it should feel free to continue turning, but I want off it.

It's ungrateful of me. I don't need you to remind me of that, Dr. Burgos. I know all about second chances and how precious they are, and how my daughter needs me despite her full-time nanny. I know, I know. And yet, here I am at half past midnight, eyes open and on the monitor showing a grainy black and white image of Gwenny sleeping with her arms thrown up in the surrender position, wishing to just fall asleep and call it a day. Kind of permanently. Peter, I feel for but didn't dare look, as he is on the other side of the bed, curled up in the fetal position. I don't need to look to know this. I'm half expecting to see him sucking his thumb if I actually turn in his direction. And I sit up and write this all down, instead.

I'm beginning to resent you, Doc—you really could be helping me with this. Sometimes a crutch is necessary; I'd give it back when I'm good and ready, I promise. I'm fully aware of how happy I should be. I should at least be happier than I am, right? Something tragic happened, but, hey, look, something good is here, instead. Take it! Let's make the best of it, no? I'm trying, I'll tell you that much. I am trying. Some pharmaceutical magic would surely go a long way here, but I can't be expected to beg. I'm just saying, my mind would be quieter, and a quiet mind is a mind I'd kill for at the moment.

It wasn't easy bringing Gwenny into this world. Harry took a couple of enthusiastic fifteen-minute amorous nights, whereas Gwenny took almost three exhausting years. They'd become mechanical, our attempts. There was some light, some humor to it when it was just us trying to become three, but, after Harry, we no longer bothered to even look at each as we fucked, there were no big productions made, no words (loving, dirty, or otherwise) uttered. Forget that, I'm not sure if we even knew why we kept going. There was a goal and we were set on accomplishing it like the professionals that we are. So, every other night, like clockwork, we each did the bare minimum we knew would get the other off before curling up on our respective sides, our backs barely touching to get our requisite six hours of sleep before having to wake up at 3:30am to make it to the studio on time and wake up the rest of Bellingham Bay. Once there, makeup would be stippled on and everyone would proceed to pretend to forget that we were the couple who'd buried their son not a year ago, not two years ago, and so on. Obviously, eventually the right sperm found the right egg and ta da— Gwenny. No, not Gwen! Never Gwen! Gwenny. This pink and translucent newborn lay in my shaking arms and all I could do was blink. She looked like Harry, but blonder. Something in my throat constricted and the rest became route. I think I'd stopped looking at Peter some time around then, too. But I can't help but wonder—what if having to fight for something this hard means you weren't meant to have it to begin with? When does determination become arrogance?

49

I'm so tired, Doctor. I am not making sense. I want to fall asleep. And not wake up. Ever. Do you have anything for that? Oh, that's right—you'd rather not medicate and mask the symptoms because you would much rather heal. Well, good luck with that. If not medication, can you at least give me a distraction? Anything to make the wheel stop.

Wednesday, October 3rd

Sioux

I don't want Mommy to join us. Peter needs support and Mommy is not good at support. Plus, she never even liked Peter so she is unlikely to be supportive now. People don't change. Especially not at her age. Especially not Mommy.

I pour myself a glass of milk and look out the window at the water droplets glistening on the back porch. It looks cold. Even the way the water shimmers makes it look as if it's shivering. Or maybe it's just because I'm cold. The windows are open downstairs, we're airing out the house. Rather, just the downstairs of it. Gwenny is napping and Gael says we shouldn't risk a draft. He is as afraid of those as Mommy is. One more check in his column.

"An orphan? Good—no in-laws," Mommy had advised Peta when she brought Peter home for Thanksgiving that one time. They'd been together a few Thanksgivings by then, but she waited to finally make the introductions. She'd always liked to sit on news of this magnitude. You'd never know given what she did for a living. I mean *does*—what she *does* for a living. Now I am thankful for that fact because it gave me a chance to actually be old enough to retain some memories of the initial meeting. We are twenty years apart-she could've been my mother.

Back then we still lived in Portland—Mommy and I. I was maybe four and had no idea what any of those words meant—orphan, in-laws, but, somehow, they stayed with me until I was old enough to look them up. That was years before I moved to Seattle for college, and she—Mommy—moved to Victoria, up in British Columbia. She was in pursuit of solitude and inspiration. She wanted me to move with her, but Peta argued that some independence would do me good. Besides, she loved going to school in Seattle and that meant so would I. I'm not sure how Mommy agreed that we part, we're very close, Mommy and I. Not a day passes without at least three phone calls between us. Peta never got this part of our relationship but there is so much talking in her life she seems to want quiet when she can get it. Ever since I was allowed to have my own cell phone (which happened literally on my way to college—Mommy pulled over by a strip mall before hopping back on I-5 N), our communication is comprised of mainly text messages. I dump out the rest of my milk into the kitchen sink as a train whistles by and my stomach sinks with alarm. The sight of this milk mixing with water and circling the drain make my stomach spasm painfully. Mommy will be here soon. Gael may need to go get her at the train station if Peter doesn't volunteer, which would probably be best, anyway. She seems to almost hate Peter. It's comical. Even the shade of his pale skin she hates, his large, moist eyes as well. Something about the aesthetics of it for her. She is an artist, after all.

The clock seems to be ticking louder today than I'd ever registered. Maybe because it's the quiet, or maybe because I'm hungry, but all the furniture corners around me seem soft and blurry. I hope Peter has news soon. He looked like a deflated balloon when he got home from the police station—a little flat, a little shabby. I don't know, I can't explain it. I'm not as good with words as Peta, but Peter's different now, anyhow—quieter. His stutter has grown worse. To think, he was so close to getting back in front of the camera again! He's put so many hours in with all those therapists and speech pathologists. Whenever I'd visit that's where he'd be. He was almost there, had almost rid himself of the stutter. I shudder to think what will happen now—this is going to set him back irrevocably. I can already hear him fighting through it again, swallowing and pausing unnecessarily, buying time. He needs good news. And Mommy is coming.

John

No, I did not notice the car during my interrogation. It's true, there was no reason for me to ever know what car belonged to a local weatherwoman, but surely the yellow tape should've been a tipoff. Dad would be so disappointed in my lack of attention to detail. Now that they were towing it, now that there was a small crowd of people gathered in a large semicircle behind the officers, less than strategically placed along the perimeter of the lot, now I had no choice but to notice. It's not remarkable, really—it's a truck, not unlike what many people around here drive. Like in Alaska, too. In school we'd all made jokes about men driving around in those monstrosities as overcompensating. But, if that were true, all men around here would have to have tiny dicks. Plus, our hypothesis lacked a theory for the female drivers.

I tried to imagine what she must've looked like driving that monstrosity. What she must've felt like. Her lanky limbs did lend themselves well to a hefty vehicle like the one being towed so it's not unnatural. When the procession out of the lot commenced, I began to slowly elbow my way toward my station. You would think everyone had gotten all the staring out of their system. Yes, I'm the guy the cops had a talking to just outside the store yesterday. Yes, yes, I'm the guy who spoke to Peta Knudsen last before she disappeared. I'd much rather they ask. I'm not foreign to being stared at but that doesn't mean that years of experience had made me a fan. Do it, ask me! Don't we learn by communicating? Isn't that how we get rid of prejudices and preconceived notions? But, of course, I just shove my backpack into my locker located in the corner of a large, bare-walled closet that we call an employee lounge. It's hardly a room, let alone a lounge, with its all of three chairs, of course, but it's there to afford a break, even if bleak and momentary, from the constant prying eyes. Maybe I should've showed it to Peta.

Peta's Journal Entry

I say this is bull, Doctor Burgos. We should probably talk about your issues, sometimes. You know, just to mix it up. I'm not saying we should talk about them all the time (I am paying to hang out with you, after all), but surely a little departure from me could prove beneficial for you. And me too, to be honest! It's pretty obvious you have issues. Come on. For example, you catch me so much as looking in the direction of your desk photos that you snatch the fucking picture frame from your desk so fast I thought I hallucinated. You threw it deep into your drawer, like hiding a joint from your dad (I would imagine)! I mean, what's that about? I mean, I get that therapists are meant to remain anonymous and a clean slate and all that, but still, this deserves a conversation. All I saw was that it was a photo of you and two men. I can only presume one of them is your son because he

54

was younger, the other—your ex? Because I heard you're divorced, right? I'm sorry if my catching a glimpse of your family is so offensive to you. Or maybe you were alarmed, or even scared. It was a passing glance, not even a stare. I'm sorry. Nothing malicious, nothing to be afraid of. It's different from when I was on, like, three different medications—then I just stared because blinking usually proved too great an effort. No, now I have some vague notion of purpose. But if I was only mildly curious before, you hurling the picture out of sight in the manner that you did surely whetted my appetite for some actual juice. Is there juice? Doc, look, I've been with my problems long enough to more than merely begin to grow sick of them—of talking about them, of writing about them. I mean, I'll continue with this journal, of course (if for nothing else then to simply keep practicing my cursive in this digital age), but there are only so many times I can talk about the root of my anxiety, the root of my insomnia, the reason for my occasional desire to take a few extra wide strides into that cold body of water located dangerously close to my house with pockets full of pebbles. Not unlike that author character from The Hours. Which one was that, again? Nicole Kidman played her, remember? Big prosthetic nose? It'll come to me.   Anyway, you wanted me to talk about my mother. Predictably, you think my problems go further than Harry but no further than Mommy. I'm surprised you hadn't jumped on the Mommy bandwagon months ago. All the others had.

Here goes, then. Knock yourself out. Though, of course, you won't read any of this. Not a word. But, obviously, this exercise is designed to outline my thoughts for the live therapy, right? You are likely to hear all this verbatim. I'm not wrong.

So… It was always just the two of us—Mommy and me. Or is it 'I?' I don't know. But yes, it was always just the two of us. Well, mostly. Sometimes she was married or had a boyfriend, but it never lasted. Oh, and, when I say "just the two of us," I mean if you don't count the other painters, sculptors, and basket weavers at one or another "commune" we used to call home at any particular point in *time. There were always men around so it's not like I grew up without a father-figure, strictly speaking, in case you're going to go down that rabbit-hole of a theory. There were enough male role models in my life, blah blah blah. It was, however, a bit of a nomadic lifestyle. We moved around a lot. Sometimes with Mommy's boyfriends, and sometimes without. And much to Mommy's recurring dismay, I always insisted on taking the last pet adopted in any one town on with us to the next. She was relieved when the last cat I took in got run over by a local multimedia artists' motorcycle and it was too late for me to adopt another before the move, especially with college coming up and all.*

I moved out of that last house weeks before classes began in Seattle. Watching me pack seemed to give Mommy a sudden onset of the maternal gene. First time in 18 years! Not in terms of raiding Bed Bath and Beyond, helping me decorate my dorm room, reminding me that I should call home soon or anything. No, nothing like that. But it was something vaguely akin to a maternal gene coming alive, nevertheless. She grew contemplative. Thoughtful. Maybe she simply grew inspired—I was finally vacating her space and she would finally be able to redecorate! I watched her grow possessed. One day, she declared that she simply had to have another child before it was too late. You know, while she still could, at least biologically, get things right. It had to be a Taurus or a Virgo and not be "spawn of Soviet filth," which was the term of endearment she used for my biological father (whom, as you may have gathered by the descriptor, hailed from the USSR, and whom I'd never met). That moniker sure was awesome during the Cold War. I don't need a shrink to explain to me exactly why I sought a job in television. Not all meteorologists have to press remote control buttons in front of green screens, of course, but those other avenues were of no interest to me. Don't get too proud of all the pretty certificates on your wall there, Dr. Burgos. Any layman could figure this one out. "See, mommy, spackle some makeup on me and my dad's genes don't look so bad." I get fan letters and everything! Creepy ones, even. Surely, that counts for something. I don't think she buys it, though. Plus, it's a scientific profession—my mind's precise-

56

not like Sioux's. That precious budding artist see's the world with eyes and mind wide open. Like her mother. Ironically (or not), Sioux never met her father either. But we do know Mommy had a list of criteria so maybe we can assemble him in our collective imagination. It was as if she were signing up for eHarmony, only she wasn't. I woke up one morning and she was scouting wherever she went—more like casting, even. It was more than a little unsettling, but we all cope in our own way and I had to get out of there despite (or is it in spite) of the drama. It was just time to leave Portland, period. Between mommy casting a sperm donor and the epic breakup with my very first boyfriend, I was pretty much done with Portland. You see, the law student I'd met waiting tables at a diner in town had just left me for a pregnant ex. It was like a very special episode of Beverly Hills, 90210 or something resembling it. It had been a lovely, desperate, reckless, butterflies-in-the-stomach, knees-grow-weak-when-he-enters-the-room whirlwind kind of a love affair. The kind you can only have at the age of eighteen. We rode Ferris Wheels, shared popcorn at the movies, made-out in both front and back seats of my car. And then it was all over, just like that. I lost my virginity one day and my boyfriend another. So yeah, I could not wait to leave Portland. Communal showers were nothing new to me, so I had little by way of freshman anxiety. And hey, it all worked out! Eventually, I met and married man who allegedly became the love of my life and I became a local celebrity by way of interpreting weather charts, a glorified weather girl. And Mommy did all right for herself—Sioux is indeed the exotic beauty she was craving when she sent me on my merry way into adulthood.

So, what's the verdict? Do we need to delve further into these issues? Should I parcel them out and unpack them in future entries? I'm not sure if I did what was asked of me in this assignment either, now that I think about it. I mean, I'll pay you either way—I need a place to go three times a week regardless of what you have me write about, so it's up to you. And anything is a break from that "let's talk about the dead son" line of questioning. Really, I can spare a few more dozen words on mommy. Maybe it'll distract me from wondering what the hell was up with that picture you hid from me today, who knows. One can hope! Oh, and Virginia Wolf is the name of that character from The Hours. There!

Evelyn

"Gwenny' is a silly name, don't you think, officer?"

"Detective."

"Right, sorry, Detective," Evelyn waved off Detective Clark as she lowered the child in her arms onto the sheepskin rug in her feet. "But don't you agree? It's just so ordinary!"

"It's sweet, I think," Detective Clark ventured having squatted down to the floor to ruffle the little girl's hair, of which she had a less than generous amount. Evelyn lamented this point often, both her daughters having been born with heads full of hair. "Of course, I understand why you'd say that. You named your girls Peta and Sioux," she tried cautiously, grinning for safety. Evelyn was used to the way people often said deriding things to her half-jokingly, as if she didn't understand that any good joke was only part that—a joke.

Her hands trembling, Evelyn took to braiding her hair to calm her nerves. It was honey brown, only individual gray hairs highlighting the mane. It had always been luxurious. She was sure Peta was always jealous of it. It was thicker than her daughter's, requiring very little product. She remembered Peta began graying early, coming back from college her first summer with dusty temples. Evelyn's fingers worked fast now, seemingly of their own volition, the fish tail descending from her jawbone down to her shoulder.

"Evelyn, Gwenny is ri— right there. Please do not ta— talk like that," Peter groaned as he poured himself a scotch before demonstratively hurling it at his throat. He always did have a flare for the dramatics. Evelyn blamed such on his scattered upbringing. Certainly, he'd had to learn a mechanism or two for standing out, getting into people's graces. She never had a doubt in her mind that this stutter was part of that too—a way to get sympathy and attention. The fact that it was now coming back so quickly only confirmed that instinct. Evelyn watched him with a merciful smile as he slammed the tumbler down on the granite countertop of her daughter's bar stand and rushed to scoop up her granddaughter in his arms, whisking her out to the deck, the door sliding closed behind them with a muted thud. He needed way too much attention; she'd warned Peta of this in the beginning. He wanted you to look—thus the floor to ceiling windows. *Well, we're in now, buddy.* Her daughter didn't have the Soviet strength her features promised. She was weak. She was bound to crack, eventually. It must've been exhausting assuring this man of his sufficiency, of the fact that he's never done anything to warrant a fate with so much death in it. Evelyn did her best not to roll her eyes when he kissed the girl's temple.

"Mommy didn't want Peta to have Gwenny. At the time, I mean. It was too soon." Little Sioux, the people-pleaser, said this loud enough for Peter to likely still hear, hurrying to finish the sentence before he could lock the door from outside and walk down to the dock. *A dock!* That was just so silly and unnecessary—they never owned a boat, what did he need with a dock?

59

"Sioux, dear, that makes me sound heartless. Like I didn't want Gwenny to be born! Let's not be selective with facts. I love Gwenny. I just wish Peta were stronger before taking on another child after what happened to Harry, that's all. And she is so pretty, she is hard not to love. That's exactly why she deserves a better name. Look at her with her big green eyes, that olive skin. Peta, my Peta, may she forgive me, she turned out more like that bland father of hers. She's got that milk-maid look about her, wouldn't you say, Sioux?" Evelyn turned to her young daughter, inquisitively. Momentarily, letting herself wonder if her first born shared her supposed revelations with Sioux, she squeezed her knee tight when the girl didn't respond right away. Her eyes, which were perennially rimmed with a messy kohl liner, were open wide. Detective Clark wondered if perhaps mother Morozova partook in something organic to help with grief—she'd never experienced such an even-keeled mother of the missing in her entire career. "Now, Sioux came out more dignified— otherworldly, even," she continued. "Her dad was much more carefully chosen. Well, to begin with—he was *chosen*." Evelyn patted her daughter's black hair, lone tears marking the length of her long face etched delicately with fine wrinkles, as if someone of her own grade in the art world had taken to her with a chisel. Only occasionally did she let her fist close on the girl's tresses before relaxing her fingers again.

Evelyn could see that Detective Foster took Peter's bait, watching him cuddle her granddaughter out on the dock. *She* was the mother, *she* needed the attention, not the overgrown orphan with mommy issues. Evelyn snorted, whisking away her tears before proceeding to stroke her younger daughter's hair with renewed vehemence. Sioux had learned not to flinch years ago; Peta never learned. This familiar posture of Sioux's calmed Evelyn a bit

"Nothing was the same with you, dear. I had a plan with you—a whole master plan. Your father modeled for me— a graduate student making pocket money."

She watched Sioux blink, wishing someone had the sense to interrupt her in time. She did like engaging in unsolicited soliloquies, which often embarrassed Peta at parent-teacher conferences. But Sioux truly was her masterpiece. She would tell this to anyone willing to listen, which, in turn, embarrassed Sioux. But she couldn't help herself. Peta had inherited her stubbornness, but it was Sioux who was the looker. Those long eyelashes, those cheekbones. The girl sat complacent at her mother's side, her arm wooden, firm in her mother's lap, their fingers interlaced. The only thing the two sisters had in common besides gender was their hair length, Evelyn couldn't help but compare. Sioux oozed exoticism—her almond-shaped eyes, soot black hair arranged in those myriad braids, skin the color of creamed coffee, curves of a dieting belly- dancer. Peta was, and regretfully so, more of that farmland beauty queen variety: all doe eyed, she was pretty in a way that wasn't as intimidating as her sister. Evelyn kissed her younger daughter on the forehead when she saw a lone tear roll out of the girl's left eye. She'd heard the story in its entirety before. Outside, Peter sat crossed legged on the grass across from Gwenny. Evelyn had to crane her neck to see anything, but she saw that his spine was curved, and his head was tilted. If you couldn't hear, which they couldn't, the picture conveyed engaged, cooperative play. Evelyn felt her eyes roll before she could do anything about it. What a good dad, ladies and gentlemen! Just look at the dedication, soak in the love. Too busy herself before she could make a bigger spectacle of herself, Evelyn reached for her phone with the hand that wasn't holding on to Sioux's with all the predictable desperation and thumbed aimlessly between icons. *I'm telling her everything,* was Peta's last message to her mother. Evelyn's stomach grew cold.

Peter

With Gwenny banging two plastic spades together at his feet, Peter tried to think past the whoosh of his own blood in his ears and the water hitting the rocks below. He felt his mother-in-law's steel eyes on him as he tried to focus on the detectives' words. They'd joined him, eventually, Evelyn having released them after holding court. The woman sat and wiped her glasses on her scarf. The mere sight of her made Peter's shoulders inch their way up to his ears.

"A journal?"

"Yes, the Doctor had her keep one for therapeutic purposes."

Peter scratched at his receding hairline. He was too young for it and looked it.

"A journal? Really? Peta keeping a journal? I understand you have no reason to know this, but that's just comical." Peter screwed his eyebrows tight in demonstration of his skepticism, a deep crease above his nose. The idea of his wife, pen in hand, writing down her innermost thoughts as part of her therapy was laughable. The same Peta who mocked the idea of therapy in the first place? The Peta who abhorred writing anything down for fear of paper trail, if not fear of commitment? The woman who didn't even keep a day planner in college, her brain seemingly capable of storing all due dates without any need for a calendar, keeping a therapeutic journal because some doctor said so?

"Yes, a journal. Dr. Burgos thought it would be beneficial—"

"Well, I don't know where it'd be if such is the case," Peter interrupted Detective Foster, proud to have uttered another sentence without having to pause, to breathe or swallow to buy time. Afraid his bravado wouldn't last under the gray-eyed gaze of his mother-in-law, Peter knelt down to pet his daughter's head. The act seemed unnatural and he was sure the detectives would think so too. Here's a dad putting on a show, they'd think. Here he is pretending to be hands-on in crisis. Impressions are just that—they are instantaneous, and you can't rationalize or explain them away. His body language was hurried and awkward. He could see now, as he cringed in a way that he hoped was as imperceptible as he intended for it to be. Changing anything now would do more harm than good. It'd be better for his image not to flex at all now.

"There is no real reason for Dr. Burgos to lie about this. It could be enlightening to the case if we could find it," the Detective noted without feigning quite enough conviction.

Peter wasn't sure why he felt his stomach drop but it did. He was afraid it'd scare Gwenny with its whoosh of a sound on its speedy descent.

"Oh?"

That sounded more unsure than Peter would've ideally preferred. He kept his translucent eyes on his daughter's fine hair. He knew every move was important now. The wrong one may indicate to them that he may have something to hide. That's how he would've reported the story himself were he in front of the camera again, or even back at the studio in any official capacity, for that matter. Instead, he was told to take it easy by a punk half a decade his junior but one step above him on the food chain. Over the phone! More specifically, he was told to take care of his child in this "confusing and difficult time." As if he needed instruction to do so. Or permission. They all couldn't wait for the body to surface; that broadcast would bring some actual ratings to their local town news. This wasn't something you had to be an insider to understand.

"If she writes one, anyone reading it would be some kind of violation of privacy." As a former on-camera reporter and producer, he was always looking for an angle. Peta had accused him of this when Harry died, too, when he wanted to sue the place and its so-called teachers. She believed he'd derive too much professional credit by doing so. And it wouldn't bring back their son. She was right.

She should've gone back to the first doctor after Gwenny was born. Sure, he medicated more and the resulting state was unsustainable during pregnancy, but were he still in charge maybe Peta wouldn't have had the energy to do something this stupid. Dr. Burgos was new in town and her headshot was plastered all over the local circulars. A blonde of an unnatural shade, she squinted thoughtfully in the photo, emulating empathy. Of course, Peta, freshly impregnated after years of stubborn attempts, was intrigued. Going off meds cold turkey wasn't something she was prepared to do, but continuing the massive doses she'd been on since Harry's death wasn't something Peter was prepared to let her do past the first positive pregnancy test. But he liked the medicated Peta, he had to admit. She was calmer, more pliable then. But no, the state was unsustainable. It was out of the question. He hoped she'd go back after she'd be done with breastfeeding, but something about Dr. Burgos made her stay. And the reviews were good. Dr. Burgos had practiced in Alaska for over a decade, focusing in family and bereavement counseling. The only complaints they had been able to find on the woman was that occasionally, though her waiting room was empty, a patient would be kept waiting longer than fifteen minutes. This struck some as mysterious, selfish even, but surely that was some country folk; city people like the Knudsen's would surely be okay having to flip through an expired magazine or two for a few extra minutes. There was also some disciplinary action in her records, but no details were publicly available. Peta's argument had been that since she was able to retain her license and work in a whole new state, how bad could it have been. Peter would've loved to say that his journalistic instincts had told him to investigate further, but he was really tired that night. And Peta really did have a point. And she was going to be the patient, after all, not him. Hers was the deciding vote. But people talked. And being a newsman, Peter couldn't avoid all the noise. A small town wouldn't be such without its residents doing some side research—a single, professional woman does tend to draw attention. Why was she here alone? Why weren't there photos of her with family on Facebook? Was she divorced? Didn't she have a son? And wasn't he black? Did she lose custody? These questions only excited Peta. In between sorting through the Weather Service updates and gagging on toothpaste, Peta Googled away. She must've reported her findings to Peter at some point, he was almost certain, but he was finally getting somewhere with speech therapy and hardly willing to spare any brain capacity on a shrink hired to get his wife through the gestation of his child with as few drugs as possible; so long as she was licensed and an in-network provider, he didn't care about the lady's personal life.

Detective Foster coughed, prying Peter from his memories. Slowly, he raised himself to his feet and pushed his shoulders back, hoping the action would win him a couple of inches in height. Gwenny continued to bang away at his feet.

"I didn't know about the existence of the damn thing. For all I know, that doctor is making it up." The last part flew out unconsciously. Poor taste, surely, to accuse the doctor. When his vision clouded by some moisture pooling behind his eyes' rims, Peter bit his tongue. He wanted so bad to rub his forehead when he remembered they didn't need him for this. They were here only to gauge his responses. As far as Peter was concerned, this was all a big test—an exercise in provocation. Just like showing him that security video.

Peter picked up his daughter and placed her on his hip. He stepped in the direction of the door, praying the gesture would read confident but not cocky.

"Is there an office Peta used that we can look through?" Detective Foster ventured. Surely these cops were seasoned enough to know that someone of Peter's education would agree to no such thing, but he couldn't blame them for trying.

"I'll do the looking myself, tha—thank you," he laughed, surely untimely. "Now, if there are no updates on the investigation…"

The detectives exchanged a look; Peter, shifting Gwenny's weight on his hip, could not decide if it was meant to look rehearsed or not.

"Actually, there is something," Detective Foster sighed, visibly weighing if this information was timely. "Actually, we can now confirm that Peta never boarded her train."

Peta's Journal Entry

I love these assignments, Dr. Burgos! Well, I don't really, but what are we without sarcasm?

So, this week I am supposed to tell you why it is that I "decided" to become a mother in the first place. Yes, those are quotation marks because I think it's funny that you think it was a choice. Was it for you? I occasionally do have to remind myself that indeed everything is a decision of sorts, and therefore a choice, but still though. No, I wasn't coerced, and yes, I could've said no, but I don't think of motherhood as a real choice. Not with my husband's background, not with my need to one-up my own mother. And don't forget that golden "it's time" line of daily questioning. Like, all of that combines leaves semblance of a choice. Though it was time, clearly. Or so they told us. Seriously, literally everyone told us this. So yes, thus the quotation marks.

Now, I already had an entry on my own mommy (kind of), and, contrary to what your stupid honor system may allow, I don't (often) cheat and go back and edit my previous entries. But this is relevant to the entry at hand, so here's some more on mommy-dearest for the context of it all—the bigger picture. What do you care so much if you claim not to read these anyway?

You see, Mommy was a busy woman when I was growing up. A self-coined Renaissance woman, it was a rare moment when she was not sketching, molding, or blistering her fingers on her banjo (which she decided to pick up along the way—somewhere between our Bumsfuck, Connecticut commune and the San Diego one). Whether I was allowed to be whiny or loud or bored depended on what occupied Mommy at the moment. If she was busy, it wasn't uncommon for me to be swatted away with whatever rag was at hand, and if she was feeling maternal—we could doodle together. I wasn't much good at that, either, so that rarely ended in cuddles. But, as Peter likes to remind me, at least I had a mother. Have. Granted, though, she truly did not come into motherhood by choice so any bitching and moaning of mine is ill-placed.

There's footage of me crying on a live-feed from my room at PeaceHealth, where I gave birth to Harry. Peter was back at work already, beaming in front of the camera—a proud father. People think I was crying those proverbial tears of joy everyone talks about, but they were mostly tears of fear. Imagine—not a week in and I was already terrified! It wasn't looking good. I was expecting to be a tireless, fearless mother, and here I was—exhausted and petrified, with sore nipples to boot. He was here—now what? I was entirely too quick to understand that I wasn't the serene, happy-to-be-up-every-two-hours-around-the-clock mother I envisioned myself becoming, and that stung like a motherfucker. Harry stayed in the room with me because Peter said that letting him stay at the nursery would cause rumors to spread. He wouldn't latch (Harry, that is), and starting formula right away is apparently frowned upon. I hadn't slept for three nights straight. Those were not tears of joy. It was just that I already knew I was my mom.

When we got home, Catriona was waiting there and paid to take over. But what prevented her from labeling me lazy if I chose to just hand Harry over the moment I got in the door? A nondisclosure agreement seemed like an overreach given that we were hardly the hosts of The Today Show. So, I stayed up some more. When I'd finally gone to sleep, I'd slept for days, it seemed, but it was only three consecutive hours. And I hated being awake the second my eyes fluttered open again. Maybe a little less so than I do now, but I'd always been too tired to enjoy my baby the way the nurses instructed me to at discharge. Nursing took hours, as did pumping. Guilt over resenting anything coming in contact with my breast took up the rest of the time. The fact that I produced enough milk to also feed the already overweight stray cat who loved to visit our deck didn't soothe any of the guilt, so as Harry grew, I eventually gave up and had begun to spend an increasing amount of time playing Trivia Crack in my office if Catriona was on duty. Which inevitably caused more self-resentment, more guilt. It was hard to win. So, what makes me so different from mommy in the end? Not much. Maybe that rag. And I wasn't raped, and Harry wasn't the product of such, so I was worse, actually! I had a husband, a nanny, my American Citizenship. I had zero excuses. Still, I couldn't wait to get back to work.

Well, there you have it: I'm just not a very good mother. I didn't have much of a chance to notice with Harry. Not after I went back to work and him dying so soon after. But now, with Gwenny... I'm home alone with her without Marsha (our new nanny) often enough to know for sure that I would've never gotten better even if Harry had lived. I'm just not very good. You'd think I'd be grateful now, that it would carry me over. You'd think that'd be motivation enough. Nope—still tired, still short-tempered. I don't want to come running with a pacifier, I don't want to sit on the floor and bang pots together. A mother twice over, I'm still not entirely sure what people mean when they say that happiness lies in watching your children grow. For me, this whole exercise has been about anxiety and resentment, and not much else. First smile, first full head support—there'd been flashes of happiness immediately followed by anxiety of the what-if-he'll-never-do-this-again variety. And eventually it did all stop. It ended. I was right. Turns

69

out, it doesn't always feel good to be right. And now it's the same with Gwenny, only more so: I'm simultaneously anxious about milestones delayed, too tired to do anything about it, with a little resentment mixed in as to why she can and her brother could not... Nice, right? Mother of the year.

I want to go back to sleep, but here she is, at the foot of the bed, unloading my lipsticks out of my dresser drawer with alarming precision. They'll probably say she too has PDD. Or maybe I have undiagnosed PDD. Or we each have our own Ps and Ds?

You know what? I've been writing for about an hour now and still haven't answered your question. Why? This big fat why. Here goes: I'll just summarize in my conclusion—the first time around, mostly it was because I was thirty-eight, and with Gwenny it was some unspoken "Operation Replacement." Yes, the sad reason our plump Gwenny came into this world is because we had a person to replace. It was important to the community, somehow, I think.

This could've been a much shorter entry, now that I think about it.

Okay, now that that's out of the way—let's talk about you! Why did you become a mother?

<u>Gael</u>

Everyone pretty much had figured that much—Peta never boarded that train. CCTV footage was spotty, as were the cops, but she never boarded the train.

"But I don't understand," Sioux whined. "She had something to tell me. She would not just leave me hanging."

The scariest thing to Gael was that Sioux believed this with every fiber of her being, with every ounce of her birdlike frame. It was both endearing and infuriating how someone in her 20s could be so innocent; it both made him want to hug her and squeeze her skinny little throat. Because *how can anyone be so stupid, so naïve?* Her love for her sister bordered on infatuation, as far as Gael was concerned. It was like when you watch a movie and become so taken with the star on the screen that you want to consume everything with him or her in it, even if it's a three second spot on *Law & Order,* and then can't stop talking about it all, bringing up the poor actor in every conversation, unbeknownst to them, until you feel like a sad little stalker. It was like that with Sioux and her sister. Only it was her *sister!* And Sioux didn't feel bad about it. That part wasn't endearing. She tried telling him that he didn't understand their relationship because he was an only child, but it wasn't that. He understood love, he understood admiration. This was worse—this was infatuation in that she fully believed the sentiment was returned fully and to a tee. From where Gael stood, not only was this disturbing, it wasn't true. It wasn't natural. He rubbed Sioux's back as she heaved, talking about her text messages as if those served as proof that Peta simply would be right back, had to be right back.

Nothing was normal about this family. For one thing, nobody cried. Not the mom, not the husband. The baby cried but that wasn't a dedicated cry. The only one who cried was Sioux and it seemed she cried on everyone's behalf. A proxy of sorts. He learned that word in his Intro to Business Law class he took as an elective.

"Any way to see where she was headed? After the train station where she didn't get her train, that is?" he heard Peter ask, his eyes on the verge of tears but not quite. They

71

were always like this. Granted, he'd only met Peter that one time, but he remembered this about him from then too. It'd bothered him then also, so the quirk stayed with him. Gael had to remind himself to unclench his jaw. Then and now.

"It's patchy. To be precise, she did appear to seem to want to go to Seattle," Detective Foster said locking eyes with Sioux. Merciful as its intention, it hurt Gael somewhere around where he imagined his diaphragm to be. "She bought the ticket but was late to board," the Detective explained, nodding emphatically at the near-shuddering Sioux. "She left the station the minute she saw the train leave the station. It'd be reasonable to estimate that she'd be looking for a different way to get there." There was so much faux compassion in that voice, it took effort for Gael not to stand in front of Sioux to serve as a shield.

"Anything more specific than an estimation?" Evelyn piped up, taking a break from playing with her hair. It was like an insecure eight-year-old girl was trapped in a body of a seventy-year old woman. Gael wasn't sure how old she really was but seventy seemed fair. Out of the corner of his eye he registered Peter begin to bounce Gwenny on his hip a little too aggressively for his taste. "Bus? Plane?" Evelyn probed.

"No, neither. We're canvassing neighboring businesses for more CCTV footage. For now, all we see is her exiting the station." Detective Clark clearly didn't appreciate Evelyn for all that she so obviously tried to be. "There is a car rental nearby, which is our next stop. However, before you get your hopes up, it needs to be noted that there were no credit card charges by a Hertz or the like. A search party is going out again tonight."

He must've missed when Peter shifted Gwenny from his right hip to the left, but when Gael looked up at him from the top of Sioux's head, she was playing with his left ear. Peter squirmed almost imperceptibly, looking as if he were gearing up to speak.

"Wha— why was her ca— car left at the store's lot? It's not that close—why did she walk? And has anyone tried her phone since the night of?" It hurt how much hope was packed into that one combative sentence: his eyes seemed to glimmer more, his voice was higher. Watching Peter speak was painful, in general. Gael felt a flush to his own cheeks on his behalf. It made you feel like averting your eyes, but he didn't.

"Oh!" Foster exclaimed, a pale finger stabbing the air above. "I meant to tell you before! The car was out of gas! She must've literally been riding on empty. The way the timeline stands now—she saw her doctor, hopped over to the store, made it over to the station on foot, and that's when we lose her."

And at that, Sioux's lanky little body folded into an untidy heap into Gael's arms.

"Oh, and the phone was inside the car. She left that behind, too. She texted both her sister and her mother often in the last few days before her disappearance now, didn't she? Not much to say to you, Peter."

Dr. Burgos

Even if all they were doing was looking for any kind of evidence of their son's relationship with her patient, Dr. Burgos's heart raced at the newfound proximity to her ex-husband. Their elbows occasionally touching was almost worth this mess. John made it clear by not returning any of his mom's calls or texts that he wasn't interested in helping. On her way from her office, Dr. Burgos stopped by the store to make sure her son was still at his station. It was of comfort to see that he was. Her son scanning coupons ten to twelve hours a day was not something she planned for him, but he wasn't with the cops and that was good enough for now.

"Are you sure you saw them together?" Andrew asked as he bent over his son's sock drawer, looking for some connection. He was dressed in what Dr. Burgos could swear were his old college jeans and a similarly aged t-shirt with cut off sleeves. No one packs like this by accident, the doctor's training reminded her.

Dr. Burgos, her back to the love of her life, knew what that question was meant to convey: was she sober enough at the time to be a reliable witness?

"Yes, I only drink at night," she muttered, swallowing saliva pooling in the back of her throat as quietly as she could. Abandoning her son's desk, she collapsed on his bed and rubbed her eyes with the heels of her palms. This was exhausting.

"Okay, so let's take it from the top—are you in the habit of stalking all your patients or just those of quasi-celebrity status?

Dr. Burgos heard the hydraulics of her son's desk chair whoosh with her ex-husband's weight, but she didn't dare move. He may still scare easy, she feared. She could already imagine him arching his brow—he was waiting for her to trip.

"You're missing out on a stellar career as a prosecutor!" she tried, anyway.

Work that day was an unproductive, distracted, fragmented five hours. Between the endless phone calls from curious spectators enquiring as to her treatment of the missing Peta Knudsen (and some called from as far as San Francisco, which flattered her, to her own surprise) and the Greens' painful marriage counseling, she couldn't wait to be back home, where she knew Andrew was waiting. She visualized him on her couch, legs crossed, a mug of coffee in hand, his laptop balancing on his knee while she listened to her patients bicker. "Not everyone who fights to stay together is supposed to stay together." Andrew had once admitted this in their own marriage counseling session and she had taken this to heart, signing the divorce papers right after their appointment at the cluttered breakfast nook in their kitchen. She couldn't bring herself to divulge this precious piece of wisdom in her own practice, of course, but she'd be lying if she said the mantra hadn't affected her treatment. The Greens didn't have anything but their bank account in common, and they may as well share some of its contents with her before realizing this much for themselves.

Andrew waited. His pauses, silences, were often the worst. He could wait you out as long as was necessary, no squirming, no breaking. This was when she usually wanted him the most. Those smoldering eyes burned hot and they burned deep. Even sober, it was all she could do not to throw panties at him as if he were some rock star.

"I had a window between clients and thought I'd stop by to say hi to your son—" It was as if she were trying so hard to stay cool and collected, she accidentally overcompensated. But Andrew still didn't bite. He continued to wait. Lying there, on her son's rented, lumpy mattress, she painted him in her mind's eye—jaw strong and flexed, eyes well-hooded. There were barely visible holes where his piercings used to be in college—right eyebrow, left earlobe, right nostril. Andrew removed those in law school, when he arrived and interning at an environmental non-profit in Portland without any pay was no longer a viable option. That was around the time when those dreadlocks went too. His tattoos were still there, of course, but she was no longer privy to seeing him in all his full, beautiful glory, and most of his ink was well-hidden. God bless him, he made money any way he knew how back then. Any side gig would do. She didn't care where the formula money came from and didn't ask many questions. He always did the right thing. Her eyes watered at the memory of his youth, as did her mouth.

"That's one lucky coincidence. Want to try again?" he led when she reluctantly sat up to remind herself of the shape of his nose.

"Look, what do you want me to say? John kept telling me about this lady asking him questions about him. Said that whenever she came to the store, she always made sure to seek him out, start a conversation. It was creeping him out! For John to talk to *me* about it, it must've really been creeping him out, you know! He said it was the lady from

76

TV so I kind of put two and two together. I wanted to go see it for myself. Can you blame me?"

Andrew shut his eyes. He inhaled deeply, his lips parting as if in inquiry. He shook it off with the slightest tremor of the head.

"How well do you know Peta?" he asked after a swallow that sounded too good to his former wife. "And what exactly did you see when you followed her?"

"Nothing! I saw her go inside. I followed. I saw her head for John's cash register right away, throw a bottle of water on the belt, along with something else. They seemed to be arguing about something. Then she left with her crap and John got busy with the next customer. I think. I don't remember."

"Did you mention this to the cops when they came to see you?" Andrew asked as he leaned back in his chair, further away from Dr. Burgos, pretending not to notice that she never answered his initial question; as if to make up for what he took away. He spread his legs wide. This game of invisible racquet ball didn't used to be their sole method of communication. She could try to parcel out the blame, but she was also aware that Andrew's only fault lay in his proficiency at collectedness and responsibility.

"No, I didn't," she sighed, abandoning the reminisce. Feeling her thighs warm under Andrew's gaze, she took to her son's walls. He'd been living there for almost half a year now, but the room still looked bare. All her furniture rented, there was a twin bed, a four-drawer chest, and a desk that served more as a repository for clutter than a place for him to do his homework. No posters, nothing to say he lived here. His room in Juneau looked different but that was home. No one made a home of a motel room, and that's all this was for John. He even left his clothes out, as if expecting housekeeping. On Andrew's watch, things were folded and put away. They were always the best of friends; she was the occasional sitter. Even when he was little, people always presumed she was hired help.

"You didn't think that mentioning that you saw the woman who's missing the day she disappeared was worth mentioning?" Andrew cocked his head to the side asking this. He could always see deeper than her skin. "What aren't you telling me? What scandalous shit did you talk about in her sessions?"

Weighing her options, evaluating her word choices, Dr. Burgos said nothing.

"Lena, you really think there are no cameras there? You think they haven't seen the exchange on tape yet? How many black young men with dreadlocks does Bellingham Organic Produce employ?"

Fuck, he couldn't know that she didn't only drink at night.

Her flush was now radiating in her extremities. She had no comeback. Andrew was right—this was inevitable. She had to come out with it.

Andrew

Andrew must've asked Lena how well she knew Peta at least three different ways. Neither one of her vague attempts at answering bore any resemblance to neither the truth nor what he was looking for. Yes, this was her patient, yes, she allegedly found her boring and privileged, yes, she thought she was interested in her son, but that wasn't it. He knew Peta Knudsen before she was a Knudsen. He did and that meant she did too.

Managing Lena used to be a full-time job. Maybe not their entire life together but enough of it, anyway, to let the rest of the memories rust. He wasn't expecting to have to continue doing this five years post legal separation, but he couldn't entirely blame her for this particular wrinkle. The coincidence of it made him lightheaded. While she was at work basking in the new fame as the Missing Woman's Therapist, Andrew put Lena's Wi-Fi to try to string together the woman's nonsensical ramblings into something cohesive. It only took a simple Google News search.

The headshot didn't quite knock the wind out of him. No, he could still breathe, he could still feel the floor under his feet. But there was a distinct buzzing behind his eyelids that he registered, this vague static of recognition. She was two decades older, a little softer around the corners of her eyes but that particular shade of brown was still in there, the same chocolate in her hair. He almost knocked over his coffee mug all over his laptop when the article finally loaded, complete with the picture.

He knew her before she was a Knudsen. She had a different last name then. She must have because, according to her channel's website, there was also a Peter Knudsen and he didn't remember her having a brother. He never knew her last name, whatever it was. She was just Peta—an eager eighteen-year-old marrying ketchups in the back of the diner. He could still picture those pink-tiled walls, smell the stench of stale carpeting. For the longest time, that's all he knew about her. "Marrying Ketchups" may as well have been her name as far as he was concerned for months. She was mousy but had spunk in that defiant way she held her chin as she held the narrow necks of the clunky bottles. Had she paid attention that day coming into the kitchen instead of him having to ask his manager for a change of clothing when she dumped a pitcher of water all over his shirt, she'd forever remain the Ketchup girl. Instead, she laughed, and he liked it—her laughter. It made her mouth gape open in the most improbable of ways, displaying her large teeth in all their brilliance. On another face, it would've been hideous, but on her, it was becoming. And so, they went to the movies. And then bowling. And then the back (and front) of his car. This was fresh off Lena and the whole thing was a breath of fresh air. It was fluffy and light. At least until Lena found out she was pregnant, and the Ketchup girl lost her mind in the breakup of a relationship that never really could've or should've been called one.

The girl didn't look as mousy or spunky anymore. It could've been that particular headshot of the plastic variety that was to blame but somehow, even with all the makeup, she looked more ordinary than anything else. Her skin blended and matted to perfection, her hair highlighted a wide range of auburn, her lips the professional shade of glossy rose. She could have been anyone, anywhere in the country. You'd want to see her rattle off the weather forecast with a clicker in her hand while you drank your morning coffee, sure. He could see the appeal and felt his lips stretch into a smile. What were the odds?

It took another mug of coffee to finally Google her name. Once he had it, though, he was done before he was through with even half of it. Not much was available by way of any interest or information—her alma mater had a small interview with her published in an alumni magazine, her channel's page, her private Facebook page. Those gave him nothing. Born in Topeka, Kansas, raised in a variety of places by a single, immigrant mother, Peta went to college in Seattle, Washington and settled in Bellingham with her broadcaster husband. He saw a picture of the husband, too—another headshot template. He was handsome, albeit in an unconventional way. Still, he was man enough to see it—a large, open smile, soot black hair, an oversized set of unbelievably green eyes, and a severe jawline. They were an unlikely fitting couple. He was happy for her.

There was another article that popped up when searching both her and her husband's name. A news piece in a local paper, reprinted by a few larger ones, it was about their son dying while under care of a day care center. He was one and apparently died of anaphylactic shock. This was five years ago. This probably explained her relation to Lena—who wouldn't need therapy after something like that. Didn't seem like much of a stretch. The question that plagued him, and apparently his ex-wife as well, was what was Peta's connection to John? Sure, he remembered her leaving an insane number of messages after he broke it off, but for a professional, successful woman to come back decades later to stalk his son seemed incongruent. Lena may have been a high functioning drunk, but it was no wonder she didn't like this woman, whether or not she herself realized that the glossy woman was the same girl who once showed up at his doorstep with tear-stained face and unwashed hair just as she was moving in.

So, while the skies outside continued to darken, he kept asking her:

"How well did you know Peta?"

Peter

Peter was never in favor of a California king. Four people could comfortably fit on that landing strip of a mattress and they were never going to be the couple that condoned co-sleeping. Not with their topsy-turvy schedule. So, what was the point of ever purchasing such an ambitious bed? It was an obligation, not a place to rest. And now that Peta was no longer pretending to be coming to bed later, like she often did, he wasn't sure he should even be on top of the blankets, let alone under them. What was he doing in bed at all? What was he supposed to be doing? There was no script for this. The cops never left him a helpful pamphlet like the ones those numerous social workers he'd encountered throughout his life often left him with—first as a boy shuffled between a few too many households, and then as a father of a boy who passed away suddenly and prematurely. Even at ten, he'd always obediently peruse those on his own time, away from the eyes of grownups who routinely asked if he had any questions. These booklets were usually printed on cheap paper with ink that stained his fingertips and made him want to scrub under his nails immediately after. But he still wished he had one to thumb through now. It's been over forty-eight hours and he has done nothing. Was he supposed be proactive at this stage? He'd be asking these questions, as a journalist. Instead, he was hiding. Gwenny was long asleep, Marsha always tucking her in no later than 7:30pm. It was only 9pm now. He was, theoretically, free to go out and join the search party the detectives so proudly declared they'd set up. Shake a few hands, put in an appearance. He could, for example, step outside his front door and make a tearful plea in an exclusive interview to one of his peers. For starters, he could simply move: swing his legs out, land his feet on the cold wood floor, brace his toes to support his weight and simply *move*. Not like he was counting on any respectable number of minutes of sleep tonight. Still, he stayed put, his arms straight like those of a toy soldier, doing what only superficially could've been described as "resting" against his body. He was not resting, but you'd never tell.

Thursday, October 4th

Evelyn

Gwenny cried more urgently than Harry had. Not that she ever babysat her grandchildren, but she believed that visiting alone was enough for a statistical average of sorts. She observed the girl now as she lay in her crib getting red in the face. She tilted her head in observation. It was as if the child was afraid she wouldn't be heard if she didn't hit a certain decibel level or pitch. She may or may not have been wrong, that was the curious thing. She was born anxious. It's not an easy job replacing a dead sibling.

The guttural cries reminded Evelyn of her kids when they were each roughly Gwenny's age. That same desperation, that same audible fear of not being heard. Infants aren't original. She even had Sioux's hearing tested back then, fully entertaining the possibility that maybe the reason for her unnecessary volume was her inability to hear herself. Something about that auditory loop her landlady told her about. She was an audiologist-turned-entrepreneur. She could not for the life of her remember what exactly this business was. Sioux's hearing was fine, it turned out; she just liked to cry. She grew out of it eventually. The trick was to not reward this behavior. Evelyn rarely responded to whining or unsubstantiated crying. If either Peta or Sioux cried when they weren't obviously hurt, Evelyn never rushed to see what the matter was. Peta was slow to learn this, but Sioux was quicker. Gwenny, from the looks of it, wasn't ever going to learn, just like her mom. Peter ran to her at any indication of minor discomfort. So did that nanny. Now Sioux and Gael waited on her, bursting into the room at the first threat of vocalization. Just like Peta, this child wasn't going to learn to self-sooth, self-regulate during that vital, formative age.

Evelyn, her fingers tangled in her hair as she braided the few loose strands that had come undone from her bun, contemplated picking up Gwenny now. The kids were supposed to go out. Peter was nowhere to be found, as usual. It was like the man wore an invisibility cloak and could disappear from Evelyn's sight on demand. And Marsha was in the bathroom; it was unlikely that she heard Gwenny's wails. Evelyn didn't have many of these opportunities. It wasn't often that she had alone time with her granddaughter, whether she was crying or not. She reached into the crib, but her arms retracted half way in. She could stand to cry a little longer. She was dry, she was fed. She was fine. Instead, Evelyn snatched her phone out of her sleeve and snapped a few pictures of the pudgy girl. She was cute. It'd be nice to show a photo of her granddaughter to show around, she figured. She'd been accumulating a new crowd of friends in Victoria and was the only one who was not surrounded by an array of family photographs in their studio space.

It was interesting for Evelyn to note that she didn't want to break out of her skin at the sound of this child's shrieks. She attributed it to maturity. She would've never been able to stand for this with Peta, even when she was in her twenties. She did not have the luxury to condition herself to ignore the wails either. Sharing a room in the attic with a screaming infant did little for the daily pulsating migraines she used to get back then. Or from having to decipher a language she barely knew. The room was small, overheated, and wallpapered, which was the room's sole similarity to the Soviet flat she shared with her parents before she escaped. Back then when she was down in bed her face was entirely too close to the sloped roof. Every time her lids fluttered open with another one of Peta's incessant wails, she endured another rush of panic. There was only a small window above her mattress for access to fresh air and, with the post-partum flush of hormones, Evelyn was almost always drenched in sweat no matter what the weather was outside. The frigid cold air outside, no matter how naked she got, did nothing to reduce the incessant heat exuding from her body. Of course, it was an ill time to complain as to the room and board accommodations, the quarters rent-free and the lady providing them living just below. Her papers temporary and still crispy and fresh, her womb still violated and shrinking, whenever she slept at all (which thanks to Peta was rare), she saw him—"the father" as the immigration authorities referred to him, in her asylum interrogations. They didn't call them such, of course, but they were repetitive and lengthy, so Evelyn knew better than to refer to them as interviews. If it walks like a duck and talks like a duck… She was a novelty in town—a much better term for "charity case." The whispers weren't quiet enough, the glances weren't ambiguous enough. A single young Soviet rape victim seeking asylum in Kansas sure made the news. And the vetting took so long that it was too late to consider an abortion. So green in her surroundings, so flimsy was her status, she couldn't very well let this child cry until she was evicted, but she also had no plans of raising an entitled brat. It was conflicting, complicated. To let her child cry without needing to stifle her own desire to make her stop forever. Evelyn went out a lot, usually walking circles around the lake at the Wyandotte County Park. The name was hard to read, harder to pronounce, but the hike was long, and the air was always crisp. Not many ventured out in the winter so she could let Peta cry it out as long as she needed. And she needed a long time, apparently. Eventually, red faced and exhausted, the infant would sleep, and when she would quiet, Evelyn would sit on a bench, her eyes frozen open, her ears ringing, her thighs trembling.

Just when it looked like the girl was beginning to make peace with having to soothe herself, Marsha burst into the room, looking flustered and disheveled in her haste. Fearful of what may come out of her mouth were she to let her lips part, Evelyn demonstratively stomped out of the room, leaving audible *tsks* in her wake.

There were no photos of Gwenny displayed on any of the many walls in her daughter's house, Evelyn realized as she stomped down the hallway to her room. Neither of Harry. There was no artistic bone in that girl's body, no matter who her father was. So much time in therapy you'd think she'd discover something about herself that would make her want to capture, to create, but no. As far as Evelyn was concerned, there was entirely too much time spent in that therapist's office. Every time they talked, granted that wasn't often, she seemed to be on her way to see that woman. She didn't understand to what end. What was the point in that constant dissection of self? Especially if, after all is said and done, one still comes back out in the sun (or the drizzle, as the case may be) and life continues unchanged. She attempted a session of her own once when she was fighting for asylum, but the exercise turned out to be simply an uncomfortable couch to cry on. And you had to pay for by the hour! The whole thing seemed unreasonable. She already had a mattress in her attic and that was pretty much the same thing. She'd cry more after the appointment just thinking about how much money that other crying session was costing her benefactors. Wasteful! Her hardened parents wouldn't have ever believed in therapy. And she knew, neither did she. That was for legitimately crazy people. Her parents, if they'd know about this, they'd knock her upside the head. So, she quit after three attempts. The rest of her recovery was spent sketching the lake. That spring, she lost the stroller and surrendered it to the original donor. Peta was just learning to sit up and was stationary so that worked for a while. When she was finally learning how to crawl and began to ambulate, she had to stop. It wasn't until she was planning for Sioux that she got another therapeutic project.

Peter

Peta's office was dark. Dark and narrow. These attributes had nothing to do with the fact that Peta insisted on only ever illuminating it with some ostensibly vintage floor lamp left over by the eccentric old man who had sold them the house. No. Rather it had to do with the redwood planks the room had for walls. Given its constricted built, the paneling did nothing to open the space. Peter tried to explain this, but Peta was adamant—she liked the small window with a view of the water, and she liked her wooden walls. This was going to be her office. Period, end of sentence. She couldn't wait for Peter to leave so the room could be hers and hers alone. He begged to at least rip off the carpet. From group homes he remembered what carpeted floors represented—the spills, the smells. He offered to replace it with equally dark and moody laminated planks, if that's what she was after, but she refused. She wanted to keep the gray shaggy carpet. She liked the way her toes sunk inside it. He'd once pointed out that were she ever to turn on her heel too abruptly, she'd cut herself. Maybe she liked that too.

He hadn't been inside Peta's office since the early move-in days, when he helped install the shelves on the opposite wall. Those shelves now hosted her framed and autographed photo of her meet and greet with Ginger Zee—a good decade her junior and broadcasted to the whole country. That always stung, no matter how much Peter would remind her that she never would've so much as consider the east coast even if it was a viable job opportunity because of Sioux. But he knew it was a weak argument. He didn't buy it when she attempted to make him feel better with his own Willie Geist comparisons. It was strange to be here now—almost but not quite inside this dim, cramped, thoughtful place. He had to admit now that it made for a nice contrast to the rest of the house boasting of its cathedral ceilings and oversized windows. It was an enviable hiding place. Peta was on to something.

The room being trapped on the landing between two floors, its door open wide, Peter straddled the threshold. This whole thing was ridiculous. He hadn't stepped foot inside the place for a decade, how would he know where to look for the journal? He barely knew where the light switch was. If the whole journal thing wasn't a rouse to begin with, he had to remind himself. It not being illegal to lie, the cops could've easily been lying now that he thought about it. And more power to them, if this brought them closer to Peta. But on the off chance they were not, Peter couldn't risk closing the door and going down two flights to his own office, which was much more familiar, and much lighter despite being located in the half-basement. This room could hold answers to questions he never thought he had.

Rolling eyes at himself and his momentary romanticism, Peter finally put his toes over the threshold, his shoes skidding on the carpet. He straightened up immediately, pulling on the collar of his shirt, as if adjusting an imaginary tie. Old habits die hard.

Peta didn't dust. That much was obvious even before Peter pulled the shades up and watched the dust mites fly. Marsha tidied up in all other rooms, but Peta must've obviously told her to stay out of this one. Their house was hardly an operating theater, but dust flying through the air akin to tumbleweed at the mere mention of disturbance was uncharacteristic. However, besides the dust and some unremarkable clutter, nothing about the room stood out in any way of note—a corner unit desk, a swivel cracked leather chair, a sofa that'd obviously seen better days, shelves upon shelves of books. A plaid blanket lay curled at the foot of the sofa; a pillow with a thoroughly worn "Keep Calm and Carry On" logo sat at the head, upside down. It was three wide strides from the door to the couch. That's it. Peter made them quickly. The floor squeaked under his left foot on the third step, making him wince. The sound, Peta claimed, made her morning sickness worse when she was pregnant with Harry, but there was nothing Peter could do to fix it, and eventually she stopped mentioning it. He wasn't even sure if she had morning sickness with Gwenny, he realized now as he lowered himself onto Peta's futon.

He heard Gwenny gurgling something in her room, the baby monitor nestled in his pocket. She was crying before, but now she was with Marsha. Having lived through Harry and all his delays, they now knew the proper term for what

Gwenny was doing—*jargoning*. It sounded like she was talking purposefully, only she wasn't—it was a pretend, made-up language. She may as well have been speaking Martian. But it was a proper step in typical development. Who knew!? As nonsensical as it sounded, as annoying as that sound was, it was good. It was proper. It was hopeful. Maybe had Harry done this on schedule, they would've never sent him to get "socialized." Maybe he'd still be alive. But then maybe Gwenny wouldn't be. Peter let himself sink down onto Peta's upside down *Keep Calm* pillow and closed his eyes. Sioux was there. And that aloof boyfriend of hers. They'd keep an eye on Gwenny when she took her break later. They would know to keep Evelyn at bay. She reeked of cigarettes and Peta would not have approved of her babysitting. And that's all Sioux really needed to hear in life, Peter knew—the girl lived her life by "what would Peta do."

The pillow smelled vaguely of avocado. He wasn't sure if it was Peta's shampoo or she just really liked to eat avocado in her office. He couldn't remember what Peta's hair smelled like, couldn't remember the last time he sniffed it or even had his face that close to her body. Without opening his eyes, he reached down for the blanket wrinkled on the floor and drew it up over his legs. He could afford a few minutes of rest.

His relationship with sleep had always been complicated. The first time he remembered having a sleepless night was the first one he spent with the "authorities." They called his aunt as next of kin after explaining to him that his parents would not be coming back and told him he could get some rest on a bunk bed in the back of the station. It was supposed to be a treat—there was swag kids were supposed to appreciate back there. He was supposed to like it. He didn't. His body shaking uncontrollably, every time he'd close his eyes, he would imagine what it must've been like for his family station wagon to drive into a truck, to feel that acceleration and adrenaline. He would hear his mom's shrieks, his dad's groans, and open his eyes again. His eyes stung from the strain to make out anything in the dark. Since that night, it'd been a straight downhill tumble for his sleep hygiene. Beds changed as often as the roofs over his head and, eventually, insomnia became more of a habit than a medical condition. It wasn't so much that he didn't want or need sleep, but anything more than five or six hours felt unnatural. Whenever he would get that occasional eight, he felt downright disoriented in the morning. He'd wake up nauseous, his stomach cramping. He'd be the natural choice for taking the night shift with baby were it not for Catriona, and now Marsha.

With a deep sigh of resolution, Peter turned over, nuzzling his forehead deep into the back of the couch, his hands blindly grasping at the cushions, suddenly desperate to hold something close to himself again. If the cops already knew Peta never boarded the Seattle-bound train, how could they not know where she went? It seemed implausible that in our day and age, people could simply disappear without a trace, Peter mused, as he screwed his eyes shut. It was then that his fingertips stumbled upon a marble notebook wedged between the pillows.

Sioux

Mommy is on the phone a lot now. She always spends a lot of time on the phone when she's not working. She speaks several more languages than I understand. I understand exactly one. I took sign language in high school, so that's one, but it's not spoken, so I'm not sure it counts as another language in this particular context. It's a visual language. I'm visual. What I mean is, mommy often *speaks* in a language I cannot understand.

She's been doing that a lot lately, these dramatic monologues with the phone wedged in the crook of her neck. She's either in the kitchen or out on the deck. She's emotional. She is loud. Gwenny has, only now just let her lids close for her morning nap and I'm worried mommy will wake her.

"Do you know what she's saying?" Gael asks.

"Not a word."

"Do you know who she is talking to?"

"There is a young Russian sculptor in Victoria. I can only presume that's who it is," I shrug.

"So, is that Russian?"

"Presumably."

"She never taught you?" There's disbelief in his voice. It's like he's shocked, though he shouldn't be—we've been over this more times than necessary. But language is important in his family. Culture is, too. Family dinners, church—the works. We must seem a bit strange to him: we don't believe in god, we rarely have Thanksgiving dinners. He claims he doesn't mind. A girl whose mother is a Soviet ex-pat but who doesn't speak a word of Russian, a girl who's never been to any house of worship, a girl who doesn't have any cousins or uncles. His family must surely think I grew up in a cult, but I've never met them so maybe it truly does not matter. Peta was it—my entire family. Peta *is* it. Why do I keep doing that? But mommy never taught Peta Russian, either. Peta doesn't know any language other than English. It wasn't a requirement when she went to college.

I hear Gael shuffle behind me. He doesn't understand. I don't need him to.

She's crying now. Not that dramatic thing she does when she knows someone's watching, but that muted, suppressed gulping-for-breath kind of cry. We don't know why exactly she's crying, and I don't want to go and ask. You'd think it's obvious, but it isn't. She has the monitor in her pocket, where I dropped it, so hopefully she'll hear Gwenny over her own voice. Peter has the other set, so one of them should. And Marsha is around, even if she is eating lunch.

Mommy is not like other mommies. Others would be worried sick if their daughter went missing, but not our mommy. She insists she is not. She's convinced Peta is just fine—taking some time for herself at some spa as far as Arizona. Being selfish, making everyone worry. Maybe she's thinking this because, probably, that is what she would've done in her place. For an artist, she sure tends to be rational when she wants to be. On the other hand, she's been here all but a day and already she is moping around the deck in her Aztec cardigan as she pontificates that it's Peter's "darkness" (whatever that means) that killed Peta. When I ask her if she really believes that Peta is dead, she snaps at me, reminding me that Peta is merely taking a "selfish break, like the selfish girl that she is." At least she says it in English, so I understand, her sweetly caffeinated breath too close to my nostrils. I bet her breast milk smelled and tasted the same. Gael jokes that I should be able to remember, given that she breastfed me till I was five. Not nurse, per se, of course; that stopped at three (and that's when bottled breast milk took over.)

"There are no pictures of Gwenny, anywhere," Gael points out to me as we carefully trot down the stairs. I hope mommy quiets down while Peter looks for some papers in Peta's office, he says the cops said may be important. Poor guy now has homework now too, as if his life wasn't enough of a test.

"Peta was—*is* afraid of getting too attached," I attempt to explain in a whisper. Peta has never confessed so much but you hardly need more than Psych 101 on your transcript to figure it out. Gael's beautiful brow wrinkles. He is too adorable. Literally—too adorable. I want to pet him half the time. There's no manliness about him. What you see is what you get with Gael, which I suppose should go in the "pros" column.

This is a strange concept, I agree—being afraid of growing attached to your own child—so I understand why Gael looks perplexed. But he didn't hear her wailing like a gutted animal for three days straight, until her throat was so dry she could barely speak on the fourth. He didn't see her eyes turn the color so raging red, it took all the self-restraint I had not to try to dip into them with a paintbrush. He didn't have to watch as she fought to keep her posture upright in front of that camera when she finally went back to work after those two months spent at home with the shades drawn, the skin on her face sagging more every day.

"Hey, I didn't mean any offense. It's just strange to me, that's all."

"It's pretty basic psychology," I pout, as we close the door tightly behind us. There seem to be more news vans here than the last time I counted. I don't want to stop and count now but it looks like there are more. It's an alphabet soup of letters and they all blend together in my head. A few reporters drop their coffees and start to approach us at a speed exaggeratedly choreographed so as to appear hurried but not intimidating. Gael waves them off before I can and presses his palm into my lower back to get me to walk faster toward the car. I comply, shielding my eyes with my braids, loosening them from under my scarf. This is another reason we should be the ones to go out if need be. Peter has enough on his plate to also have to deal with colleagues out here, and I don't trust mommy. She'd make for a great sound bite, but it wouldn't help anybody—not the case, not Peter. And me? It's hard to stay inside knowing there are always that many eyes on the house. On the door, on the windows. Just yesterday, we ventured to the backyard when talking to the cops; we wouldn't dare now for fear of those massive mics picking up our voices. Walking through the mob now is nothing because I know the fear is fleeting. I know they won't follow us. And then it'll be easier to breathe knowing there are no lenses on us.

"She's in therapy and everything. I think she's trying someone new now—some woman who'd moved here from Alaska or something. She felt too medicated before, with the old guy. She knew she wouldn't be able to take all that crap and carry Gwenny, and this lady is allegedly more holistic. She's really working on herself," I finish when we're in the car and the reporters finally step back enough to let us safely roll out of the driveway.

I see him nod out of the corner of my eye, steadying his old car as we pick up speed. I know he'll be afraid to ask me much else on the subject, but Gael's quiet is better than mommy's noise back at the house. And quiet it is—all the way there. He knows where "there" is, but that's where we are headed, anyway. Peta always shops organic, especially for Gwenny, and short of resorting to Google, we do not know any other stores in town. Somehow, it doesn't occur to either of us to exert any effort into looking for another. It seems like that would've been wiser, but it's like I'm drawn to the place that last saw my sister alive. Maybe it'll be like picking at a scab, like sucking on a toothache. It must be done. It'll be satisfying, rewarding somehow. I close my eyes, but Gael's driving brings on motion sickness even faster that way, so I let them open and see exactly where we're going.

"That's where they'd discovered Peta's car. Or, rather, that's where she'd left it," I hear myself practically whisper, my throat small as we pull in. He knows, but I have to say it out loud anyway. Just to hear it. I pet my insulin pump for comfort, as I'd been known to do since the early days of its installation.

"Maybe—"

"What?" I challenge at the sound of his perpetual need to placate me, make me feel better. This feels good—like a much-needed cough that seems to clear your throat, if only for a second.

He hesitates but parks with precision between two oversized SUVs.

"Maybe your mom is right—"

"Which part? She has so many ideas!" I pretend to laugh. This scoffing is almost therapeutic.

"Where she thinks that maybe Peta is taking a break. Maybe things were getting too much with Gwenny getting to Harry's age when he— You know what I mean."

"Yes—died. It's okay, I'm aware. You can say it."

Gael swallows audibly as he pushes the gearstick into park.

"Well, maybe she needed a little escape."

I shake my head so hard, I feel more braids break through the confines of the scarf tied tightly around my neck. We'll have to leave this car sooner or later. I screw my eyes tight and answer.

"She wouldn't do that to Gwenny. Don't listen to mommy." I'm practically growling. He's the last person I should be growling at, this much I know, but his proximity makes it easy. "Did you know she didn't even want to keep Peta? She almost brags about this every chance she gets! She was her golden ticket to get a visa, she just couldn't get an abortion in time."

"She's been crying—"

"That's how most of my needs were met as a child— she'd cry, and a neighbor would pay for my ballet lessons. 'My little girl doesn't have a daddy! Boo-hoo!' Did you know that? Don't buy into her crap. She's an opportunist."

Gael avoids mommy like the plague despite her verbal approvals of my choice in partner. "Partner"—that's what she calls him, as if we play tennis together. She doesn't like to use many other terms. At least she doesn't call him a *subject*, like she did many of the men she hooked up with after sculpting their forms. Not that she hadn't tried to wrangle Gael into modeling for her. But the idea of him disrobing in front of her gives me the hives, even if he'd be in his "swim trunks," as she puts it.

"So, you think Peta is dead?" he asks.

I swallow for what feels like the first time in a short lifetime. It hurts.

"Well, she's not hiding out voluntarily, this much I know." When I feel tears threaten, I pull the lever to open my own door. The air feels thick around us, the color of it turning milky. The fog is rolling in. Before Gael can say anything, I slam the door shut with him still inside. I shouldn't do that to him either, but, again—he's right here.

"Are you absolutely sure you want to shop here?" he asks the second he catches up to me at the automatic sliding doors. "We could drive around and find something else." Not stopping to reconsider, I say nothing. I have to keep moving or else. Or else what? I don't know, but my breath is growing shallow and my pulse is painful. I walk on. Gael tucks his hair behind his ears and nods in the corner of my eye. He's compliant like that. The moisture in the air is beginning to make his hair frizzy, which makes him look younger than his already boyish genes. I pick up speed with no intention.

"Do you know what we need?"

"The basics—milk, cereal, apples, bread, bananas. Some granola bars wouldn't hurt," I rattle on as I pick up a basket and begin throwing things into it haphazardly. My vision a tunnel, I toss a few oranges in and steer Gael toward the cash register. We're not here more than a minute and, I don't know why, but I must flee. Maybe it's not like sucking on a tooth that aches, after all. There is no satisfaction here and sucking on a toothache does give you a perverse one. No, here I'm just lightheaded, wondering which aisle my sister walked up or down before disappearing. It's becoming harder to breathe. *Smell the flowers, blow out the candles.* The large warehouse is at once too cold and too stuffy. There are too many options of every item. The prices are outside our student budgets. It's too loud. It's too bright. I want to get back to the house, even if there are twice as many cameras as there are men outside it. My stomach is growling those loose, watery growls that threaten projectile vomiting. "That's enough for now. We can come back tomorrow if Peter wants us to." I grow dizzy as I look for the fastest route out, for the nearest exit. There is no such path lit up for us like there would be on an airplane in an emergency landing. I feel people begin to stare but there is no way Peta and I look alike, nobody can possibly know we are related. Somehow the local meteorologist's black sister doesn't really come up during the weather report. And still I see people looking in our direction. This must be simple paranoia. Again, no need for advanced psychology courses. I pull on Gael' sleeve harder, and he doesn't resist. He never resists. It usually makes my blood boil but not right now.

We're close. We're really close now. There are four registers open and there are very few people in each line. We can be out in minutes. My sudden vertigo seems to pick up a notch at the sight of the proverbial light at the end of the tunnel. There's no logic to this. No rhyme, no reason. I don't like it when my heart races this fast without an obvious reason or permission. It feels like what I imagine a bad car crash would feel like—that involuntary propulsion. Only there are no seat belts or air bags. I want out. Somewhere between the soda aisle and the dry goods, my eyes on the scratched toes of my lace up boots, I trip. In the effort to stay upright, I latch onto Gael and my head is thrown upward by some instinct encoded for self-preservation. *TVs.* I hadn't noticed screens mounted all over the place before, but I don't know how I could've missed them. There are so many. They are lined up along the perimeter. My mouth stretches open, but air seems unreachable as Peta's headshot materializes on all the screens simultaneously, staring us down from every which angle. Mommy says she isn't beautiful, but she is. It's an old photo—her hair is chocolate and sleek, clearly recently highlighted. Her lips are on a brownish side of taupe and lightly parted, different from the other headshot I'd seen floating around. Her teeth have always appeared large, but it's their impeccable shade of white that is so striking. I know there is a screen between us, but she seems to be looking directly at me with those big smiling eyes of hers. I must look away as I feel my stomach gargle harder, my esophagus contracting.

I rip the basket out of Gael's grip and slam it onto the conveyor belt hoping that Peta is no longer looking down at me. A guy no older than me immediately proceeds to unload our scarce, random items onto his scales, his focus enviable. He pauses between bananas and bread to pile his dreadlocks on top of his head and my eyes catch a tattoo of a butterfly on the back of his left elbow. Mommy would find him stunning.

"Find everything you need?"

"I'm not sure what else to look for, quite honestly," I hear Gael say before I can.

John

The first thing I ever said to her was, "I'm sorry." It was also the last thing I said to her. What a stupid thing to say. Truly. Unoriginal, at best. That's how everyone had been greeting her for years, I bet. I should've just pretended I didn't know who she was, didn't know anything about her son or how the entire town pretended to be personally affected by his death. The day care was promptly closed, though, so I guess, at least in terms of full day childcare, little Harry's death had indeed impacted a few infants and toddlers and their parents, but still. This was years before either I or even mom had moved down here, but my manager says that that place was the only one in town to open at 6:30am, ready to receive kids aged seven weeks and up five mornings a week. And they were open as late as 6:30pm, from what I understand. Can't argue with the convenience of it. But you kill one kid of a quasi-public figure, and BAM—you're out of business and half the town is upset.

Anyway, if she was bothered by our introduction, it didn't show. I should've stuck to "find everything you were looking for?" and called it a day. Or maybe just nodded sympathetically while bagging her groceries, but that's it! Five whole years ago—I was in high school, for fuck's sake. Far from here. What the fuck did I know? What the fuck *do* I know?

It's strange seeing her on TV now. And we have TVs set to the local station plastered all over the place so she's hard to avoid. As if people come here to catch up on the local news rather than to pick up milk on their way home. Often, it's only an old headshot of "the town's beloved meteorologist, Peta Knudsen"—a still. But she's more animated in real life, even when she was sad. More attractive, too. You need to see her in 3D. A still is just not that accurate. Occasionally, they air her old segments—the occasional heavy storm, a particularly strong aftershock— but knowing that they are running these in a manner that visibly shows their restraint in not officially calling the thing posthumous, it's just not the same. It's not flesh and blood and these TVs don't exert as much heat as the old models used to so there's no hope for any resemblance. God, it's the local channel and they don't spend nearly as much time on the national news as I'd like at this point. I'd kill for a little Trump update right about now. But no such luck—it's all local attempted sexual assault stats and the missing meteorologist. Her doe eyes, her full lips. Suddenly, I realize that I miss them. Her chocolate hair, her alabaster skin. If I screw my eyes shut, it's like she's right here, asking me where my father is and why I live with my mom. And she was, just a couple of days ago. So, I try to keep my head down and speed-scan the countless expensive food items as fast as I can. *Find everything you were looking for?*

I only occasionally bring my eyes up to the screen now because I know that the odds of seeing her up there at any random point in time are high. I'm not sure I need to see her that often. It's bad enough I had to see her right before she fell off the face of the earth. It's bad enough I'll have to forever wonder why she wanted me to drop everything and go with her. Why would a woman I only knew as a fan of overpriced kale ask me to cut my shift short and blindly board some train with her? Why the fuck would I want to meet her sister? What a weird way to propose a setup?

"Find everything you were looking for?" I ask on autopilot when a thin girl with ass-long hair materializes in front of me as if out of thin air. I'm grateful she does; now I can focus on her carton of 1% milk. The dude next to her mumbles something about not knowing what else to look for, but my question is rhetorical. I'm not looking for an actual answer. I don't care. My sole focus is on avoiding the TV sets along the perimeter of the damn place, so I glance at the girl, smile, and nod. Her eyes are down, her fingers fiddling with her change purse. The pretty boy just stands next her—an accessory; I presume that's her boyfriend. Out of the corner of my eye, I see him place his open palm on the girl's lower back and I can't help but laugh. Internally, at least. By the time I scan all of their five items, Peta is no longer on the screen, I'm relieved to notice. Now they're talking about some local kitten adoption drive. But the girl is still fiddling with her coin purse. Of course she has a coin purse! She's clearly the poster child for what people visualize at the sound of the word "hipster." She's either from Brooklyn or Portland, I presume.

The couple hurries out the automatic doors the second I toss a receipt into their bag. The girl leads the way, her braids swaying, and her boyfriend follows on her heels. We used to have a dog that followed my mom around like that—wherever she went, he followed, his tail wagging. I wonder if this guy whimpers when his girlfriend leaves the house. With the fog now thick outside, I soon lose them. Much like mom had lost that dog.

I still can't bring myself to go home. Going home to face her inquisitions wasn't something I was eager to do that day, and I still am not. I get dad's texts; he says he's here. He wants to talk but doesn't want to pressure me. She must've summoned him. This is both comfort and alarm. Once she'll hear that Peta was asking about dad, she'll go into one of her hysterical fits of jealousy. Anybody who dares to breathe the same air as dad wants to fuck him, according to her. It's suffocating even for me and I'm not him. No, nothing good can come out of it. Certainly nothing productive. Too many things would be said out loud and then there'd be no taking them back. Answering the cops' questions was bad enough. "Did you see Peta Knudsen that day?" "What was the nature of your exchange?" As if they hadn't already seen our brief exchange play out on tape every which way 'til Sunday. Going home for more? I'm not ready yet.

Dr. Burgos

"Wait, she was the girl you broke up with that day at the diner?"

"Yes."

"The same one who showed up at the apartment that one time?"

"Yes."

Dr. Burgos made a show of not being able to wrap her mind around this.

"How can you be sure?"

They sat across from each other in the kitchen, her rented barstools tall. She didn't go into work. She cancelled all her clients—all three of them, the Greens making up two. Her voicemail reported lots of inquiries, but she wondered how many of them were legitimate and how many were trying to fish out a quotable line from her. She felt it best not to follow up just yet for fear of saying something just off color enough to lower the client roster. A grown woman was pursuing her barely legal son, for God's sakes, and no one is the wiser! That's your story! But all the attention was now on the fact that she was missing and on rehashing all the wonderful, fabulous things she's done on air. Being dead does that—it makes you infallible. And being the disappeared is just as good. No, it was best not to answer phone calls, it was best not to go into the office. She had the right not to take on any new patients, albeit her bank account wouldn't have agreed. Instead, she stayed home, her robe over her pajamas, and stared at Andrew from across the kitchen island, his laptop between them, as she drank one mug of coffee after another, hoping that the rum she would occasionally sneak in there was not giving off any traceable aroma.

"Are you sure?" she asked again.

Andrew sat dressed in a wrinkled t-shirt that'd seen whiter days and pajama pants. It was noon. Dr. Burgos was surprised he'd packed for this many overnight stays. When she drunkenly called him that first night, she didn't even realize he'd call her on her bluff and actually come. Well, not only did come, but he also brought pajamas! Today, when she first came out of her room, her hair in a precise top bun, she interpreted this as a good sign, making coffee with a smile on her face. It was only when she turned to face him, with a carafe in her hand, that she realized he was

106

engrossed in his laptop and unlikely to had showered. They'd been sitting on opposite sides of the kitchen island for hours now, making no headway.

"Yes! The name didn't sound familiar because I knew her before she was married."

"What was her last name before?"

He rubbed his stubble. When that didn't help, he rubbed his forehead.

"I don't know."

She thought to say something sarcastic like, "what, it never came up?" but she remembered that this must've been long before social media. Their relationship, if she could even call it that, could not have lasted long enough to enquire as to last names. She and Andrew were apart for no more than two months, so that's roughly how long he could've possibly known Peta. Unless they overlapped, of course.

"I know. *Morozova*."

"What?"

"That's her maiden name."

"How do you know this?" Andrew perked up, his back straightening behind his laptop, his glasses off the bridge of his nose and up on top of his head. Dr. Burgos read his look as curious, but it just as well could have been a challenge. She chose to respond as if it were former. Sure, the odds were that he'd already found her maiden name online, but this was all part of some exercise Andrew was keen on playing out.

"She is my patient. Or is it 'was'? I'm not sure. I'm privy to a lot of intimate information. When exactly did you go out with her?"

Andrew rubbed his face as if to waken it just a nudge more. Dr. Burgos couldn't believe he lost sleep over this. Peta's tentacles reached even her ex-husband. What was that magic she possessed?

"But you didn't know we went out until like five minutes ago, no?" he challenged, suddenly flustered. "Total coincidence of her being your patient, isn't it so?"

Dr. Burgos wasn't used to seeing Andrew fluster. He was confident; cocky, if you didn't know him, even. His frame didn't lend well to "fluster," and neither did his cheekbones. And yet there was an obvious fluster to his complexion.

"No, my patient intake form does not call for a list of all prior relationships," she quipped, egged on by the unfamiliar. She shifted on the stool, suddenly aware of the time.

Of course, she knew. And, of course, he now knew she knew. There was no way she was a convincing actress. It was true that Mrs. Knudsen walking into her office as a patient was indeed a coincidence, but on the second look, if not the first, she recognized the girl behind that thick layer of makeup—that same scared, pathetic little girl, all doe eyes and flat hair. She bet there were still freckles on her nose were she to take a makeup wipe to her face. A few carefully phrased questions and she had her confirmation:

Portland was where she grew up, Seattle is where she went to school. They managed to talk about her previous relationships simply by way of delving into trust issues (she made sure it sounded relevant at the time, even encouraged journal keeping to get her to open up afterward, in therapy), and sure enough she'd dated a law student before heading off to college. That was her only boyfriend before her husband. She didn't seem to have much to say about Andrew, claiming it was a short, immature relationship, but Dr. Burgos suspected there was more, especially when she noticed the woman's usually distracted stare grow focused when she registered a photo of her family on the desk.

Andrew sighed as he scratched his head. Maybe the fluster she picked up was actually a reminisce.

"How did you guys meet?" Dr. Burgos leaned forward on her stool, elbows on the cool surface in front of her.

Andrew scoffed, waiting out the thunder rumbling outside. Dr. Burgos knew he was on to her, but the foreignness of it all was so refreshing. Arousing, even.

"She worked at the diner where I tended bar, remember? I worked there between second and third year in law school. I worked there when we broke up—"

"For a month."

"Six weeks."

The nostalgia in his eyes made the blood inside Dr. Burgos' veins boil. She was afraid she'd bubble over if she didn't breathe just right, letting some air out.

"Right," she breathed. "And what was your relationship like?" she continued her line of questioning.

Fixing her gaze on his heavily hooded and clouding ones, Dr. Burgos tried not to let her own eyes tear. This was a personal challenge. Any intimation of personal offense and she'd feel needles in her nostrils, that stubborn prickle that added vibrato to her voice and made her eyes water. This wasn't a problem at work because nothing was ever personal there. Not her. Not until Peta fixated on a goddam family photo, at least, and started asking all those odd questions. Before, she found it easy to listen to other people's problems, wallowing in someone else's insecurities, phrasing inquiries just so that they answered their own questions, veiling her own opinion just enough to get more five stars on ratemymd.com, so that the person on her carefully picked out couch was none the wiser. But personal matters were different. At every parent-teacher conference she spilled tears. Not angry or sad tears, really. Just whenever she didn't like what she was hearing, the sting would be back, and before she'd know it, she'd be reaching for a tissue. No one takes a crying woman seriously. No, this was an impediment. She was educated, she was professional, she was paid to watch others cry. Why couldn't she talk her way out of these involuntary tears?

"Oh Lena, cut your shit. Like you really want to know. We dated. I was twenty-three or some such. She was eighteen. We made out by the dumpsters a lot, smoked weed. It was over before it started—"

"Did you sleep together?" That was it—the trigger. The tears were now out and rolling down her bare face. Outside, the rain pelted the window. "Did she have your daughter?"

110

Peter

Peter swirled a spoon in his tall mug of coffee. There was no actual need for the spoon at all, given that after finally uncorking and swallowing whole two bottles of wine they'd been storing for a worthier occasion over the years, he was now taking his coffee night-black. No cream, no sugar. There was no need to stir anything.

He tried to think clearly but the caffeine was neither strong nor fast enough and the haze was far too thick. He lowered himself to the floor and sat cross-legged across from his daughter, who was up now from her twenty-minute nap, according to Marsha. The kitchen tiles were too cold. Peta wouldn't like her sitting there, but she was crawling now, so it was hard to keep her confined to the area rug in the living room. And he didn't feel like locking her down in the playroom so soon after her nap. He missed her. Surely, she needed human contact too. Marsha was folding laundry—how much attention could she pay her? Evelyn was not an option, not that she ever volunteered. He listened to Gwenny babble and watched her drool away as her rice cracker as it melted in her mouth. Peta was late to introduce solids. And after Harry, who could blame her? So here she was, gibbering on whilst trying to down a rice cracker. Between the slobber and the nonsensical syllables, the sight was yet another distraction from Peter's goal of clarity.

Reluctant to face his infant, Peter was slow to look up from his cup after gulping down his scalding hot coffee. The skin on the roof of his mouth peeled on contact, but he didn't blink. Ignorance is bliss until it's not. Eyes on the refreshingly cool tile floor, he stood up on unsure legs and threw the mug into the sink, immediately feeling a ping of guilt for the clamor it caused. He glanced at Gwenny over his shoulder, but the girl barely winced. He was relieved until it dawned on him that it might mean that he would now have to check her hearing.

Leaving Gwenny where she sat, with his stride less than precise, Peter walked over to the kitchen counter. A marble notebook—that's all it was. When the cops first mentioned a journal, he envisioned a leather-bound, traveler-type of a logbook, but no, it was much more generic than that. She must've picked it up at any random corner grocery, not some stationary store he initially imagined. This was a disappointment in itself. If he was already confronted with the idea that his wife was a person who kept a journal under doctor's orders, he would have an easier time coping with an image of a wife who scouted boutiques for paper quality and hard binding. This was another let down and they were only two days in. *Was* it two, technically?

Peter fingered the pages, the wide college ruled lines. The edges were frayed, bent every which way. It was sloppy. Some looked like they had liquids spilled on them and then air dried, the ink runny. Another strike.

Scooping Gwenny under one arm, the diary in the other, Peter plodded into his office. The floor here was warmer, the office carpeted wall to wall here too. In no time at all, Gwenny's foot was in her mouth, her sock just as soaked as her rice cracker had been back in the kitchen. Peter wondered if it constituted a choking hazard but decided against it, leaving the child to it. She seemed amused enough.

The curtains thrown open against his half-basement windows, Peter let himself watch the storm, the horizon bleaker, not as peaceful as the day when they put in an offer on this place. If Sioux was still out there with her boyfriend, he hoped at least one of them was familiar with driving in such thick fog. Sure, they lived in Seattle, but that was a bigger city, much better illuminated.

He heard Gwenny cry but stayed put, eyes on the glass that could've used a more thorough cleaning. A nanny and a cleaning lady would seem too extravagant to the town, he thought, so Marsha was paid to do more than just make sure that Gwenny wasn't ingesting anything that could've possibly come in contact with a nut. He thought to call her in now to take Gwenny, but he was afraid he'd stutter if he tried. It would be a good idea for both of them to learn to separate a little better. Peta, too afraid to get attached again, had done this early, almost preemptively. She'd even nursed with her eyes on TV and not on the girl's blonde hair. Peter, in spite of himself, did the opposite with Gwenny than he had done with his son—he cooed and cuddled, making up for lost time. He, of all people, should've known better.

Peter weighed all this as he pulled the blinds shut against the thunderstorm outside and cracked the spine of the black marble notebook.

Entry One.

Peta's Journal Entry

First love? Have I ever been in love? Is this a trick and/or an existential question? That sort of thing? I don't know. Have you ever been in love? Who is your first love? Who gives a shit—I'm over forty, married, with a child (and then some), so what difference does it make if I had a high school sweetheart?

To be honest, I'm not experience-rich. A weird girl who spoke too impassionedly about thunderstorms in science class and lived in a weird art commune, I wasn't exactly popular. It was only after graduation, when I took a job waiting tables at a pub downtown to try to earn textbook money that I even got my first (and pretty much only) "boyfriend." And that only lasted a few of weeks as it was. After him—Peter. And he was cute, and our names were a match and I was still bitter about my last almost-boyfriend, and I knew mommy would hate him and so...BINGO! It was the perfect storm. No meteorology pun intended. I didn't give myself the time to try many others. Just those two. So, who was and/or is my real love? Or first love? Those are different questions, but the answer is the same: I don't know. I don't think it's Peter. But I don't think so now, as I sit awake in my office and hear him snore all the way from half a flight above me. We've got two decades under our belts—two births, one death. The account of my feelings now may not be completely reliable. And Andrew? I was eighteen—that's not even fair! It was all black and white photography and coffee shops for us back then. Remember those? It was butterflies in the stomach, dizzy at the thought of him kind of a thing. But again, I was eighteen. That's hardly reliable either.

Let's just go at it chronologically then, shall we? It's not a long roster, anyway.

There weren't many kids my age in the commune. Mommy had me kind of young, in my opinion, although not exactly by choice. And when I say "commune," don't worry, it wasn't like a "culty" commune, or anything. No, nothing creepy. I just like to refer to it as such. Why? No clue. Shock value? Maybe. In reality, it was like ten artists who banded together for some reason and relocated for inspiration every few

114

years, taking a vote as to the location every time. They'd rent a house together, do their thing. Most were single, fucked around. Sometimes with each other. I don't have any dark tales about being seduced by an older friend of mommy's or anything like that, so don't let those salivary glands loose just yet. Haven't I told you all this before? But yeah, mostly it was adults around me growing up, not many kids. In fact, I was literally the only child there until roughly about the age of seventeen. And then this one oil painter got knocked up by her model and had a baby boy. I was going to become its natural sitter if I didn't do anything about it, so it was time to get another job. I say another because I'd always had at least one. Since I was old enough for a work permit. Started at the local library, moved on to summer camps and after school programs, and eventually—waiting tables. It wasn't that I had such enviable work ethic or anything. It's just that there was never anything to do at home other than to ingest improbable amounts of weed (both contact and direct), watch my mom sketch horses with tireless abandon, and see the occasional nude model who made you question the term "model." And homework only took so much time. So, yeah, I got another job simply to appear busy and not get suckered into babysitting. This particular gig was at a local eatery doubling as a bar. A pub, it called itself. I was hardly of legal drinking age, but so long as I only worked the morning and afternoon shifts, never evenings, Courtney, the owner, was cool with it. That's where we met— both working brunch shift on a Sunday in July. Andrew was making whatever was in before mimosas became all the shit, and I was pouring coffee and buttering toast. I used the wrong door coming out of the kitchen and bumped into him on his way in. Very "romcom" of us. I spilled half a tray of water on him, making his white button-down shirt cling to him in a way that was not unsightly, to say the least. Awkwardly, I patted him down with a wad of napkins. He laughed, ticklish. Just so precious. It was not a bad day for this virgin.

It was all pretty typical, at first. Maybe not typical (because, who knows), but it was surely anticipated, imagined, whatever synonym you want to insert here. We flirted, told jokes. Mine were more unsure and generally dumber than his, but he had a few years of experience on me so that was to be expected. He was in law school, apparently, so obviously he must've been smart. Or at least educated. Because that's a whole other conversation—education versus intelligence, am I right? Anyway, I'm guessing he was 24-ish? So, like a six-year difference? No biggie. Nothing pervy. Besides acne ridden high school boys, I'd never really been in such proximity to a member of the opposite sex so close in age. It was exciting. Enamoring. There were giddy butterflies in my belly every morning I knew we were both scheduled to work. In fact, they were so crazed, I often felt I was going to be sick, but no— it was just all my senses getting overwhelmed, overloaded, system going into overdrive. I wasn't entirely sure when he stopped humoring me and his interest in the cloistered high school grad with a strange choppy bob became genuinely piqued, but I can't say I cared one way or the other when I accepted the pathetic dare to take the gum he was chewing out of his mouth with my tongue. Of course, that led to my first kiss. First kiss that did not involve spinning empty beer bottles, that is. Needless to say, I mused over what our kids would look like as early as that night and all those many nights I was too excited to sleep after our near touches by the dumpster after work. And, sure, I perused bridal magazines at any checkout line I would find myself in with all the teenage prematurity you may expect. Mind you, our total dating period was roughly about a month. I cringe thinking back to this. Thank God this was before social media or else I would've surely made quite a Pinterest vision board after week one. See, I was crazy before you!

I lost my virginity to him. It seemed like a good idea to do it with someone clean, smart, and attractive before going to college with all that pent-up sexual energy. I was convinced I'd waste it on some idiot otherwise. After all, it was what you did if you liked a boy, TV had me believing. Wouldn't Kelly do it on 90210? Brenda would consider it. Although Donna Martin definitely wouldn't. But I definitely wanted to be Kelly, so it was decided. One morning I told mommy I was going to go to the library to get some guide books on Seattle in order to be ready to explore the city the moment I got there, but instead

116

I drove to Andrew's apartment upon a throaty invitation to fondle in a place that wasn't dumpster-adjacent and in between shifts. I'd all but lost my mind shaving and re-shaving everything I'd imagined would make a difference in whether I was going to get a regular visitor when I finally moved to the State of Washington. Mommy was only then establishing her relationship with the university, so I knew she hadn't yet had a reason big enough to warrant traveling there often. But if I had a boyfriend… I'm not sure why I'd lied to her about where I was going to be that day. She knew I was "dating" someone. She'd come by the place under the pretense of getting a meal or a drink about twice a week, but everyone including Andrew knew she was there to check him out. "He's cute," she told me after the first time. "He can probably do better," she pretended to joke, nudging me in the ribs as I pretended to laugh into my glass of coke during my lunch break. Maybe that's why I told her I was going to the library.

Being with a man a whole six years my senior sure did make me feel mature. And important. It hastened my pulse, fragmented my breaths. It was easy to grow dizzy with…something. Love? I don't know. Infatuation? Obsession? Maybe. I honestly don't know but something sure did run rapid in my bloodstream. Does it matter to you what it was? Whatever it was, it was intense, I remember that much. Just the thought of him walking into a room made my head spin, made my stomach feel as if it were growing concave, and made my legs weak. It was intense. The kind of intensity that eventually makes you lose quite a bit of self-respect and your grip on reality.

How did it end? He broke up with me because his ex-girlfriend turned up pregnant. That was it. One day my toes flex and point under his weight, and the next day, it's over. Not literally the next day, but you get the point. Being the honorable law student that he was, he was all set to marry the girl, which meant I was out a boyfriend. It stung like a motherfucker. Not that I expected to marry the first man to come inside me, but still—this was just mean of the universe. It was too soon, too quick. I got no say in it. Plus, the idea of him fucking

117

someone without a condom sent me reeling because he was a bigger stickler for protection than I ever was. So, I proceeded to call the poor guy nonstop. I was relentless in the two weeks I had between quitting my job on account of it being too painful to be near him and driving down to school. I still cringe thinking back to those tear-streaked fourteen days. I think I might've even showed up at his door once, I don't even remember clearly now. Did I? Oh God, it was probably awful. I'd only stopped calling Andrew when I got to Seattle—those calls were long distance calls then and I did not have the means. My scholarship didn't cover phone expenses. Though the number of messages I left before I left…and his ex had probably moved back in by then so major embarrassment right there. I was eighteen—that's my defense. I don't know what I was mourning—a six-week relationship or my virginity. I couldn't imagine it was the latter, then. Now I can't imagine it being the former.

So yeah, I got to college with exactly two goals—reaching enormous success with the sole purpose of some sort of revenge and getting a boyfriend who'd find me hot enough to last more than six weeks. Very important. Imperative, even. Unfortunately (or fortunately), it took me more than a year to find Peter (and if I know you at all, there will be a separate assignment on him. Or multiple.). There were a few false starts. Do they count? Should they?

When I'd gone home the summer between my first and second year of college (mommy was very pregnant by then), I went back to the restaurant (for lunch! Ha!), but Andrew was no longer there. No one knew where he was, either. He was supposed to be done with law school, according to my calculations, and likely had nothing left tying him down to Portland. I don't remember where he was from, but he wasn't from Oregon. I can only presume the pregnant girlfriend (who surely wouldn't have given birth by then, I would imagine) moved on out with him. Wherever that was. And lord knows where she's from. It was a relief he was gone because I would've surely come by every night, otherwise. Groveled all over again, needless to say. Asked all the "whys" that truly, honestly had no answer. It would've been tired and unbecoming. It was good he was gone. It helped. It wasn't really that I wasn't over him—it was just that I hadn't found anyone who'd pick me yet. That had to have been it. I understand that now. So, when I'd gone back to school that August and met Peter and he invited me to that international night at the cafeteria, it was a done deal. And when, that same night, weighed down by mass-produced burritos, I wrapped my legs around his pasty hips on top of his lumpy dorm bed (taking advantage of the fact that his roommate was busy researching a fraternity to pledge, gloriously unaware of the fact that his efforts were unlikely worthy of the objective), it felt like a bit of payback, or that elusive revenge, even. I'm not sure against whom, though. My opponent wasn't aware of the fight.

That's it. My two lovers, my two great "loves." I guess. I honestly don't remember the thesis statement now.

Gael

Gael knew he should've known better. He was there to steer when Sioux could not. Agreeing to take her to that store was very clearly poor judgment. It was too much. This isn't a small town with one corner grocery shop. They could've Googled, They could've asked Peter. Yes, Sioux guarded his privacy with the same vigilance she seemed to defend Peta's honor, but surely going behind her back would be warranted in this case. The ends would've justified the means. Instead, now there was Sioux, comatose in the passenger seat of his father's old car. She wasn't medically comatose, of course, but the lax body slumped against the seatbelt may as well have been. No words left her slightly parted lips as she stared aimlessly out onto the road, so what was the functional difference? Gael didn't know. And it was probably best not to focus on that for the time being, if he was being honest with himself. He needed to get her home, regardless. Period. With the fog slowly enveloping his small vehicle, his focus had to be elsewhere. The Echo was reliable, but it was too old for such a change of climate. It had a good run back in Sherman Oaks, where the weather was stable and dry. He inherited it when he was sixteen. He delivered many a pizza with this thing in high school. Taking it so many hours north for college was a risk, though. And then a few more hours on top of that? He had to be extra careful. Dad may not have wanted this slowly rusting Toyota back, but he sure wasn't in a position to get a replacement mode of transportation were this one to crash. Not like the Knudsens would cover it. So, Gael knew he had to keep his eyes on the road, not on Sioux, for once. That was the responsible decision. Sioux was still going to be Sioux when they got back to the house. He wasn't sure what stood more of a chance at changing that—Peta coming back or not.

Andrew

The connections were made slowly. Too slowly, one could say. Having now seen it, he could not make peace with not having figured out his ex-wife's riddles as she less than soberly doled them out over days. Not sooner. No, Peta did not have his child, but her mother may have. Lena, who was now sequestered in her room after storming off there when Andrew refuged to engage, changing the subject with ease and eloquence, left him the rest of the house that was both hers and not hers to try to piece together something that happened to him in his twenties and that he hadn't thought about since. Before collapsing on the couch with his laptop tucked under his arm, Andrew drew the curtains closed with gusto. It was dark out now, so it wasn't immediately apparent if the fog outside was thickening or lifting. It didn't matter with the curtains drawn.

Begging John to finally come home because he was upsetting his mom was still proving to be a futile exercise, but Andrew was happy enough with that remaining so just for tonight. He needed to make space for his past, before there was an Andrew. His abdomen already seemed to be on fire; he didn't need to be answering questions right this moment. Instead, he took a few calming breaths his quasi-spiritual students have taught him how to take and loaded his computer. Before he could lose his nerve, he tried running a Google search. Proper keywords were something he prided himself on, what he drilled his students on. It's all about how you frame a query. Still, Andrew's hands trembled at the realization of the simple fact that he had no memory whatsoever of the name of the woman who used to pay him more money than he could make in a month of tending bar to model for her as she sketched and sculpted his form. The same woman then proposed to pay double that amount if he agreed to "help her have a child." That was the exact quote, he remembered now. Suddenly, as clear as day, he heard the woman's voice. It was lightly accented but precise and self-assured. It was a matter-of-fact kind of a transaction, the way it was presented. And he was shocked, at first, he was sure of that now. He must've been, at least. Surely. He couldn't imagine it being otherwise. But he agreed. He was certain of that, too. He needed the money. *They* needed the money.

What was her name? Did he even get her name? He'd recognized her as the mother of the girl he dated briefly that summer—Peta. The woman had come to visit her daughter a few times, he remembered. They must've been introduced then. He was probably given a name, even, but like much else back then, if any particular piece of information thrown his way didn't seem like it could help on his road to a bright and shimmering legal career, it'd immediately gone over his head. That was probably it. That early fall, then, when the same woman came in for a drink, she must've introduced herself again; why didn't he remember her name then? By that time, he knew he was going to be a father before the end of his third year of law school. That was his answer—he simply could not have possibly had enough brain capacity for a name. He was lucky he wasn't forgetting to breathe. He recognized her and that had to be good enough.

Andrew groaned at his own stupidity when he realized the simplest way he could finally Google this artist woman to confirm this hypothesis. He nestled himself into the very corner of Lena's rental sectional. All it took was a search of Peta Knudsen to find her maiden name. Lena just told him what it was, but fuck if he remembered it now. Google it was. And it wasn't hard—just a couple of clicks. *Morozova*. Bingo! Yes, that's what she'd said. He almost proclaimed Eureka. From there, it was simple: images returned just the likeness he was looking for.

Was this nausea? He couldn't tell, but as the images loaded, something lunged itself from the pit of his stomach with the target of the back of the throat. Was he going to vomit? This was rental furniture. Sure, it had Lena's wine stains already, but that was on her. He could never lower his standards to fit in with hers. He clasped his hand over his mouth, prophylactically.

He hadn't known the outcome; he wasn't meant to—that was never the agreement. There was no outright agreement, just a tacit one. One week, his services simply were no longer required. A polite "thank you" accompanied the last installment of the payment he was promised. An unmarked white envelope, as usual. The door was shut and bolted behind him and he was free. Did a child result from those clinical thrusts? He didn't want to know then. He didn't really want to know now, either, but the "now" was different, unexpectedly complicated. Now there was a woman missing, and this same woman was sure that her sister and the son he didn't need a DNA test to confirm was his looked a lot alike.

Evelyn

Evelyn kept no routine. No, that isn't entirely true. She did and she didn't. She was routinized about her work, but not so much about anything else. Sleep was a free-for-all. At home, she could go to bed at 9pm or 4am, it didn't matter. Alone for the first time in a lifetime, she could read, draw, play whenever she pleased, all walls, all corners, her own. Here, in her daughter's house, it was different. Nothing was hers here. Like before. Sure, Peta was considerate enough to dedicate a room to her, but the gesture reeked of passive-aggression. They didn't have a relationship to warrant an exclusive guestroom. It made her uneasy.

Still, confining herself to a room as early as possible was better than staying in the living room where the windows faced the front of the house, where dozens of cameras and men congregated. Their presence made everyone anxious, prompting endless tears from Sioux, more back rubbing from Gael. No, she could not stomach being captive audience to that grand performance any longer than absolutely necessary. Then there was Peter, but Peter was a ghost, appearing and disappearing soundlessly, talking only to the cops. He lugged that baby around like a rag doll, but she was yet to hear him utter a syllable in her direction. That left Marsha and Gwenny herself. Marsha too never spoke. Evelyn wondered if she was hired on the condition of muteness with the exception of the occasional report as to Gwenny's wellbeing. She couldn't remember if she ever heard the woman's voice. No, the only voice that could still be consistently heard doing something other than crying was Gwenny's. And it was mostly nonsensical babbling, at that. If not for the small circle of creatives back home she would've lost her mind already, she was sure of that. Her phone was all she had to connect her to the world outside this house. And she tried to talk on it as much as she could. But night was a different matter. Everyone she knew accumulated relationships just as she managed to shed them. There was no one to talk to past 9pm, Pacific Standard Time.

Evelyn arranged her body on Peta's crocheted blanket and redid her loose, graying braid. Who did her daughter think she was when she picked that horror out of a lineup of mass-produced duvets? This would've been the last thing she would've picked for herself. She sighed once, twice, before getting up again to draw the shades on the sole small window in the room. It faced the backyard, where there were no cameras, but it still made her feel better. Curtains seemed the common denominator in her life: they were with her when she needed privacy from her parents when they shared a room inside a larger apartment housing four more families, they were there when she needed privacy from her five roommates in college, their beds lining the perimeter of that cold, high ceilinged room, they were there when she was stuck with Peta in that attic in Kansas, and they were there in every house she shared with her friends. In her first apartment with Sioux she finally had a door. She no longer needed curtains.

Where was Peta? She didn't have to wonder about her whereabouts when she lived under her roof; it was unfair to have to do that now. She was supposed to be done. Done ages ago! Peta—forever the stubborn attention hog. Maybe she was more like her mother than Evelyn had given her credit for.

The plan was never to have her; to have kids at all, for that matter. Evelyn did not hide this fact from either one of her children. Maybe a little bit from Sioux, but certainly not from Peta. No, the plan was to simply try and run at the first opportune moment. It wasn't every day that a Soviet theatre got to tour the United States. Of no political convictions of any kind, Evelyn merely wanted to be free. The art she wanted to make and the way she wanted to make it at home—even at the age of twenty-one she knew she wouldn't be able to make it. She didn't want to mend dresses for ballerinas for a living. And she didn't want to live with her parents for lack of housing options either. Her parents nodded solemnly when she'd told them of her plans, though they didn't understand. They would never see each other again; neither understood that.

It was all set. Only she kept losing her nerve once across the Atlantic. Boston, New York, Washington D.C., Chicago—she kept getting cold feet. She had her script committed to memory, planning to report exactly what she logically thought the United States would love to hear from a citizen of the mighty Soviet Union who desperately wanted to stay: she was seeking artistic freedom, political freedom, religious freedom or some such. Still, though she practiced her speech in Russian nightly and her desire to stay grew with every city, her nerve to make a run for it weakened as the tour rolled on. Then came Topeka... That's where it happened—the one unplanned, unexpected thing. When he entered her room with her roommate's key, when he climbed into the shower with her. When he held both of her wrists with one hand and parted her legs with the other, his fingers fat little sausages. That was when she'd stopped trying to remember the frame by frame. When he left, she was face down on the bed with no recollection of how she got there. No words were exchanged. Drowsy and sore, she knew she wasn't going to make it to Los Angeles. Instead, she'd wrapped the many wasteful towels that the hotel staff left in the room for her and the other seamstress she roomed with, and stumbled downstairs. She'd asked the reception to call the cops using all the English vocabulary she could summon under stress. She'd asked for an interpreter, she'd given a statement, she'd asked for asylum. She was going to do that all along just not as rape victim; simply a Soviet citizen feigning oppression. When, two weeks later, she tested positive, her case suddenly began to move with such ease, it was as if the bureaucrats' desks were suddenly greased—*1971, a young Soviet aspiring artist is raped by her artistic director while on tour and is now pregnant?* Now that was a story! She didn't have the heart to see what would happen to her case-file if she would inquire as to abortion. In Soviet Union, she'd already had two abortions by then and firmly wanted another. But what would happen to her case? Would she be sent back, like her rapist? And that's how Peta came to be. She knew she should've been grateful, but she hated that child for growing, for trapping her just when she finally had her freedom, when she finally could envision living alone, taking an art class that wasn't censored. She tried to stunt that growth as best as her own mother taught her—hot baths, headstands, jumping jacks. Nothing helped. She lived. An uncomplicated birth, she came out a puffy cheeked newborn. Sometimes Evelyn liked to pinch them just a second too long, just a smidgen too hard. When she was older, she'd sometimes hide a toy the girl particularly liked, or a blanket. Once, it was a book report she knew she had due.

Evelyn felt her eyes draw shut and remembered that she was still wearing her clothes and shoes. She's always hated this about American TV—the actors always lying down on their bed with their shoes still on. It was disgusting. She felt too close to sleep to wrestle out of her clothes, but she managed to kick off her shoes without much of an effort. Then she re-braided her hair and gave in to sleep. Her girl had to be all right. She'd survived everything else.

Friday, October 5th

<u>John</u>

It's 7:05am and I have already snoozed my alarm twice. I need to get up. I have a sociology class at 8:26 and my commute from here is almost twice as long. 8:26…who comes up with schedules like this? Why not 8:25? Why not 8:30?

This couch is lumpy. It was lumpy the first night, but four nights is entirely too long. I can go home, of course. I know I can. But somehow going to the police station yesterday was an easier task than entering that house. It was just for an official statement—the whole thing took roughly an hour. I was more nervous about it than I had to be, as it turns out. Foster and whatever the other one's name is sat in a windowless room with me and recorded my account of Peta's pretty much last accounted for interaction. To be completely honest, I expected them to be a little more tense, a little more preoccupied, but no, it was all bureaucracy for them. The tall gray one chewed his lips a lot, watching me write. The blonde lady kept checking her watch. It was as if I was wasting their time. If they had realized how inconsequential my presence at this station was, why did they even ask me to come in? They could've typed up what I had already told them and brought it over for me to sign at the store. Nope—one's day must be interrupted.

Anyway, I didn't have to lie. Peta Knudsen came to my register at such and such time, with such and such items, she invited me to go with her down to Seattle to meet her sister. Why? I have no idea. Honestly. Truly. That's all I could put to paper because that's all that I did. The only thing I omitted was that mom was hiding behind a stack of bagels capping off the bread aisle. But Mom did this with some regularity. When I first got the job she showed up without silly disguises: she'd just buy something and make sure to check out with me. Then, eventually, a few months back, she started playing detective—showing up and lurking in the background. Mom's a shitty spy and I'm not convinced Peta didn't see her, too. She dashed when Peta did, presumably betting on me not registering her now that a new customer was tossing something on my conveyor belt. But my god, mom is such a terrible spy, it's embarrassing. It's no big deal for me to omit this little piece of chronology from my nothing of a statement. There is no way mom did anything worthy of further examination. There is no doubt in my mind that all my mom did upon exiting the store that afternoon is go out to her truck, light a cigarette that dad and I both pretend we don't know she occasionally lights, drove home, got drunk, and called my father. I know this with a degree a certainty I'd take to Vegas. This had happened so many times, it is so much an educated guess as it is conceited certainty. Mom is not violent—she is a drunk (and not a violent one, at that). She gets weepy and sleepy—that's her drunk M.O. Mentioning her would not only be a waste of police time, but also drive mom to drink more, and for more of dad's papers to go ungraded. It just wasn't worth it. I signed what I could and left. As far as I know, I'm done over there.

God, I need to get out of bed. Off this *couch*. Whatever. I'm going to be late. If for nothing else, I need to move back to mom's to take advantage of that slightly shorter commute time. I check my phone. It's already 7:18. With a sigh I know I'm too young to justify, I land my feet on my friend's very much visibly dusty carpet and slide my thumb down my phone screen. Maybe if my eyes focus on something, my mind will wake up and my body will follow. Avoiding social media, I check CNN instead. It's official— Peta is national news.

Sioux

I'm breaking out. There's a painful pimple right on my chin. Every time I move my jaw, I feel my skin stretch and pull. It feels like it's the size of a small planet. It's gross. My fingernails itch to pop it, but mommy says I must never. I try and try to look away. It takes considerable amount of energy to pry my eyes away from my reflection so I take to washing my hands with Peta's soap. I wipe my hands with Peta's towel. We still haven't washed the towels in Peta's bathroom even though they say we all really should every couple of days. Dead skin cells and all. For further distraction, I open lotion after lotion on Peta's impeccable vanity and rub them on every bit of exposed area of skin, of which there isn't a great amount given that October is not what you would call warm up here. Scents of vanilla are predominant among the many salves my sister keeps by her sink, as if intent on proving mommy right on her choice of descriptors for her. I get dressed before the steam from my shower can fully dissipate.

Peta's bathroom is of that steam-punk variety. Does this cancel out all the vanilla? I wonder. It's all cold industrialism. This is and isn't a stark contrast to the rest of the house. It's weird. How can something be so incongruent and not? Like—her bedroom is all whites and Tiffany blues with all the foot rugs and intimidating, oversized upholstered headboards. And the downstairs is a wannabe Gaston's hunting lodge sans LaFau, with all the exposed wood beams and cathedral ceilings. But here is Peta's bathroom with its pipes, its wooden shelves, its unframed mirrors. I don't know whose idea it was or how it came about. The faucets, the shower stall, the Jacuzzi. But they are all shiny. Maybe that's what the common theme with the rest of the house is, shiny. It's like a studio set prepared for multiple projects at once.

The idea of starting my day is excruciating. My lids are heavy and swollen from sleep that's been fragmented for days. All I want is sleep. I sit down on the edge of the tub and cradle my head. I let my eyes close. I know I have to get out of here but I can't just yet. I hear Gwenny from down the hall. I hear Gael. I haven't seen Peter since last night. He hasn't been using this room. It's pretty much mine now. And none of us have heard from Peta in days.

I take out my phone and look through my texts. Is she safe? Is she alive? Then I check my missed calls. There is no purpose to this, it's just that I feel a sudden desperate need to make sure I hadn't accidentally missed any calls from Peta, haven't missed any texts. She was coming to see me— is this my fault? My thumb is shaky. I pull the screen down, refreshing it over and over. I'm dizzy within moments. I should probably eat. Or, at the very least, measure my blood sugar. There's nothing new on my screen. The last time Peta's number appears in my missed calls logs was the day before she was due in Seattle. The last text was the morning of, telling me she's on her way. Before I can turn the screen off, my thumb slips and I'm in my voicemails.

Peta.

It's a bad habit. Gael always tells me this. I'll get your message but not delete it. "How can you even keep track at the end of the day," he asks every so often, my phone never locked.

"I'd ask you about Seattle weather but that'd be silly. I'll see you tomorrow, lovie. I got some hardcore intel for you…do kids say that nowadays? Let's just say, you'll see mommy-dearest in a whole new light."

My heart is pounding, as is my head. The pipes, the mirrors, they begin to undulate before me. I play it again.

"I'd ask you about Seattle weather but that'd be silly. I'll see you tomorrow, lovie. I got some hardcore intel for you…do kids say that nowadays? Let's just say, you'll see mommy-dearest in a whole new light."

Peta's voice is tinny and the acoustics tricky in this room. She is speaking as if she were there. It's uncanny. Still, I'm not sure why, but my thumb won't move from the icon. I play the message over and over again. I swallow down bile and try to stand up again, make my way back to the mirror, my thumb still on "replay." I have to stop. I turn on the faucet to drown out my sister's shimmery voice. Maybe that will help. I splash cold water on my face as Peta talks of some intel, she was so proud of herself to bring my way. What "intel?" What could she possibly need to tell me that would make her plan to come to me off schedule instead of waiting for me to come up for Thanksgiving? Was it something she didn't want Peter to know? Otherwise, why not wait until they both came down, as they did at some interval, even if she did not feel like waiting for Thanksgiving? Was she pregnant? Was she leaving Peter? And what does mommy have to do with any of that?

Mommy is convinced that Peta never loved Peter, convinced that their marriage was nothing but a product of Peta's spiteful nature in the first place. Then again, on other days, she is convinced Peta married him because of her pragmatic nature. They are a marketable couple, after all.

Her deeply held opinions depends on her mood. I suppose it's not that unusual; it has to be part of human nature. What does and always has surprised me about mommy, though, is how she was always so tough on Peta. Sarcasm oozes out of her when speaking to her first-born. It's the opposite of what you'd stereotypically expect. She's spent a whole two decades longer with her than she has with me. Shouldn't she love her that much more than she loves me? Shouldn't there be some bonding in place that I should be jealous of? Still, I guess, the reason doesn't matter. Mom's tough. Maybe it's because she thinks she's more capable. Who knows? But she likes to fantasize and I have to eventually come out of this bathroom in order to stop her from telling any of her stories to the police now. That's where she's headed soon, demanding updates, refusing to "stoop to depending" on Peter. He and mommy never did get along, so I'm surprised it took this long for the line of communication to finally break.

She's waiting for us now, mommy is. She's downstairs, probably braiding her hair. She does that often and seemingly without much intent because her braids always wind up loose. Not that it's of any consequence, but she simply can't say any of her crap to the cops. It's not true and would cause Peter quite a bit of unnecessary embarrassment. He's been through enough as it is. And she did too love him! She *does,* I mean. Why do I keep doing that? No past tense! But seriously, maybe not the way I love Gael, but our love is more primitive, basic. We're young, we're art majors—we're supposed to be all poetry, black and white photography, bands that no one has ever heard of, and Yerba mate. With Peta and Peter, it was more formal, maybe brutally practical. They were on TV and it was their job to make the other look better, complement each other. Yes, they were "marketable as fuck" as a pair (mommy's words), and they knew it, but that does not negate their feelings, of that I'm sure. At their wedding, both were giddy as children at the altar. I saw that on video. And when Harry was born, he thanked her on air, those wet eyes of his barely containing the saltwater inside, while she, on a live-feed, wept with joy. That I saw on TV. You can't fake that sort of emotion. Yes, they were TV personalities, but they were not trained actors. No, *are* and *aren't* respectively. No one acts with that level of proficiency without proper training. Now that I'm thinking about it, no, I don't think she was about to tell me she was leaving Peter. Even if their lives now are different, even if she maybe doesn't like him as much as she did at some point in time, I don't think she'd do that to Peter.

I turn Peta off. She's been repeating the same thirty-seven words for a length of time I forgot to measure. My chest is burning, I look at my reflection. Water is dripping down my cheeks. I've been eating chocolate if I'm eating anything at all. That's why I'm breaking out. Smelling of five different creams, I can't resist it anymore—my fingernails reach up to my chin and proceed to pick at the whitehead of my zit before I can do anything about it. In no time, I feel it begin to drain, my fingertips now moist, bloody. It brings me back and I remember that I must never. My eyes search the mirror. There's blood on my skin. Mommy will see it, there is no question about it. There's no rubbing alcohol in Peta's bathroom. Not that I can find, anyway. I hear a train whistle outside and run the tap again. It's a soothing sound, both the train and the water. It almost allows me to forget Peta's voice even though only a minute ago it enveloped me. I almost don't care anymore what intel she was in such a hurry to deliver my way. I just want to stare out this window. Bellingham is beautiful in the morning. But I have to hurry. Mommy can't go to the cops alone, but someone else will have to drive. I'm too lightheaded. I have to get Gael.

Peta's Journal Entry

The longer you live with somebody, the stranger it feels to look back, to remember that the world somehow managed to spin before they entered your life, that somehow your lungs were always able to expand and contract with the intake of oxygen. It was like that when Harry turned into dust and was returned to the earth. Peter used to have to remind me to breathe in that fragmented way, like his sudden stutter made him do it. He was taking plenty of unnecessary breaths for us both. I kept waiting until I'd imagine my skin turning blue before eventually parting my lips and gasping for air. It seemed unfair that I should or could.

You asked, Dr. Burgos, so get the tissues out. I'd much rather talk about my most effective distraction—waiting to spy that family picture of yours on your desk again just so I can rack my brain trying to figure out how I know that boy and the man to his right. I assume he's your son (and the other man, I also assume, your ex-husband, the boy's father, if my logic doesn't fail me). I've seen them both before somewhere, I want to say, but I want another clue. Can I call a friend? Use a lifeline? That's the thing about motherhood—becoming a mother messes with your perspective. Something tells me you can relate. Anyway, here goes...

We put him in day care because he wouldn't hold his cup on his own. And because he preferred the bottle over the straw. And his hands were still mostly fisted. He was one. Literally—he'd turned one just two weeks before we had "the talk."

"Put him into day dare—he'll be holding his cup in no time. You're too easy on him—too gentle. And I am, too, on your behalf. Mr. Peter is right—he's not a baby anymore. If you want a baby, have yourselves another one. This one needs structure, and we are not authority figures simply because we are primary caretakers." Catriona. Pretty much a direct quotation. I'll never forget it.

The idea of Peter and Catriona discussing this without me made my neck itch. That was my first thought, my initial reaction. Catriona was our nanny. She no longer works for us or else I'd introduce you. She was cute—an au pair from Belfast. Redheaded and downright adorable.

"Isn't it some kind of abdication of responsibility?" I'd asked her over our 3:45 A.M. coffee, my damp hair in a bun piled on top of my head. I always wait to get to the studio to look presentable. At least back then I did. Strategic mistake, if you think about it. If I was afraid that my husband's eye would stray off my auburn hair and onto

her fiery red mane of breezy waves, I should've probably been at my best to compete with my 25-year-old nanny. Well, maybe you could say I asserted my rightful place as the boss—I didn't need to impress her, she needed to impress me. Right? Right!

"I read about PDD online and I just don't want it to be that."

"Pervasive Developmental...something? Because he's not holding his cup at a year and two weeks?" I'd almost spat out my coffee. I should've fired her on the spot, but I was too tired. My eyes were burning. We'd had this same routine for a decade, Peter and I, but I never quite got used to it. Staying home with Harry those seven weeks had set me back, if anything. And Peter was just jogging down the stairs, I could hear, so we had to go. There was no time for a properly articulated firing. We were due at the station at 4:15 A.M., and it was already likely that we were going to be late. I had no time to remind Catriona that, before discussing my son's cup preferences with my husband, she should talk to me. I was his mother. But I was pissed mostly because I knew I'd have to hear all about the benefits of institutional upbringing from Peter now. You'd think he'd want for his son to have a life that resembled his own as little as possible, but I guess his son's potential deviation off the developmental milestones timeline was scarier than his own fate. Peter was a self-made man, after all, and appearances were important. Still are. Of course this was what we were going to "discuss" on our drive to work. The houses are planted sparsely, most of them ranches, so the drive at that hour of the morning is always romantic bordering on eerie. You see, the moon reflects off the water, the sycamores just grazing the dark clouds above. All this always makes me speed just a little to get on the freeway, but Peter, on the other hand, seems to relish it. He'd always rather take

138

his time on this drive and I dreaded that talk. Maybe had I dreaded having to have it less, it'd be harder for me to acquiesce.

Predictably, Peter liked the idea of day care. He'd found group homes better than the fosters he'd got put in, believe it or not, so if I couldn't be the primary caretaker, why have a twenty-something Celtic beauty queen do it? he reasoned. Why not just have trained professionals do the same? And a group setting would be great for his delayed socialization skills—behavior modeling or some such. Yeah, they'd already agreed his socialization skills were delayed when I wasn't looking, you read that right. He claimed not to blame me for returning to work when Harry was just seven weeks old. It's not like I had any real choice in the matter. If I didn't want our whole viewership to forget my face in favor of Lucia's (who wasn't even a meteorologist! She just read the teleprompter!) in the brief time that she covered for me, I had to go back. Peter got this like no one else could have. And, despite my jokes and petty insecurities, Peter never did hit it off with Catriona. He understood that her presence was an important one, but there was something about her being there that he just never got used to; it was like a guest came to visit overnight and never left. It took a short lifetime for Peter to afford his own space and he didn't need her crowding it. That's how I understand it, at least. Who knows, maybe she reminded him of one of his temporary moms, though surely Catriona was too young to evoke childhood memories he'd long ago packed up, duct-taped, and left in storage in the darkest corners of his mind. If a stranger was going to be raising his child, he told me, it may as well be in an organized fashion that would leave his son ready for school. Now, what school was he preparing him for?! I never asked. He also thought the city would appreciate this token of trust, the example it would set for the other working parents to have two TV personalities entrust the life of their baby to the educated, trained teaching personnel at the Bright and Early Development Center. That was his other argument. I don't blame him, of course, but I guess I don't not blame him either. I'm pretty sure there's an inflated sense of ego at play there, too. Maybe you could evaluate him.

So, as history now has it, Harry's death made the news. Peter okayed it. He had to. We were those adorable, super local celebrities, after all. Our Chamber of Commerce sponsored both of my baby showers, and even the Mayor attended. When he'd told me (over overstuffed containers of Chinese food that no one was going to touch) that the morning show was going to talk about it in the morning, I'd said nothing. Peter said we owed this much to the community—that they had the right to know. They'd grieve with us, he'd told me. I never said anything at all, as if pretending that if nothing was ever said on the subject, it would make it go away. Instead, that night, mute, I twirled my fork around in the thick noodles I knew I would not be able to swallow even if I were at gunpoint. Harry's throat closed, and mine, it seemed, would remain forever tighter. Poetic, right, Doc? I do try. Peter was going to sue the day care, too (also on behalf of our small population, no doubt), but I'd asked to be kept out of it. The sight of the place alone used to give me such vertigo that about four months later I actually passed out at the wheel and drove into a lamppost across the street from the daycare center. Peter obliged and settled on the city authorities taking matters into their own hands. We can only hope that the center's worker and proud holder of the associate's degree who did not know the difference between "you're" and "your" in her daily reports on our late son, but fed him nuts is now…well, we could never agree on what fate we'd wish upon her. Some days we wanted the place to spontaneously combust (but only when the owner and the teenager who called herself a teacher were in there alone). Other days, we wanted her truck to roll off the road. It really depended on the day. Still does.

So, sad yet, Doctor? No? Let's see what we can do about that.

Check this out. It turns. The world, I mean. Is that an idiotic observation? Like, it insists on turning, regardless. It dares to turn. Sun rises, sun sets. I could go on with meteorological references here, but you get it. Life—it moves on! A grief counselor (or whatever that lady's title was) warned me about this. Was she a bereavement specialist? Some shit like that. I remember she came into the patient relations conference room where they housed us and rubbed my forearm. Maybe she was called a life expert? I don't remember. She said that eventually everyone would be ready to move on and expect me to as well, even though I wouldn't be ready. It made sense. She kept saying how it was normal to have a mourning period. And that that period is of a non-uniform duration. It's personal. Everyone is different. There is no shame in it, she assured. It's okay to be sad over the fact that you will never see your child grow up, she said. Like I needed her permission. I remember trying to focus on the bitter coffee that Peter kept landing in front of me whenever I dumped the previous cup he left in a fit of violent denial that my son lay lifeless in the basement morgue. But I should've paid more attention. Asked her what "mourning" is, exactly. Surely, everything I've been feeling all these years and to this day can't be called the same thing. I suppose I could ask you, you're a shrink, but I don't want to. The trouble is that it's been four—five years (or something) and I'm still not ready to part with this feeling.

Mourning. What is it, really? That something she said—the thing about being sad about not seeing your kid grow up—does that mean that we are all just that inherently selfish? Because, if that's what we

141

call mourning, then I haven't been sad about my son all this time, I've been feeling sorry for me. And holy fuck, is that even more depressing or what?! It got me thinking—not a soul out there mourns because they feel bad for the deceased. And what is there to be sad about— they don't have to live anymore! They aren't in pain, they aren't upset. They aren't anything. They simply aren't… Aren't anything at all. So we're mourning us. Essentially. Missing "us" in some fictitious alternate universe we will never know. Shouldn't there be some shame attached to that?

But I am not ashamed. Just like that expert said I shouldn't be. So yay, I guess. Good for me. But I do keep thinking about all the things he would've been. On those nights, I can't sleep. Every time Gwenny reaches a milestone listed on the poster pasted on our pediatrician's wall, it washes over me, pulls me under. It's an outdated poster, with pictures of babies from the '80's. The milestones are still accurate, I presume. And here is Gwenny, not one yet and already ahead of her fourteen month old dead brother. Instead of celebrating, I stand there fantasizing, wondering at what age he'd catch up. Is that mourning? And is that selfish? Some combination of the two? It's something. I'm too tired to figure out what exactly. But I can't stop. I keep thinking. When I shop online for Gwenny I keep looking at boy clothes and almost click on them, wondering what would've been Harry's likely current size. This isn't about him. It's about me and my imagined motherhood. Selfish! It obviously has nothing to do with him! He has no clue I'm mourning! He has no clue who I am because he's dead! But here I am lamenting, feeling sorry for myself for not being able to dress what now would've been a preschooler. Tsk. Mommy did say I'd always been self-centered. Always. I guess we all are inherently selfish. At least I hope we are and it isn't just me. We are selfish and vain. Even the act of having a child—you do it for you, not for the unborn child, am I right? The sperm and the egg don't give a shit. The embryo unlikely does either. But you have all these fantasies about being an awesome parent and teaching a son to fish and a girl to shave her legs. For mommy, I guess, all this was a little different. But for me, for your average Joe, your average Jane, is it true? If you really wanted to impact a life of a child and have it not be about you, you'd adopt. You'd foster. Though, I guess that'd still be about that heroic "you." So maybe there is no winning. You know, Doc, this is a good exercise. When I started this entry, I had no idea I'd be talking about a win/lose situation of child bearing.

That's it, I think. I mean, I'm told to be thankful to have known little Harry at all, but I didn't know him, did I? Not past hospital discharge, really. Catriona met us in the driveway of our house and moved out only the day of the funeral. And I had gone back to work after seven weeks, returning home during a late afternoon nap and retiring to bed in order to be up way before dawn at the same time as his bath time. There was no time for knowing so there isn't much to be grateful for.

So can we talk about you yet?

Peter

Peter knew this was his doing when he refused to go to the station without an arrest, but now they were here, crossing barricades of journalists. Bursts of flashes washed out their suits and badges on their approach to Peter's heavy wooden door. The two shielded their eyes, their mouths moving, intermittently; Peter wasn't good at reading lips but it wasn't difficult to see all the right shapes of "no comment." Every hour, it seemed, more and more cameras parked just on the edge of his front lawn, careful to err on the right side of trespass. He knew them all, those mannequins, but it didn't make it any easier to look them in the eye. The words got caught in his throat whenever he tried to say hello when picking up the mail, let alone anything of substance. He never did get around to making an official statement.

This was Peter's third sit-down with the police in three days, though he wasn't sure exactly where the clock started—when Peta left the house, when she didn't arrive in Seattle as planned, when her car was discovered, or simply when Peter first reported her missing.

Nobody was offering Peter coffee this time. Instead, wordlessly, Peter made three mugs himself and placed them on the butcher's island separating him from the detectives. He attacked his own with gusto, savoring each scalding swallow as he tried not to give credence to the pain. He waited. He was good at this. People in Peter's life tended to die, and in masse, at that—waiting for "what happens next" came with the territory. Mother, father, the second cousin twice removed who'd taken him in when he was nine—they all died. Even his first set of foster parents—they died too. Peta, of course, was well aware of his history. He believed in full disclosure and laid it all out there as early as their first date. *Peter and Peta*—it seemed to be written in the stars, after all, and he wasn't about to waste time leading her on. She deserved to know what she was getting into. But she didn't like it when he talked like that. "You're not cursed," she'd groan then and with practiced regularity thereafter, smacking him playfully upside the head each time. Then Harry died. And now she's missing. She should've taken his word more seriously.

"To what do I owe this pleasure?" The roof of his mouth now numb, Peter allowed his eyes a long blink. Detective Clark blinked in return. She probably wasn't used to men being so abrupt with her. Peter had the instinct to apologize.

Detective Foster took the lead.

"You asked us to come to you instead of inviting you over in the future in the absence of an arrest warrant so here we are. We are not technically uninvited, you can say."

He must've thought himself clever, this cop, Peter smirked. Maybe even fancied himself a comedian. A man of his job, he likely wasn't used to contradictions. A man unlikely to be any older than sixty, but he was obviously either a smoker or a drinker and looked it—the creviced forehead, the tip of his nose with red little veins adorning it. He was likely going to be the "good cop." Naturally.

"We are here to go over a couple of things. Update you, while we're at it." Clark. She was going to be the bad cop.

"Appreciate it. Shoot." Peter shrugged. He sat down without offering the detectives a seat.

"Have you given any thought to making any sort of a statement?" Foster leaned in on his elbows, matching his height to Peter's.

"To the press?"

"Wouldn't even need to leave your property."

"Would that help?"

"Well, you tell me. You used to be on the other end of that barricade, no?"

Good move, Peter had to admit. His arms now folded across his body, he wondered why he'd previously decided to take such distaste for the man. And the woman to his left, for that matter. Weren't they looking for his wife? Was he so immature to take such offense to the fact that he was so obviously a prime suspect? That was protocol. He knew that. They'd be bad cops if they didn't suspect him. Was he so bitter that they brought up the existence of the journal that was currently causing so much heartburn? It wasn't their fault.

"Touché. Look, I'm not against it, De— Detective. I'll make you a deal—give me your latest and tell me what to say. Much like a doctor, I can't treat my own."

Detective Clark grinned.

"Good man," Foster concluded after a moment's thought, tapping the table twice with his palm flat. He nodded in Clark's direction, as if passing the mic. This was all careful strategy, Peter had to accept.

"Right, well. We know Peta missed her train to Seattle. She remained on the platform after the train left the station. We see her leave the station entirely about twenty-minutes later. The cameras lose her about a block away. We've checked the cameras of the businesses nearby but nothing seems to pick her up. There are no credit card charges anywhere. We don't know if that's intentional and she's making cash purchases or she lost her wallet. We do know she had to leave her car at the Organic Produce lot and walked to the train station, which is a hike. Either that or she paid for a cab in cash. Again, there is no credit card trail. Not even from Organic Produce. Was she a runner? Was she athletic?"

Peter shook his head. No, his wife wasn't athletic. He couldn't be sure but what he saw on Foster's face looked like sympathy and felt a faint twinge at his heart. Now this man thought he meant his wife was lazy. Before he could take his implication away, Foster continued with something else.

"You know that boy from the store? The one your wife went to see before leaving?"

Unable to compute this sharp turn in the conversation, Peter did something akin to both a nod and a shake of the head.

"I mean, do we know if she actually went to specifically see him…"

"Yes, we do," Clark assured. "He made an official statement—Peta wanted him to come to Seattle with her to meet her sister."

Peter chewed on his lips so as not to let anything escape from them. Her unplanned visit to Sioux did sound off to him, but he'd grown past questioning his wife's relationship with her sister. She picked up the phone at all hours of day and night, texted her incessantly. You'd think she didn't have her own daughter to raise.

"Why?"

"He claims not to know."

Peter breathed slowly, methodically.

"Like, to set them up?"

"Your guess is as good as mine."

Peter mulled this over. Sioux had a boyfriend. And as annoying as Peter found Gael, what in the world would possess his wife to drag a boy from Bellingham to meet her sister in Seattle? Is this how undone she'd become? This was her new pastime?

"We believe this guy?" Peter questioned.

"'We don't anything," Foster laughed. He sounded younger than he looked when he laughed. "But yes, Clark and I do. You? That's your business."

Readying to busy his hands, Peter reached for a mug and ran the tap for some water. He hadn't noticed how parched he'd gotten. If he didn't know any better, he'd think his mouth was agape this entire conversation. The implications were unnerving and, as the icy water hit his throat, Peter swallowed them all. The idea of his wife cheating with someone half her age was ludicrous. The woman wouldn't have the energy. And why would she want to bring him to Sioux.

"There is something he did not mention," Detective Foster added when enough time indicated Peter was not taking bait.

"Yeah?"

"His own mom was inside the store at the same time. Imagine that!"

His heart jolted. Was this a clue he was meant to process?

"But, it seems of no consequence so we can't really hold it against the young man, now can we?" Foster said this as he walked around the kitchen island to clap Peter on the shoulder. The paternal approach he was now taking wasn't welcome. Peter swooshed the last of his water in his mouth before gently shrugging off the man's palm and hurling the rest of the water into the sink with substantial propulsion. Foster was not moved. "The two left the store separately and seemingly in different directions. And then we have footage of your wife at the station and questioned the kid's mother's neighbors and confirmed with the GPS location on her leased car—she'd gone straight home. The lady was probably just looking at her kid from afar. I guess that's what adults with grown children have to do in order to gauge anything at all about their day, am I right?"

Nobody could confirm or deny. Nobody present had grownup children.

"So, what you're telling me is that you got nothing—still at square one? But I should make a statement?"

"Well, there is one fun note—the cashier's mom is your wife's shrink. Small town, I guess."

Peter's head was spinning.

"Son, look, we are canvasing the area, searching the college campus nearby, parks, the waterfront—"

"The waterfront? You think it could be suicide?"

The detective sighed, shrugging his shoulders. Was he old enough to be Peter's father? He was hard to read. Gray hair was deceptive that way.

"Look, I don't know. I'll be honest with you. It's been three days. We're looking. It's too early to give up hope, but we could use whatever help we can get."

Peter couldn't help but let a scoff escape his chest, as his face flushed and his stomach filled with dread. He'd been so busy reading Peta's journal and fending off Evelyn, he hadn't even realized that it's been that many days since Peta sent him a flippant text of, "Going to see Sioux. Marsha is here early. I'm out," and walked out of the house. He didn't sleep enough nights for this period of time to seem right. He was hoping the tremor taking over his body wasn't obvious, that his breath suddenly more shallow and rapid wasn't audible.

"That's a lot of honesty. Doesn't leave me with much faith."

He glanced at Clark, but her expression was blank. She definitely drew the "bad cop" straw on the way over.

"Okay, I'll do the press conference. Set it up," Peter announced with a nod of approval. A shudder finally escaped his shoulders. He needed to change his position, get some circulation in there.

"Anything the matter?"

His fingers trembling, he hid them in his hair, remembering that that's the only brushing they'd seen in days.

"Last time I was in front of the camera was after Harry died."

"Can you tell us how Harry died?" Detective Clark was tall—taller than Peter, who himself was squarely average. He remembered his dad being tall but his perception must've been off then, being six and roughly four feet tall.

"The entire state knows how Harry died," Peter scoffed, his face flushing. "He died of anaphylactic shock at 15 months of age after partaking in his teacher's almond croissant."

"I heard about that," Detective Clark nodded.

"I'm sure you have. It made the news, after all—I produced the segment! The Bright & Early Center was supposed to be a nut-free facility. No foods containing nuts were allowed to be brought onto the premises, but this was a policy that apparently only applied to paying patrons. Teachers were still entitled to breakfast, the director informed me when I barged into her office the morning after leaving Harry in the morgue." A fit of nervous laughter erupted out of his throat, flavored with a bit of pride for having said all that without stuttering.

"You must've been a scary sight, because she called the police after you left. Did you know that? We have the report. Did you or did you not threaten to kill Ms. Chernoff that morning?" Detective Clark asked as she sat on a bar stool opposite Peter and crossed her legs in his direction, hugging her top knee. "Do you often threaten to kill people?"

"It was a matter of speech, give me a break. As you know, she's alive and well. She killed my son. You see, Ms. Andi was having breakfast. 'Harry exhibited interest as to a new food—were Ms. Andi and I to deny it to him, you'd call us cheap!' That's what she said when I'd burst in that morning. There was no note of allergy in his file because he hadn't had the chance to even try nuts when we put him in day care. We had no idea! So yeah, I fucking yelled at her. I hadn't slept in almost thirty hours by then. Hadn't shaved, either. My eyes were rimmed red like a high rabbit's and there were scratches on my arms from where Peta had clawed at me all night." Not a single stutter! He was ready for this statement now.

"Peta Knudsen had clawed at you?" Detective Foster piped up, leaning his head to the right, his ear to his shoulder, like a curious parrot. Surely this wasn't their usual modus operandi. Surely this was just a tired, desperate attempt at getting him to lose his temper. Just when he thought they could be friends.

"She was hysterical, De- Detective. They'd just put her so- son into a refrigerated drawer. You'd claw at whoever was nearby too. Especially a spouse. I'm no- not accusing her of domestic violence, Jesus Christ!"

"I'm not married."

"Ha- hardly the point." And there it all went. The moment he'd think he was doing well, he'd jinx himself.

"Mr. Knudsen, we're very sorry for your loss. Really. The whole city—we all were and are sorry. It was tragic—a death of practically an infant. People of means, such as yourselves, I'm surprised little Harry was in day care to begin with. Though the whole town was split over if we are being honest."

Peter sighed and rubbed his stubble. He had hoped to show his face at the studio after this, but he now realized he needed to shave first.

"I don't know why we are talking about that awful morning at all. Weren't you going to set up my press conference?"

Detective Clark re-crossed her legs again and leaned further in Peter's direction ever so slightly. She sighed emphatically, as if she felt sorry for his lack of understanding of such fundamentals.

"Fine," Peter barked, standing a little straighter and crossing his arms just a little too tight across his chest. "She was tall and massive. A mountain of blown-out blonde hair on her head, a heaping bust. Her makeup was on, as per her usual level of upkeep. I remember wondering if she'd slept. *How* she'd slept! I wondered how *anyone* at all could sleep now. Peta and I were unlikely to sleep for at least a month, I knew that for a fact even then, and there she was—smug and clean. An- and I was wrong—it took three month to get to the point where we could actually stay a- asleep for more than fo- four hours," he scoffed. Maybe this was a tactic aimed at breaking him down before going on camera. Maybe they were banking on emotion—maybe he'd come across more genuine, relatable if his emotions were raw and on the surface. "The place was quieter than usual. Many parents must've heard about what happened the day before. They probably stayed up all night and waited all morning to hear an update from their trusty morning anchor—*me*! Little did they know; I was busy filling out my son's death certificate as they sipped their morning coffee. I- I haven't been on ca- camera since." Peter could feel his eyes begin to fill and took a breath before it was too late to swallow his tears. "'We're very sorry this happened,' she told me, 'but this wasn't something within our control. May I remind you that you first brought Harry to us when he wouldn't hold his own cup. I believe the term PDD was bounced around—" Peter's impression of Mrs. Chernoff always irked Peta.

"PDD?" Clark asked.

"Pervasive Developmental Delay. It was bullshit. He was fine! He was even beginning to speak when that bitch fed him the damn almonds. This was just her idea of shutting me up, keeping me quiet. 'He'd blossomed here in such a short period of time,' she kept telling me. 'And here he was—wanting to try something *new*! How could we not oblige?' 'And now he's dead!' I'd screamed back. I actually

155

remember my throat closing then, so I couldn't say much more than that." He touched his neck now, stroking it.

"What did she say to that?" Detective Foster looked genuinely engrossed. For a second, Peter almost forgot that this wasn't a regular friendly conversation—he was still a suspect in his wife's disappearance, and though he wasn't technically under arrest, surely his words could eventually come back to bite him in the ass. He had to pick them wisely. There was no teleprompter to help him out here.

"She said that they certainly didn't mean any harm, that it was all an accident. Same as before. All I tried to tell her was that they blatantly violated their own rules—that they claim to be a nut-free facility and yet they bring foods containing nuts there and feed them to children. But my throat was too dry from too much overnight talking. It needed a break. I was cro— croaking. I'm sure I could not have sounded that con— convincing or intimidating—"

"Did you want her to be intimidated?"

"Well, she did say that the twenty-year-old who was my son's teacher had called her when Harry reached for her croissant, seeking permission, and she was the one who encouraged the transaction. She wa— watched him eat it. She watched him die!" Peter took a deep breath when he felt a lump settle in his throat. The tightness was back. It hurt. He massaged it, fearing it'd constrict altogether.

"And neither you nor Mrs. Knudsen ever told them about little Harry's allergy?"

"Again, he hadn't yet had the opportunity to try nuts, I told you! 'He was 15 months, for fuck's sakes!' That's a direct quote, by the way. And that's also where this infamous stutter that cost me my job first began to kick in."

"The stutter?"

"Ye— yes. After Harry died, I'd dev— developed a stutter. The same one you've been listening to all this time. I stuttered as a kid but then it got better with age. And then it got wo—worse again."

"Right! That's why you were no longer anchoring!" Detective Clark nodded helpfully.

"Tha— that's correct."

His throat, his chest. He couldn't understand what was happening. His words seemed trapped as deep as his lungs. Just like that morning in that overly lit institution that was really a day care but insisted on calling itself a "school."

"It's stress related, then?" Clark inquired.

Peter nodded, feeling his temples sweat.

"Are you okay, Mr. Knudsen?" he heard them ask when he didn't say anything further, echoing Ms. Chernoff from many years ago, his limbs too heavy to move or rearrange.

"N— no! I— I'm not okay! My s— s— son is d— de— dead! An— and my w— wi— wife is missing!" he barked.

"Do you think your wife's disappearance is causing you another setback, then? Are you angry at your wife?" Detective Foster asked.

Peter considered this. This wasn't an unreasonable question. In his business, not unlike that of Foster's, he knew that truth was rarely something that was commended or appreciated. Still, feeling his words about to catch in his throat, he bit.

"You'd have to narrow down your query first, but wouldn't you be? She's not the only one depressed. She's lost a son, but so did I! And I also lost a wife in the pro— pro— process. And then a career on top of th— that. She gets to glum about, go from therapist to therapist, drug herself into stupor, and I have to pretend I'm perfectly fine behind the scenes, my speech therapist repeating the sa— same mind numb— numbing exercises, week in and week ou— out."

While Foster let an obligatory pause settle between them, surely in the hopes that Peter would let absolutely anything else escape his lips despite the speed bumps, Peter breathed through his nose. He had to remind himself that the relief he'd feel by getting it all out there wouldn't be worth it. If he wanted to talk about his feelings, maybe he could go visit Peta's doctor.

"Right. Well, are you ready to pop out there, then? Say a few words to the press? Maybe make an appeal to anyone who may have seen your wife?"

Evelyn

Bellingham Police Department was not aesthetically pleasing to Evelyn. Too angular, too beige. The blue sign out front—too dingy. It was altogether too cold a building to arouse much of anything by way of any emotion but her lip curled on approach, anyway. Gael's car hit the park gear pretty rough, as if it too was expressing its distaste. This was a town of roughly eighty thousand residents—surely they could've gotten away with something more authentic to the Pacific North West. Something more rustic or quaint. Something inspiring openness and conversation. This box didn't inspire any confidence. She wasn't an architect, but a few of her friends were designers and she was sure any one of them would love to lend a hand in redesigning the space. How could she expect anyone to comfort her inside the building that screamed "Medical Arts Plaza" more than anything else. Appearances matter. Clothes matter, business cards matter, your children's upkeep—it all matters. Like it or not, the cover is important. People judge you on it. Same of buildings. They should've thought of that when they approved that cover, Evelyn thought. Someone had to initial that sketch. They couldn't expect a mother to present properly bereaved when the space was so clinical. Was she there to demand more information on the investigation of her disappeared daughter or to get a mammogram? She could no longer tell as she unclicked her seatbelt.

"Are you ready, mommy?" her little girl asked from the back seat as Evelyn tried in vain to find her glasses in her bag. If she could find them, she could rent her own car and not have to drag these children around everywhere. This was already burdensome. She's never really had to juggle two of her children simultaneously so the idea of sharing Sioux now was still uneasy. Peta was long gone to college by the time Sioux was born. And she never so much as visited any other time besides that wasteful five-week winter break once a year. That was all the bonding the girls got. Because of this, Evelyn never understood Sioux's infatuation with her sister. How much of her did she even see growing up? How much of her did she really know? She didn't have them to be buddies. They weren't strategically spaced 18 months apart or anything of the sort. One was an accident, at best, and the other meticulously planned. Now one was nowhere to be found and the other one was flirting with a coma on hourly basis. Evelyn had no time for herself anymore. She couldn't even find her glasses, for goodness' sake. That's what it'd come down to.

Having a second child at her age, what was she thinking? It seemed to make perfect sense at the time, but now, it wasn't so important. She hadn't thought everything through clearly she hadn't had the reason to look this far into the future. But whoever takes the potential of their first born going missing into account when hand-picking a man to father her second?

"Yes," she sighed. "No use delaying the inevitable."

"It'll be ok, mommy," Sioux tried to comfort. Her speech was slow. She needed more than oxygen for her sustenance.

Evelyn landed her cowboy boots on the blacktop and eased herself out of the car. Gael's sedan was too low, and her age was slowly beginning to show itself, she hated to admit. She missed her truck. After a slow stretch, she led the children inside. It hadn't been a long ride—fifteen minutes tops, but it was too long a time spent inside a stuffy vehicle that was as quiet as a tomb: Sioux in premature mourning, Gael too afraid to breathe for fear of taking any oxygen away from Sioux. Stepping out onto the outdated plaza that contained the police department was somehow refreshing and invigorating. It was just what she needed.

"I need to see Detective Clark or Detective Foster, please. Now."

The boy who'd likely only recently begun to shave sat mute behind his desk for a second too long. This was a common reaction to Evelyn, her age ambiguous, her body breathtaking. She reveled in this as long as she could; any longer and she knew it'd read inappropriate.

"Foster or Clark. Now."

The bulletproof glass between them seemed excessive. Evelyn tapped on it when the man was slow to pick up the phone. She could feel Sioux tense behind her, forever embarrassed by her eccentric mom, her strong jaw taking on a masculine form for a moment. She was glad the girl inherited the feature from her father. Gael likely stood behind Sioux, his disproportionately large palm on her daughter's bony shoulder for a split moment before taking a nonchalant trip down to the small of her back. Evelyn did not need to turn to confirm this. They were predictable. And the reflection in the glass in front of her was clue enough.

It didn't take the boy too long to hang up the line and she could tell that there would be no detectives coming. Before he could even part those precious lips in some sort of bullshit excuse, Evelyn felt her blood pulse harder in her temples.

"Is there a problem?" she asked with her head tilted in mock inquiry. "I'm not leaving until I speak to either one of them." She turned to look for a chair to pull up to the window by way of illustration of her intent but saw none in the immediate vicinity.

"Yeah, ma'am, I get that, but it may be a while. Apparently, Detective Foster and Clark are currently at your daughter's house. In front of it, actually."

Somehow, before she could process what exactly was the meaning of the boy's self-satisfied grin, Evelyn felt her daughter's hand wrap around her shoulder. Out of the corner of her eye, she saw the color drain from her face. And before she could ask for some sort of clarification, the boy behind glass aimed a remote control at a TV-set nestled in the corner of the olive-walled waiting room, waking it. Preset to the local news channel, it came to life with the image of her son-in-law, flanked by the two officers whose faces now ignited nothing but prompt nausea within Evelyn. They stood so close to Peter, she wondered if he were feeling faint and asked him to secure him in that rigid, upright position. His eyes were loaded and ready to go. They wouldn't of course; they wouldn't go anywhere. They didn't back when Harry died and they wouldn't now. He was good but he wasn't that good.

"I love my wife. I have not seen her since Monday morning nor has she gotten in contact with me. This is becoming a nightmare come true, and our family is familiar with nightmares."

Evelyn bit her lip so hard she could taste copper. Was this doubling as a new audition tape? Who talks like that when speaking about his missing wife? She was happy Sioux couldn't see her skin begin to flush. The girl's knee-jerk reaction has always been to defend the poor orphan boy.

"The police department is doing the best it can. I am working closely with these detectives. They've worked with K-9 units and have canvassed neighborhoods, but it's like my wife disappeared without a trace."

For a man who'd been fighting a stutter for years, Peter's production sure sounded a lot like Standard American English to Evelyn. Her heart vibrating, Evelyn could no longer resist stealing a glance at Sioux. Gael had the girl under his arm, her face dangerously close to his chest; his own eyes were narrowed in concentration not required for this material. If it weren't for Peter's infuriatingly smooth delivery on the cop's screen, she would've wrestled her child from his grasp. Instead, she brought her gaze back to the screen where Peter continued to slump against Detective Foster like some prodigal son, his eyes moist, his limbs unnaturally long.

"If any— anyone has seen Peta, please, ple— please call the police." The precise timing of the return of the stutter made it feel as if Evelyn's heart was ready to eject itself right out of her body by way of her mouth. "An— and Peta, if you're watching this, if you— you're listening, please call. Gwenny and I miss you."

"You've got to be fucking kidding me!" she barked when it was over and Foster announced that no questions would be taken by the husband at the present moment. Her voice hurt her own ears. Success. She couldn't disappoint her baby girl, after all. Surely, she was counting on mommy losing her shit. The boy jumped, as did another officer to his right, and Evelyn couldn't help but grin. It was fun to still be able to instill fear using only her voice. It had always been a useful tool in the arsenal. Too bad that one night that she needed it, the night Peta was conceived, she did not have it. Her work here was done but seeing the young man so shaken, she couldn't help but smack the thick glass separating them. "Let's go!" she barked at Gael, who practically hopped at attention.

She wasn't sure if Gael's Echo could survive a bang she was about to impart but she did it anyway—she folded herself in the front passenger seat and slammed the door so hard, she was sure she saw the glass shudder. No matter. She could always replace the window, if need be. The door, too. Still, likely unnerved not just by her but by Peter's impromptu press conference, the children waited a beat too long to follow her inside.

Motherfucker. Couldn't Peter have let her know that the cops were on their way? How important could this address have been at this point? Why exclude the mother? Petty little man, she'd always known this. She needed to speak to these cops herself, without Peter. She'd tell them everything she thought about him, finally—what an attention hog he was, what a control freak. She was the mother—she needed the updates, not the incidental crumbs she was getting. Enough was enough. She felt her blood thump in her temples and burn through her stomach. She felt the sting of tears but those were not allowed out here. She was a grieving mother, yes; and a grieving mother cries, yes. However, a weeping woman, mother or not, is rarely taken seriously. No, a different emotion had to be demonstrated.

"Let's go," she hollered a little too loudly now. There was no need for the strangers passing by to stare. "Get in!"

Evelyn closed her eyes so as not to watch the two approach in with feline caution. It would only irritate her further, and "any further" could lead to spontaneous combustion.

"Home, I assume?" Sioux volunteered, not unreasonably, from the backseat. She could not have been comfortable back there, her limbs long and lean, but Evelyn often felt sick riding in the back.

"No," Evelyn announced with her fingers twisting this way and that, braiding her graying hair. "Take me to the store. The one where Peta went before running off." Predictably, the children tried to talk the silly old grieving mom out of such a traumatic trip. Certainly this could only end in tears. Sioux already teetered on the edge of tears, Gael flexed his jaw and patted Sioux on the knee from the driver's seat. The tears long ago preloaded in Evelyn's eyes nearly escaped. "I don't need to justify myself to either one of you. I need to go there, okay? It's bad enough no one thought to ask the mother to make a statement! Don't make this worse. No, we're going. I'm her mother—I need to see what she saw." It was hard to argue with that. Generally, it was hard to argue with Evelyn. She closed her eyes and the car began to move.

Dr. Burgos

They needed to talk. She knew it. She hoped he knew it too. All she had to do was stop kicking herself for calling him that drunken, desperate night and move the fuck on. This was going to drive her liver to the brink. It was too late. He was here now. She had to deal with it. Once and for all. It would maybe be better this way. Like pulling off a

Band-Aid. Like she used to tell Johnny when he was little, when the doctor would paste a piece of plaster across his chunky thigh after one shot or another. He'd cry when he'd see her go for it, but she'd bite her lip, pull his skin taunt, and quickly peel it off before he would even notice. Then she would kiss it. That's what she had to do now.

"Do you have a child?"

He looked up from his stack of papers, brow and lips contorted in that same casual disdain that was commonly reserved for Lena. She could never quite understand why he hated her so much. Perhaps, she considered, while she was at this, she could ask for more information on this matter, too. And maybe hatred was too big a word but that look on his face had been there since the day they exchanged their vows at City Hall. She wore that floral maxi dress and combat boots she borrowed from a former roommate, while he wore his only suit—the same one he wore to his law school clinic hours. He used to smile before, she was sure of that, but his face somehow soured after they traded rings. It did, at least, whenever his gaze landed on her.

"Yes. His name is John. You've met."

Before Dr. Burgos could think of a clever comeback, Andrew was back to grading papers written by his adoring students who were likely wondering why their disciplined professor was out for so long. Was he sick? Did he need nursing? Surely, they'd be volunteers. She shook her head.

She should've gone back to work today, caught up on paperwork before seeing the Greens again. She knew she needed all the prep she could use before their session. Each one of their sessions brought with them so much tension, she needed to stretch each time they would finally leave and she'd deposit their check into her locked desk drawer. Instead, she was still wearing her robe over her wrinkled pajamas, her hair in a messy bun. This wasn't what she was planning to wear when confronting her ex-husband with this question. Yesterday, she chickened out, let him change the subject, let him escape into his work. But today was it. They had to say what had to be said out loud. Tomorrow she was getting dressed and going to work. This had to be it.

"I know my son's name, Andrew. Any others?"

Finishing up something in front of him, Lena couldn't seem to will Andrew to look up at her. She tried staring intently, she tried sighing, she tried coughing. These strategies never worked for her when they were married and there were not working now. In her practice, were she wearing her signature pantsuit and glasses, she'd recite the age-old motivational quote that defines insanity as pursuing same methods whilst expecting different results. There was a reason it was frowned upon to treat yourself. She continued to stare, sigh, and cough. She wanted him to pound his fists on the table, tell her how stupid he thought she was, how hysterical…*something*. Instead, he continued to read as Dr. Burgos watched, her eyes narrowing, her vision blurring. She breathed intently trying to suppress the desire to hurl the French press that was brewing her coffee at his head. Smelling the flowers and blowing out the candles, she chose to make him coffee rather than causing him bodily injury. It was a better choice, a wiser decision.

"What are you talking about?" he eventually asked with a sigh so tired, Dr. Burgos considered offering him a blanket and a pillow. It was well past noon. Maybe she could abandon this quest and settle for a nap. Tightening her robe, Dr. Burgos didn't know what to do with Andrew's attention now that she had it.

"Did I tell you that she came to me before she went to see John. That day, I mean. That's why I followed her." She swallowed hard, feeling her legs begin to grow warm and soft. She reached for a bar stool of her own, coming down to her ex-husband's eye level.

Andrew rubbed his eyes with the heels of his palms.

"How much have you had to drink today, Lena? It's barely lunch time!"

Before she could do anything about it, white noise flooded her ears, her arm swung high and landed on the stack of student papers weighed down by Andrew's elbows. Before he could protest, she flung them off the counter.

"What the fuck is the matter with you?" she heard him cry, bringing her back to the kitchen.

"I'm not drunk!" she retorted too late.

"I swear you need help. You, of all people, should be able to recognize that…"

"She said that her sister looks like you. That her sister and John look alike. What does that mean? Tell me what the fuck that means!"

Peta's Journal Entry

Strange, I've seen this face before.

No, I'm not just singing that charming vintage classic. No, no, I mean it—I have literally seen this face before! What am I referring to? I thought you'd ask. Or rather, imagined, as you will allegedly never read this. But really, it's much more exciting to write this thinking that you will somehow get your hands on my innermost thoughts. And regardless, you bet your ass this is what we're talking about my next session.

Any-who, you want the short story? You must've forgotten to lock your desk. Silly, silly Lena. You had to have known that I'll look again. You saw my interest. You must have! That last time when you hurled the photo out of my field of vision, you seriously should've anticipated that I'd be back for it. Why did you even hide it back then? Did I creep you out? Was my looking at your family inappropriate? Well, anyway, if you were indeed uncomfortable with my level of interest and failed to straight up remove the picture from the building (or even worse—failed to register that very real aforementioned interest), then this is on you. If anything, this leads me to believe that you wanted me to get my hands on it again. Subconsciously, maybe? Did you? And to what end? Ooh, I love puzzles.

So I've been staring at this damn photo for hours now. There were two, apparently—one tucked behind the other in the frame. At first I thought they were doubles that you got free of charge at some one-hour photo service, but no—they are slightly different. My guess is that you just couldn't make up your mind between the two. Been there. Guilty! Well, now if you look back inside that magic drawer of yours, take out the frame and open it, you'll see that only one photo remains. You're not missing much—again, they are pretty much identical. You won't have reason to miss it. Other than the fact that, you know...I kind of stole it.

I've been staring at it since yesterday. You're in the middle, between two men whose arms drape reluctantly around your shoulders. One I recognize! He's the kid from Organic Produce! That's your son? Contextually, it would appear so. He's nice. He talked to me once— expressed his condolences. Not super original but nice, anyway. If I didn't know any better, I'd say he has a vague crush on me. He always attempts to smile while bagging my groceries, jerks as if stricken by lightning if our fingertips touch when he hands me my receipt. It's cute. He's what—under twenty-five, right? He looks so much like my sister. She's twenty-two. It's fucking uncanny. I'd write it off to vague, undetected racism if it weren't for the other man in the photo...Well, here's the thing—the other guy is Andrew! My first boyfriend Andrew. The same one who left me for a pregnant ex. I swear! I was trying to find an old Polaroid I had of him before going to college earlier but I couldn't find it in any of my old boxes. I had a couple, I think. I didn't take them or anything—mom had a camera but I wasn't to use it. No, I begged him for some photos to take with me to college before he dumped me. I may have left it back at mommy's house. The whole thing was so humiliating and painful, I probably didn't want to take a reminder with me to the dorms. Maybe I even tore it to shreds. Who knows now, but that piece doesn't even matter. Because it's him, Doc! I swear, it's him. What are the odds of that? I don't give a fuck what's on your agenda for tomorrow, because this is what we'll be focusing on.

Andrew

Andrew couldn't tell Lena what it all meant even if he wanted to. And he didn't want to, so there was that. Instead, he shoved his papers into his bag, graded and ungraded painfully crinkled together, shoved the bag under his arm, and left Lena to reel alone, finding refuge in his rental parked outside, unwilling to have even that temporary vehicle share shelter with Lena's. He heard items thump and clatter behind him, but he had a rule about not engaging his ex-wife whenever she was like this. She wouldn't hear him now, no matter how hard she implored him to talk to her, to be honest. She didn't mean it. It was a trap. All that could result from this was more dishware broken. He'd be called names she'd later beg to take back, he'd be left to clean up the debris in the wake of his wife's rage, his fingers in nicks and scrapes. Leaving was an easy decision. This wasn't about her twenty some years ago and it didn't need to be about her now.

Emptying his lungs with force, Andrew backed out of the driveway with slow, measured pumps of the gas. A street so empty it reminded him of a recurring dream he had after watching *Vanilla Sky*. A ghost of a feeling filled his chest while his mind reminded him that he wasn't as alone as it appeared; Lena, after all, was just on the other side of the wall. He paused there, at the curb, realizing that he had nowhere to go. Going back home now, without facing his son, would be unbecoming of the father he was. He owed Lena nothing, he was certain of that, but John deserved better than that. And he did not know where the nearest Starbucks was so if he wanted to wait out the storm grading his papers, he'd need to do it in the car. No, he was too old for that. His right hand on the gear stick, he settled the car into drive and began to roll down the block. Lena couldn't watch him hesitate through the window as he typed in the name of John's store into his phone.

Evelyn

It wasn't much of a surprise for Evelyn to see that her daughter liked to shop in places they could never have afforded back in the '80s were it not for their multiple benefactors. Moving in with adult roommates had turned out to be a wise move, Evelyn had quickly learned back in 1970-something. A young mother adapting to a whole new way of life whilst tapping into her creative essence had hit all the right notes. Still, even when pooling their resources together, their village was not a rich one, but it was luxury next to what Evelyn had been accustomed to growing up. But of course the girl wanted to feel rich the moment she could afford to. It made sense, even if it was a disappointment of a revelation. Evelyn too could afford these prices now, but who would want to spend $7.99 on a carton of milk? Maybe it wasn't a surprise but it was a letdown. Her girl should've known better. She could've learned a thing or two from her mother.

Evelyn had nothing in mind by way of actual shopping. To be honest, she didn't quite know why she insisted the kids bring her here. It wasn't like the place claimed any kind of significance. It was simply a place her daughter was seen visiting last, the place where her car, apparently running on empty, finally refused to start. That's all. That was it. It was just a store. Eggs, milk, bread—all overpriced. It was just that even she could not put Sioux through staying at the police station waiting for the detectives for however many hours that would take, and she couldn't bring herself to go home (Peta's home, that is) and face Peter. She couldn't go *home*-home, that she knew. But every minute spent in that glass house felt like a short eternity. Every time she bumped into Peter, every time Gwenny cried, she felt a stab of guilt. She couldn't quite put her finger for what, precisely, but as far as she could tell, it was indeed guilt. That proverbial pull at the heartstrings, that heaviness in the stomach—that was guilt, right? Guilt for not being out there looking, guilt for her part in her daughter's existence, guilt for being there at the house when she was not. Maybe some of that. The kids trailing behind her, Evelyn tried to throw items her baby had to eat more of into her cart. All she'd been eating was whatever random crap Gael fed her, she knew. Her skin was breaking out, it was getting obvious. Goodness, she had to at least take care of this one. The girl need more fiber, some berries.

Above them, all alone the perimeter of the store's ceiling, TVs spoke of the impending fog and rain. Just yesterday it was all Peta, all the time. Peter was too late with his press conference—the interest was already fading. Of all people, she expected him to be familiar with the timeline. The idea of it sent a jolt through her bloodstream. This was enough shopping—time to go rip him a new one.

"Find everything you were looking for?" the young man at the cash register asked, and all the fight went out of Evelyn.

Gael

The idea of Gael and Sioux trailing her only egged Evelyn on. Her shoulders looked squarer, her hair had more sway to it, Gael was certain of it. He was beginning to suspect that the woman had eyes in the back of her head. There was pep in her step with them on her heels.

The purpose for this trip remained a mystery to Gael. It certainly wasn't about the two of them, which was fun in it of itself, he mused to himself. The trouble was, it wasn't about Peta either. Not really. As he watched the woman examine the various prices of apples, Gael wondered how many sins the woman in front of him could serve as the embodiment for. This little side trip was, of course, about Evelyn and no one else. Pride, at particular, was at play. Peter's statement must've been like a scalpel was taken to it—if you squinted, you could imagine it bleeding, a wet, soggy gash increasing in radius with every inhalation, Gael was sure of it as he continued to study the woman as she hunched over the pears. How dare he go on TV, syndicated and all, and talk about missing his wife? How dare he not say that his mother-in-law was the true victim of this circumstance? How dare he not stutter enough for the woman's satisfaction? So, a panacea for her hemorrhaging ego, of course Gael and Sioux simply had to deliver the woman to this store, which was so wastefully outfitted with too many television sets.

With every step Evelyn insisted on taking in order to advance deeper into the cavernous warehouse, the tighter Gael's jaw got. He was sure it was visible now, that bulge on the right. His teeth screwed tight, he was afraid they'd soon begin to crack, audibly. The woman seemed to be taking random turns, walking up and down aisles, toward and away from the exit, taunting them with release. Sioux was practically dragging her feet now. He had to bring her home. And just as Gael readied his lips to proclaim just that, having followed the woman obediently back toward the front of the store, the bitch dropped everything, stiffened her already statuesque posture, and stomped out without uttering so much as a syllable.

<u>Peta's Journal Entry</u>

Falling asleep next to my husband is a competitive sport. If I don't fall asleep fast enough, if I come in second, it's too late and I'm a sore loser. Once I hear the snores, that's it, I'm done. I'm not sure what that has to do with anything, but I'm awake so why not reminisce whilst practicing my cursive even though I'd already written, right? Right!

Guess what? I used my sleepless night to go looking for that old Polaroid of mine. And I found it! I had more, I know for sure, but for some reason, I can only find this one. And that's A-Okay! Because that's plenty. My God is that plenty! I'm pumped but I'm also tired. I hope my shuffling won't wake Peter because I dragged my past into our bed and am now writing balancing my marble notebook on my knees.

My goodness, I'd completely forgotten how beautiful this man was. Everything about him oozed sensuality. I don't think I appreciated this at the time. I don't think I knew how. I was eighteen, for fuck's sake! They say youth is wasted on the young and, boy, are they right! Plus, there's no accomplishment in youth. Everyone has that going for them at one point in time. This, of course, comes with smooth skin and toned arms, but time has a way of wrinkling your forehead. Nobody survives this youth. From what I remember, I don't think I ever even hugged this stunning man properly. I didn't know how to hug either. Mommy never taught me. I'm still a limp hugger. I lean more than I hug, really. I never quite learned how to wrap my arms around another person, if you can believe that. I can reciprocate well enough to fake it but I can't initiate. It isn't natural. Even when someone cries, I just want them to stop, I don't want to pat them on the back. What does this all mean? And I don't mean the fact that four of these sentences begin with the word "I." That's a whole other can of worms. But yeah—regrets! Major regrets now that I am looking at this picture. I should've really hugged him. At least I now have it on good account that you likely enjoyed this man longer and a riper age than I did. Lucky lady!

But you know what—forget all that! That's not why I've spent a solid hour studying this old, faded photograph. No, the reason for that is the sharp stab of pain right in my sternum at the realization of just how much of an idiot I've been all my life. Seriously, it made it hard to blink for a while there. To soften up my muscles, I explained to myself that it hadn't been exactly all my life but a solid two decades. Jesus! It's so obvious. Has it always been this obvious? How did I not see it before? Or did Sioux really not look like her father until recently? I mean, she does have her hair in braids nowadays and it certainly contributes to the resemblance but, again, it's not just that, that's not all. Your son is...their resemblance is undeniable. I will bring you Sioux's picture so you can judge for yourself. I can't wait to see you!

<u>John</u>

I know it's my dad simply by looking at my manager's face. She appears to be seconds away from drooling. She keeps pushing her hair back behind her ears, her hands trembling, as if, were it precisely set in place just so, he would drop to his knees and sweep her off her feet (maybe not in that order). This is a pretty common reaction to seeing my father. His students (of both genders) can attest to this. I think that's what drove mom to guzzling wine straight from the bottle whenever he stayed on campus an hour too long. Not that dad ever acted on all these plentiful opportunities, I don't think, but no matter the self-esteem, seeing everyone melt around your spouse must chip away at you. And, despite all the white pantsuits she wears to emulate such, mom isn't known for self-esteem to begin with.

"I believe your father is here," my manager pants as she rushes through the double doors while simultaneously finger-brushing her bangs, her tongue practically hanging out. I all but roll my eyes. I suppose there is a resemblance between us, particularly when my dad was younger, but I doubt she'd asked for a birth certificate to confirm our relation. We are both black.

"Thanks," I mutter with my mouth full of the overpriced, dry sushi I'd purchased with my employee discount. I'm not sure I am going to be able to swallow it now.

I drag my feet as I head back out of the closet that is our employee lounge. I motion for dad to follow me outside and he obeys without so much as a nod of his head. His features are more sculpted than mine. Mom isn't the only one jealous.

"Where have you been staying?" is what I expect him to ask, but instead it's "What does your mother think she saw?"

First my head grows heavy, and then my stomach.

"I don't know what mom thinks she saw." I blink too rapidly for this to be an acceptable answer.

"I'm trying to help. I'm listening. Talk to me."

His stature makes him look taller than his height strictly allows. He's certainly too good to be doing what he does for a living, but it was my untimely arrival that hindered his career ambitions. So says mom. Theirs was a shotgun wedding without the proverbial shotgun.

We walk to his rental and silently climb inside. Pure muscle memory makes me click the seatbelt in place even though I know we aren't going anywhere.

"How did you know her?" Dad asks, his eyes on the rearview mirror. He never was good with eye contact. He is good at staring you down, that's true, but he's unlikely to look you directly in the eye unless he absolutely has to. It's an oxymoron of sorts. Maybe *that's* what drove mom to drink.

I scratch my head as if the answers will reveal themselves if only I do it hard enough. Buying time, I gather my dreadlocks in a heap on top of my head.

"We were friendly," I say with my mouth dry. I had more soy sauce than actual sushi—my first meal in days.

"You were friends with a woman twenty years your senior? Well, look at you!" he teased. "Discussed books together, or mostly fucked in motel rooms?"

"Neither," I say honestly. "She took some kind of an interest in me toward the end there. Said I look like somebody close to her—like her sister." I am suddenly happy to be talking about her. About all of this! I tug at my seatbelt. "She's clearly not okay, dad. She lost her baby a few years back. That has to mess you up."

I hear dad sigh. I don't want to look, and I don't have to; I already know he's stroking his stubble as he does without a conscious thought when something's on his mind. He often does this while grading papers. He'll probably take off his glasses soon, I predict, and then wipe them on his sweater. In response, I grind my teeth, wishing I had gum.

"What else did she share with you?"

I don't know if I should tell him. I don't even know why this is such a problem for me. The soy sauce rushes back up to my throat as the thought formulates.

Dad's finger is tapping on the wheel. Left hand, index finger. I watch it. It is pristine. For a man who never gets manicures, his nails always seem to stay well shaped and clean. Not my luck. My cuticles grow as if some kind of yeast is involved. Or full on fungus. I guess the two aren't that different. I bite into my pinky nail contemplating

181

whether or not I got my mom's genes when it comes to cuticle growth.

"She said I have a sister," I eventually say in between bites.

Looking at dad proves difficult. More difficult than I imagine it would be had Peta Knudsen not gone missing and I was able to simply travel up to Alaska to clarify my family tree. Instead, I'm staring at a glove box, heat rushing to my head, instead of studying my father's face for micro movements. I realize soon that he is not refuting this. I feel a flush coming on. If Sandy wasn't either hyperventilating or masturbating (or both) in the employee lounge right now, she'd come looking. I actually wish she'd pull herself together and do her job—discipline her employee for taking too long of a break.

Dad uses his words carefully, much consideration given to most syllables. I don't expect him to react to this information casually. He was a lawyer. I guess he still is. He went to law school, he passed the Bar, but he doesn't practice. After law school, he insisted on moving back to Alaska to be closer to his folks to purportedly have help with the infant me while mom completed her degree. Dad's ethics being such, a job in anything related to oil or hunting was out of the question on principle (and tending bar only paid so much), so when he heard of an opportunity to start a prelaw program at a local college that had never heard of such, he took it. It came with health insurance. Can't blame the guy.

He shuffles in his seat now. Out of the corner of my eye, I see him looping his scarf an extra two rounds. He hasn't hugged me yet, not even a fist bump. This isn't like him. He may be about as under-slept as I am. Who knows what junk my mom has already fed him. As the light outside slowly grows murkier, I realize how ready for sleep I am.

I shuffle in my seat, following dad's lead.

"I never met her," he finally admits.

Sioux

I exfoliate no matter where I am. It's a habit instilled in me by mommy. I've been doing this every four days since I turned twelve. We are not Jewish, but mommy picked that year for my official entry into womanhood, anyway. Somehow she was right—I inexplicably began menstruating that same year.

So I exfoliate even here, even tonight—even after that disaster of a trip to the police department, the awfulness of Peter's statement that seemed to delete both mom and me from the equation, and a waste of a trip to the grocery store. It began to snow earlier, just after we finally got home from the godforsaken trip to store where mom had inexplicably dumped everything she'd thrown into her basket on the floor last minute and bolted for the door as if she'd seen a ghost without saying a word. We all knew this excursion wouldn't end well. Mommy talks a big game but of course she's scared—it's her first-born. She's not made of any of the hard material she loves to painstakingly sculpt. She'd locked herself in her room the second we came back here, whereas I ran back to my favorite place of refuge—Peta's bathroom, where I exfoliate and try to make out the dark outside the window above the sink.

I see them now—they are small, delicate snowflakes that float over the bay in a way that would surely make me want to compose a song were I musically inclined. Instead, I massage the exfoliate atop my damp face, in circular motions, just like I'd been doing for years, just like it says to do on the box.

Mommy says maintaining routine is important. And even as we wait on Peta, there's no sense in letting my looks go (again, as per mommy). She says I look more like my dad when I take care of my skin. She busts this out every so often—my dad. All I've ever seen is a dusty, faded Polaroid roughly my age. She claims she only has the one. All you can really still see are dreadlocks and abs. The features are blurry. He was mommy's model, apparently, and she doesn't fail to remind me of this factoid whenever I come home from school with an extra couple of pounds. Peta thinks I'm mommy's sculpture, and she that treats me as such. But I'm not convinced. I'm a romantic, not as jaded as my sister just yet—I'm hoping I'm her lost connection to my father. Maybe she really loved him. Maybe preserving me a certain way eases something for her. Maybe she didn't have that with Peta's dad.

It doesn't matter, I sigh. The sky is thick; it's hard to see much of anything at all. Has been for hours. Fog is more commonplace in this place than I would've ever thought visiting. Whenever I'd come before, I'd never paid attention to the weather. They say not to confuse tourism with real life and I'm afraid that that is exactly what I'd done all those times I'd bounced up here like a child into a candy store (or so the expression goes; I wouldn't know about candy). It's colder here than I remembered. The picturesque snowflakes don't help. My God, it's been over five days and here I am talking about condensation. Five days without knowing if she is alive or dead (minus mommy's ever changing speculations on the subject, that is), five days without knowing if she's hungry or fed, cold or warm. I'm a terrible sister.

My hair in a towel, Peta's robe tied around my waist having been looped around it twice, I finally emerge out of Peta's room, my face raw. Gael is there. Gael is always there. He has a glass of juice waiting for me, like a masseuse waiting with a cup of tea or a glass of cucumber water after a massage treatment. I don't eat enough, nowadays—that explains the juice. I don't sleep enough either, but he can't give me sleeping pills to help with that. He doesn't have access to those, or else I'm sure he would. I give him a peck on his clean-shaven cheek and gulp down the juice with my eyes open. I see Peter down the hall as he ascends the stairs and heads into Gwenny's room. I know the cops were here again, and I saw the press conference, and want to ask him where we all stand. Instead, I don't dare move my glass from my face. I don't want him to know that he's being watched. He looks almost as if he's levitating, his step simultaneously heavy and ghost light. He's not himself. I would've thought that this, if anything, would breathe life into him—give him a purpose, but it's done the opposite, from the looks of it. It seems that with every hour more syllables get stuck in his throat. As I swallow the last of my orange juice, I wonder if he still knows how to talk any differently, anymore. Before he can spot me and make legitimate eye contact, I yank Gael on his sleeve and slip back into Peta's room.

"Hey, what's that about?" Gael dares to let a chuckle escape his artfully pigmented lips as he trips on his feet by my sister's side table.

"I didn't want to make Peter feel like he needed to talk to us. He's got enough going on."

"Peter was out there?" Gael asked with a wrinkled brow. "I didn't hear him. Are you sure you didn't hallucinate?"

I'm sure.

I slump down on what I know is Peta's side of the bed and throw my towel off, my braids lose and heavy on my shoulders. I'd cut them off and go for something more natural, but mommy insists I keep these. My father had dreads; I guess this is another point of similarity in her mind. It's only hair and I'm not defined by it, so what harm is there in my carrying this weight around? I consider sharing this with Gael but bite my tongue. He already has plenty of bones to pick on my behalf so I won't give him another. Instead, I cross my legs and drive my knee into a drawer.

"Fuck!" I yelp, my hand immediately clasping my mouth.

"Shit, are you okay?" Gael is at once at my feet, stroking and blowing at reddened skin. He's always *right there*. He's too good for me. Men in our lives tend to be, I'd once noted to Peta, but she'd laughed. I remember it like it was yesterday—we were out on their deck, hot chocolates in hand, my last night of summer vacation before going back down to Seattle. This was just a few months ago. Her laugher rang loud and crystal clear with the humidity in the air, my observation so silly to her decades on me. Something about my not knowing about her father.

I wave Gael off, my lips painfully bitten to prevent more expletives from escaping their confines, and absentmindedly paw at my sister's side table. Inside her drawers, I find mostly receipts and old daily planners, for which I too have an affinity. I wanted to study anthropology but mommy thinks I'm an artist. I pick one out and leaf through it. It's not a diary, it's only a planner so Peta wouldn't mind. Gael, as I eventually notice, gives up on my knee and sits himself down to lean against the table, taking my cue for some friendly snooping. Leafing through random appointments and notes on wind condition, I slowly let go of my lips. It's almost fun to be in on

187

something together with Gael. For a moment, I almost forget why we are all sequestered here.

"What is this?" I hear him ask and pry my eyes away from Peta's meteorological short hand. They mean nothing to me, anyway. I remember, once she read one of her high school science reports to me before bed when she came home to visit over Christmas break in grad school and I got sleepy really fast. If her goal was a soporific bedtime story, it worked, I guess, but this may or may not have been what she really wanted out of the experience, now that I think about it. Was I to be impressed? Interested? Inspired? It was about thunderstorms. I remember being scared right before my lids drew together that night. Maybe that's why I'd fallen asleep so fast—defense mechanism. There was something about crystals inside clouds crashing against each other and producing this charge, this little fire. Or something like that. I'd always kept meaning to ask her about this—about thunderstorms—about thunder and lightning—as an adult in college. On a less sleepy and scared mind, this time, that is. Whenever I'd be in bed during a thunderstorm and the thought would enter my mind, I'd make a mental note to call her in the morning and ask, but then, in the morning, I would forget all about it, our schedules never matching, our lives decades apart, and move on with my day.

"What?"

"This!"

Gael's eyes are bright, like those of a child. They are big—too big for his face. It's like his face never quite grew into them. Harry had eyes like that, I catch myself thinking. Before I can melt into a puddle of salt water, he hands me a sheet of tablets.

Wellbutrin.

I shrug it off. Never heard of it. We were never big on medicine growing up. Besides an occasional Tylenol, our remedies of choice had always been herbal. The first time my system had to digest an anti-biotic was in college, upon the onset of my very first UTI. I can only imagine Peta's experience was vaguely similar to mine. I don't know where or when in her life my mom picked up her horticultural lifestyle. This was another thing I'd meant to ask Peta about. I want my bullet journal so I can make note of all these things now, in case she comes back. *When* she comes back.

"There's more," Gael gasps, utterly giddy now. He's been cooped up in this house for days and clearly needs a distraction. "A bit of an odd location for a medicine cabinet, no?"

"Maybe this is the safest place away from Gwenny?" I say with audible doubt and sigh again. I really do need some sleep and calories, but I can't seem to neither quiet my mind nor make my jaws cooperate long enough to chew. It's the not knowing—that's the worst part. I think I could stand the idea of swallowing if I had something concrete to chew on.

Gael keeps rampaging through my sister's drawer, paying me no mind. I twirl the sheet of tablets in my hand, watching him. He really is a precious boy, as mommy refers to him. Everything about his features is delicate—his slightly hawkish nose, his perfect eyebrows, his thick, crow-black hair. With a wide smile now plastered on his face, he continues to go to town. We make a gorgeous, androgynous couple. We're made for photographs. I used to love sleeping with him. I would just picture the way his body would contour mine and drift to sleep easily, quickly. But sleep has become painful and scary, my ribs rattling so hard, I fear they'll break if I don't move to at least mask the sound. Even Gael's safe arms can't keep me safe. I cannot stay in bed because if I move, my heart is not so loud and my ribcage seems less braced for impact and thus it hurt just a little less. So I don't lie down much anymore.

Bile begins to burn in the back of my throat. It hard to decipher if it's hunger or dread, but I decide it doesn't matter. These pills are long expired. They must be from her old shrink. Gael's giddiness aside, there's nothing here to salivate about. We didn't just stumble upon some deeply hidden secret, and suddenly his smile is wearing a little thin on me. Time to get out of this room.

But Gael is relentless—he keeps looking. He seems to have suddenly decided that he needs to have a project on his hands, to be occupied. They say kids have to be bored in order to be able to create their own fun. We're missing a crap-load of school, but mommy was commissioned for every little bust and sculpture at the place so all will be forgiven so long as we complete a few independent study assignments that nobody will ever read if my sister indeed never comes back. I'm not sure when we'd even get those assignments and when we'd actually begin working on them. I may as well begin to wonder now because my heart is already in my throat. Should I tell Peter?

"Who's this?" Gael asks, forcing me to bring my eyes back to him, away from the thickly shaded window in my sister's bedroom, where they'd wandered. He hands me a photo and it takes a moment for my pupils to adjust.

I shrug. It's a photo of a woman and two men—one older, one younger. It's probably father and son—they look alike. And the woman is probably the mother. Or so logic would dictate. The younger one looks like the kid who checked us out at the store the other day; the guy who seemed to send mom into a trance with his mere presence. He is cute, I guess that partly explains mom's instant infatuation. We sort of look alike, if you squint just so, it's funny. But the older man reminds me of someone else. Someone I must've seen once, in a dream or a photo. I screw my eyes shut trying to bring up the image in my mind's eye. It makes the nausea worse but I can almost see it. I must look like I'm in pain because Gael begins to rock my knee as if to bring me out from whatever this stupor he must think I've just fallen into.

"I think it's my... I think it's my dad."

Peter

Peter lay on the floor in his daughter's room. Peta was a big proponent of getting at least an area rug for the room when Harry lived there but with Gwenny she hasn't been a strong proponent of anything by way of the décor. This is why, instead of being remotely comfortable on some thin carpet, he kept pressing the small of his back into the hardwood floor. Given Harry's fatal allergies, maybe it was a good idea to keep carpets away, allergens and all. He hadn't craved a cigarette since graduate school but he wanted one now. Staying in his daughter's room was thus strategic—he knew he couldn't smoke here.

He didn't want to rouse Gwenny. Turning on his phone briefly, he tested the effect of the screen light on his daughter's sleep. But the almost toddler lay still on her belly, the Minnie Mouse bumpers guarding her against accidental head bumps, not bothered in the slightest. She was a solid sleeper. She was probably old enough to safely sleep on her stomach, but he couldn't for the life of him remember the exact cutoff. He could Google it, and he could also probably turn the child over on her back. Instead, using his phone as a flashlight, he went over Peta's last journal entry. He leafed through the rest of the book but there were no more scribbles—not a date, not a phone number noted. Not much by way of allowing Peter to feel like a moody, solitary detective.

What a fucking soap opera. He was to understand the boy at the store was the son of the shrink and Peta's ex-boyfriend? And he has some resemblance to Sioux? What was the implication? He didn't get it. Was Sioux really Peta's? No, that didn't make sense—he knew her then. No, that wasn't it. He could almost wrap his mind around it but every time something concrete would come into focus, it dissolved again. Did Evelyn fuck her own daughter's boyfriend?

Gwenny stirred. The light was probably getting too much. Finally.

Saturday, October 6th

Dr. Burgos

A day out of heels routinely meant swollen feet for Dr. Burgos. Still, stuffing her puffy flesh into a pair of suede pumps felt like the sweetest of victories. She winced as she felt the leather contour her skin, wishing she'd get over her distaste for stockings. If her mother was to be believed, they made wearing tight shoes like this bearable. One day she'd test that for herself. Sucking in the smallest reminder of child bearing, Dr. Burgos zipped up her high-waisted pencil skirt and checked her reflection in the mirror. She thought about her mom. She wasn't around anymore (neither was her dad), but the older she grew, the more she'd randomly, seemingly out of nowhere, vibrate with the memory of one or another phrase her mother liked to overuse. For example, when John was just a few months old and she considered taking some time off before finishing her degree and going back to work. Dr. Burgos remembered that her mother had told her growing up that being a fulltime mom was always a poor choice. "A woman needs a purpose outside the home—a reason to get dressed in the morning.

Trust me." She was a housewife with a drinking problem, thus in possession of all qualifications needed to dole out such advice. Lena's postpartum mind took the words she heard repeated throughout her childhood for gospel. John was placed into day care at four months. Or was it seven? She couldn't remember. But whatever the exact age was, Andrew couldn't stomach full time enrollment and would pick him up at whatever hour he could, thus giving John no consistency. It took the boy forever to get adjusted to "school." She never told him this, but she swore half his issues stem from those early day rescues. Her own mother wasn't around to get an earful about the shortcomings of her advice now. True, it wasn't really her advice that was flawed but the manifestation of it in her life that was the culprit. Still, it'd be fun to rip her mother a new one over her son's subpar academic performance and his downright noncompliance and disrespect when it came to his mother. Not that she even remembered what her mother sounded like. In fact, she tried to remember why it was that she chose to move to her childhood town after her divorce, but she couldn't come up with one plausible explanation now. It seemed romantic, perhaps. Dramatic, maybe. She hadn't seen her parents since she announced her pregnancy but knew they were dead long before packing her bags and returning to her hometown. What was she trying to reclaim here?

Now that John was home, it was time to go back to work. It was a brand new morning, a brand new day. And Mom was right—all this pajama wearing had to end. Time to suck it up, suck it in, and go do something with a purpose. Something that earned her money, respect, and usually a thank you. Taking a full day off was a lot as it was. She had a business to run, an appearance to maintain. And neither of her men wanted to talk so what was the point of wasting another day sitting around the house? They didn't want to talk to her. Communication between her son and ex-husband seemed continuous, telepathic even. It was of no consequence, or so it seemed now on a sober mind. He was home, he was safe. She'd known he was fine, yes, but now he was under her roof and that meant more than just texts sent to his father and then relayed to her. John was home. That's all that mattered. Whose brother he was wasn't particularly relevant, at least for now. This Saturday morning she was returning to work. It was time for rational decisions. No more choices made on a whim, out of emotion. Those other types took too long to get over.

Sioux

Waking up in Bellingham refuses to get easier. Each morning seems grayer than the last. I can't remember if it's always been like that whenever I visited. On this trip opening my eyes each morning is a letdown. That's assuming that I actually sleep at all these days. Which I know I did last night, judging by the drool on my pillow. Gael is still asleep. I guess I can't expect him to stay up for days and days on account of my missing sister. Apparently, I can no longer expect my body to either. When Harry died, my guidance counselor insisted on sitting me down for grief counseling having heard I postponed my SATs because of the funeral. She warned me that everyone grieves differently; some may be ready to move on before others and that is okay. It was not a slight, nothing to take personally. That's all fine and dandy, but apparently, I'm crashing first. I *slept* last night. Am I over it? Am I over my sister? Or am I mad at her for having a picture of my dad that she knows I don't have.

I halt my breathing and listen. Besides Gael's soft wheezing, the house is quiet. I don't want to know what time it is. Gwenny usually wakes up around eight and Marsha was usually invisible until then. And I've given up trying to track Peter's routine. Mommy? I can only presume she is in her room, unlikely to venture outside alone no matter her oral bravado. She's asleep also after yesterday's events. Maybe that's why we are both sleeping today.

I pull the covers up to my chin before I notice that I left Gael completely uncovered. He shivers. My goodness, he is lovely. All scrawny, his features are both crude and delicate at the same time, he's like a child you want to nurture. Which is funny because I don't remember the last time I did anything for him. I cover him with my part of the blanket and call it even.

Even before he developed that stutter, it is beyond me how Peter could ever start everyone's day with a good natured "Good Morning, Bellingham!" When has it ever been good?

Peter

Her office was less clinical than Peter had imagined. It was all couches and miniature tables and candles. It was more Pier 1 Imports than an office. It was like a set for a TV show. The magazines and catalogues lay fanned out just so, they looked untouched, their covers and spines pristine. There was a design catalogue, a Psychology Today, and a Psychological Review. Peter considered fingering through a magazine just to busy his hands, but he folded them, instead and laid them on his lap. The one-way window to his right provided enough by way of distraction and he turned his attention there. Every person passing by seemed to pause and look inside, as if hoping to see the disappeared Peta Knudsen hiding in her shrink's office. Peter suppressed his desire to throw one of Dr. Burgos's many paperweights strewn throughout the room through the window. He commended himself on refolding his hands instead of succumbing to that desire. He wasn't sure why she had this many paperweights on display. Surely, they created a hazard with at least some of her clientele. This was a liability waiting to happen.

"What would you like to talk about?" the Doctor asked when she arrived. It almost felt like a date when she sat down across from him in her high-backed chair and crossed her legs, her skirt rising ever so slightly up her thigh. She wasn't too hard on the eyes, this Doctor. Her hair was obviously highlighted blonde, the roots of it dark brown.

He'd say black, but he remembered learning in high school that black hair doesn't really exist...or was that black eyes? He couldn't remember. Her eyes were a variation of green; maybe they were hazel. It was impolite to stare, and his own eyes were already burning from the strain and the many hours of missed sleep.

"I don't know."

Doctor Burgos rearranged her legs.

"Surely you want to talk about your wife."

This wasn't a question and Peter complied with a shrug. He wasn't sure if he was completely sober. It required courage to plow his way through the journalists outside his door this morning, and he still felt warm in the chest. Peta's last journal entry boasted of a revelation she was to share with the doctor; before showing up at Organic Produce in a rush mad enough to not notice that her tank was empty, it was confirmed by the cops that his wife saw her therapist.

"Let's do it."

Marks were made on a notepad in her lap and Peter tried to guess what they were by the strokes the doctor was making.

"Any developments?"

Peter shrugged, his head involuntarily falling.

"Nothing really. They've canvassed all relevant areas—dogs and nosy volunteers and all. It really is like she vanished into thin air. Went to the sto— store, bought no groceries, and *poof*," he scoffed from nonsensical self-imposed pressure to keep things light. "Well, at least that's all I've been told. Probably because I'm their fa— favorite for it."

"That's standard protocol. It isn't personal," the doctor smiled what Peter imagined to be her most practiced smile as her scribbles increased in speed and intensity. She was probably leaving marks on the page below. Her eyes narrowed and widened as she neared what Peter imaged to be the end of a sentence. He wondered what she was writing about; he certainly hadn't given her any information worthy of such rigorous note taking.

"This is hard on everybody, Peter. Believe me, I understand. Peta has been an interesting and challenging patient. I'd be lying if I said I hadn't grown attached to her over our time together. Look, it'd be my honor to offer free sessions to her mother and sister. Her sister in particular. They sounded close. This is probably agony for her. It's the not knowing, right?" Her gaze continued to be down as she made this offer and Peter almost chuckled out loud at its transparency. "I imagine Peta's family is staying with you?" she continued, eyes still cast down. She was a shitty actress. To Peter, she just appeared to be doodling. This wasn't the fun he expected it to be. "So, tell me. How is everybody?" The moment her eyes shot up at him again, Peter regretted ever wishing they would be. Sharp and defiant, they seemed to shine in the morning light.

"Ye— yes, the whole circus is in town—her mom, sister, the sister's boy— boyfriend," Peter answered with renewed difficulty.

"Lots of help with the baby, then?"

"Some. Mostly from Si— Sioux, Peta's sister."

"I see. How old is she again? She and Peta are quite a bit apart, aren't they?"

"Roughly twenty years."

The shrink sighed. Peter was no longer sure whom this session was for. To get any benefit from it, and to get his money's worth, he knew he had to get talking, but, suddenly, nothing came to him.

"So, you had her keeping a journal?" he hiccuped.

The doctor blinked. Then swallowed. It was of comfort to see that he wasn't alone in finding its existence painful.

"I did," Dr. Burgos admitted, her tongue getting ahead of her brain. "It's a tool. A vehicle to get a patient's thoughts out in a completely judgment-free environment. Not all patients are comfortable speaking their whole truth to me, no matter how I try to put them at ease. And they shouldn't.

I get it. But they still need to get it all out. It really is a great tool, believe it or not—"

"Right, I'm not here to debate your treatment methods. I'm here about the contents."

He blushed at the sound of his voice. Was there a way to make this sound less accusatory?

"You read it?"

"Have you?"

Shit, he was now past pretending this was a legitimate therapy session. It was as if years of keeping syllables in for fear of stammering meant that now they were all rushing out too fast, too forceful.

Doctor Burgos showed no signs of replying. Her eye contact was now impeccable. No one would ever be able to attempt to place her on the spectrum. She blinked once but that was the extent of the break she was willing to afford him. This was probably a technique of sorts.

"I never read my patient's entries. Those are all strictly confidential," the doctor eventually defended. For all Peter knew, she was telling the truth. It didn't matter though. Knowing his wife, there was no way she hadn't taunted the doctor with whatever she discovered before he lost her. "Have you read this diary in its entirety?" she asked, her pen in perfect tripod grip of her right hand.

"I felt like it was an invasion of privacy but I overcame it," Peter scoffed. "Most of it was not an exciting read so you didn't miss much—we lost a child, we lost ourselves, very poetic and statistically likely. Then a lot of 'Mommy this' and 'Sioux that.'" This was a lot for him to get out without stopping to regroup. He made a mental note to report this to Janet—his speech therapist.

"I see," the doctor nodded.

Peter couldn't be sure, but he thought he heard her voice quiver. She was probably tired. Everyone looked tired in this town now. As if they were all out looking for his wife.

The Doctor looked expectant of him to continue, her chest even, no breaths taken. A few beats she waited. Then she moved on. Now, this was a technique he was familiar with—prompting. It was the same in journalism. He took his cue.

"Is John from the Organic Produce your son?" he asked, leaning in closer to the doctor, who remained stoic. "He is a nice boy. Very courteous and professional, too. You must be very proud."

If he squinted just so, he could just begin to see what Peta was getting at in those late entries, but, zooming back out, the image would again become grainy. He wasn't sure. But Peta was.

"And Andrew? Tell me about Andrew. Did he tell your son that he has a sister yet?"

<u>John</u>

Mom is never inconspicuous when leaving in a huff, which is often. The door slamming shut behind her downstairs shook my bedroom window so hard it had me worried about mom's security deposit for a second there. But my mattress is so much more comfortable here, I was pretty sure I could overcome the concern. Regardless, though, she won—I'm awake. I'm yet to tell her I saw her that day, yet to ask her why she was following Peta. I'm yet to talk to her at all. It's my day off and I can afford a few more hours of sleep, or at least a morning of quiet solitude.

It was time to come home, dad was right. To be honest, I'm not sure why it wasn't time earlier. Well, I do, I guess. At first, it was the idea of being home alone with mom after seeing her hiding behind that bagel display. It reeked of some kind of crazy; it just felt safer to sleep on a foldout couch across town than risk both asking and answering nonsensical questions. Even when I knew dad was summoned down here and I had a buffer. Makes little sense now that I think about it but that's why they say hindsight is 20/20.

I turn over on my stomach and bury my head in my pillow. The pillow is better here too. I try to hang on to sleep but I feel it draining, slowly making its way down my limbs and out of my toes. I kick at my covers. Dad is up, no doubt. He's an early riser. No matter what time a night he ever goes to bed, he's always up early. And the clock on the wall directly in front of my face reads 11:15. Of course, he's up. I'm suddenly happy at the thought. Happier than I've been in days. I don't know if it was my comfortable bed or finally getting some clarity, but I'm suddenly excited to go talk to my father.

I shower and am feeling cleaner than I had in days. I make my way to the kitchen more reluctantly than I should. Mom's car is not in the driveway. The coast is clear. We can pick up where we left off.

"Hey," I hear my dad. He isn't looking at me, his eyes on the screen in front of him. His job is important, I've always been told. I fold my way in a stool in front of him and sink into my elbows. "Sorry, one second," he mutters with his eyes still squinted in the direction of his phone.

"No worries," I shake my head assuredly as I chuckle for levity. To busy both my eyes and hands, I head over to mom's fridge. It's empty but for a random speckled apple and some hard cheese. Our household has always been mostly coffee and alcohol. I choose coffee.

"Right," dad says. He rubs his face with impressive vigor. I'm not sure what he's trying to rub out—his students' e-mails or the memory of a daughter he did not know exists.

"So…"

"Yes, sorry," he groaned. "Mind if we take this from the top. I haven't slept a wink last night."

I'd love to say "ditto," but I slept okay, really. I have a sister. What's wrong with that?

"Whatever you say, pops," I shrug. "Peta was your ex-girlfriend?"

"If you can call it that. We dated for a few weeks in law school. Then mom found out she was pregnant with you and I broke up with her," he shrugs, summarily, visibly wanting this to truly be it. I can't help but giggle at dad's discomfort. I'm not sure why he's so shy about this. We've never been prudish.

"Wouldn't it be something if that temporary girlfriend found out she was pregnant after you broke up with her to marry your pregnant ex-girlfriend?" I try to lighten the moon.

Luckily, dad agrees to see the humor in this.

"It would sure make this simpler."

The coffee is still hot. I wonder if mom made a pot before she left or if dad threw it on. I take a few gulps while dad's eyes dart like those of a high rabbit. I mean, I can only presume, because fuck if I know what a rabbit under the influence would look like. He's thinking, but I, for one, am hopeful that this sister of Peta's really was a sister, and not a daughter she had too young and out of wedlock and had her mother raise or something. That would be too creepy. I can't recover from that. It's bad enough that she'd fucked my dad! That, by itself, I can try to get over. Having my father's baby would be entirely too creepy. Even I don't have enough mommy issues to feed that monster.

Dad had told me on our ride home that mom was concerned that Peta expressed "unhealthy" interest in me. Thus, the clumsy spying. That was the best news I'd heard in days. I loved seeing Peta's smiling brown eyes at my register, her perfect nose, her perfect lips. Even when she was sad (which was always) and had her ear pods in (which was often), she was beautiful. I don't find older women attractive but something about her toothy smile gave me goose bumps. The good kind.

"So why is there a girl my age who Peta thinks looks like me?"

At this, my father takes to his own mug of coffee.

Andrew

Andrew never shied away from difficult conversations with his son. He prided himself on being able to have open sex talks with his son when he was sixteen. Went out and bought condoms with him, even. He was a cool dad, a solid dad. And yet, this was hard.

"We needed money. When mom and I got married, and you were on the way, we needed money. I tended bar and that was shit money. I had an internship but that didn't pay anything. Literally. We needed something quicker so I did whatever I could—retail, gypsy cabs, some modeling."

"Modeling?"

He'd laugh this off were they discussing his past jobs under any other circumstances, but for reasons he could not explain, his son's laughter made his blood boil. Taking particular pride in never letting his rage boil over at his son, Andrew took a few deep breaths. Slow and deep. When that didn't work, he closed his eyes and counted to ten.

"Yes, modeling. You got a problem with that? Because you didn't latch apparently so we needed that formula money, my friend. I also painted houses. Does that bother you too?" It was a testament to his level of overwhelm that his damn breaths and counting didn't work for the first time in twenty years. He heard the resonance of his voice and immediately wanted to vomit.

"Sorry, I was kidding," John laughed with his hands thrown up. "I just never pictured you as a Fabio type," John continued to prod. Jesus, the kid was a little prick. Maybe he should not have spent years agonizing over how not to raise so much as a decibel in his direction. He was an adult now—arguably too late to reprogram him.

"That's because I wasn't, asshole," he barked now. To hell with his self-imposed discipline; he needed to get this shit out. To this, his son continued to hold his arms up in surrender. He tried so hard not to screw this kid up that he might actually have despite his best efforts. He wondered how his daughter turned out. Was she better or worse for not having had him for a father?

When nothing but proverbial crickets filled the silence, Andrew chose to continue.

"If you're ready to listen, I modeled for a local artist...who also happened to be Peta's mother."

John's eyes opened so wide, it halted Andrew for a second. Was he disgusted? Surprised?

"Did you know that?"

"What?"

"That she was Peta's mother?"

He sighed. There was no right answer to this.

"I did. I met her once when she came to visit Peta one night at the restaurant when she worked there."

Pausing for a gulp of coffee that was now cool, Andrew could see John weighing his life-held view of his father. He had to speak fast, fill the quiet.

"She came into the restaurant one night long after Peta had gone off to college and started up a conversation with me at the bar. I vaguely remembered who she was, but she reminded me, anyway. She told me she was a sculptor and was scouting for models. Named the sitting fee she was willing to pay, and like I said—we needed a whole lot of formula money. It was a no brainer."

"It does not compute, dad," John said with audible suspicion. "How does one get a baby by modeling?"

"Well, the fee for getting her pregnant was higher than the sitting fee, if you catch my drift. I had the Bar Exam coming up in about half a year and if I wouldn't have to work while studying, I'd fuck anything!" As soon as the words were out of his mouth, he could practically see John begin to feel sorry for ever asking, but it was too late now. A woman was missing and somehow his gig well over two decades ago was related. It had to be discussed.

"Wow, dad, I always knew you were a dedicated father, but holy fuck! How old was she?"

"I have no idea. Probably as old as I am now," Andrew shrugged, glad some levity was finally entering the conversation.

"So how long did this project take?" John's face was scrunched up to such a degree, Andrew wondered if his lips hurt and whether his face would ever regain its previous shape.

"Oh Jesus, it was not that bad. I mean, I guess it's cheating but it was for a good cause—namely, you. It honestly, hand to God, did not seem unreasonable. An older single woman wanted another child. She was paying! I'd get way less working at a clinic. Two months later, I was done, and I could now afford Bar prep classes."

The two men sat a long few minutes without saying anything. Andrew could only presume that John was painting a variety of pictures in his mind. Andrew, for his part, was trying hard to remember if he'd ever again heard from the woman after they'd said their goodbyes. Come to think of it, he didn't even remember her first name.

"I never heard from her again," he said out loud.

Evelyn

Evelyn did not remember ever being particularly interested in any one man. Sure, she's been attracted to many and lived with a few, but none of them were ever of specific interest. It wasn't that she was asexual, it was just that male company was never an intimate necessity. If there were no other needs to fulfill, she'd be perfectly content without men in her life at all, but there were needs and there were men. Had they met under different circumstances, perhaps she'd see Detective Foster in a different light, too. Tall and brooding, Evelyn was almost tempted to flirt.

"Peter is out, Detective," Evelyn informed him dutifully, hearing the children's shuffling feet rushing to the living room behind her. God-forbid crazy mommy would be allowed to talk to an authority figure without supervision.

"Well, that's okay, but I was told you were very insistent on seeing me at the station yesterday so here I am." Tall and dignified, he stood over a full head above Evelyn.

"Touché, Detective. Make yourself at home." Evelyn made a vague gesture toward the couch, but the detective made his way toward the bar stool at the kitchen breakfast island. Evelyn followed. The crowd outside hadn't dwindled, she could see through the window, but it also hadn't grown. It was plateauing, which was good, she supposed. Depending on the perspective, of course. It was a conflicting game, wanting the interest not to wane but privacy to restore. Even she was starting to feel bad for Peter. Just to imagine stepping outside your own front steps and seeing colleagues, former interns even, gleeful for any hint of suspicion thrown your way. Maybe he wasn't the villain she'd so painstakingly crafted him to be. Maybe he was indeed just a boy who refused to be lost by the system. Maybe it was time to cut him some slack. Of course, Evelyn wasn't naïve enough to believe her own sudden onset of empathy; it was just that her former preoccupation with Peter was temporarily overshadowed by the beautiful boy who she could swear was her daughter's brother.

"Hey, can you do me a favor?" Evelyn threw the curtains closed and sat across from the handsome detective. He was unaccompanied today and that, she was sure, could not have been a coincidence.

"Shoot."

And just like that, like a schoolgirl, she took to her braid again. She saw Sioux and Gael settle themselves on the couch. She waved at them—a promise she was going to be on good behavior. It wasn't fair—Sioux needed to eat and here she was hogging the kitchen. But this was in her best interests, too.

"You actually want me to believe that you came here just to pay me a visit on account of my paying you one yesterday?" Evelyn couldn't help but smile, so tempted to jump right into it but unable to bring herself to do just that. "Where is your partner, detective? Is there a reason you're visiting me alone?"

"You're charming, you know that?" The detective didn't skip a beat. He reached into the inside pocket of his jacket and pulled out a bottle of water. As he took an enthusiastic swig from it, Evelyn wondered if it was indeed water inside. "Between us—it's good optics for us to parade back and forth in front of those reporters out there. It's just the way it is. Believe you me, we are doing our job, but unless we stay visible…well, Ms. Evelyn, we need all the help we can get. Your daughter did a mighty good job at falling off the face of the earth, if you would forgive my being so blunt. Whether Peter likes it or not, he'll have to host us here until there is resolution. Is that insensitive?"

It was, Evelyn assessed, but it wasn't untrue. Detective Foster's thin lips were folded in respect and sympathy, but his eyes still held a trace of a smile.

"I got you, no worries," Evelyn nodded, genuinely getting it. "Now, any of those updates I came knocking on your door about?"

The Detective sighed and the air seemed thinner.

"We… we got a hit on her credit card. I just got the call. That's where my partner is—chasing that down. From the sound of it, we aren't sure it'll turn out into any kind of a lead so don't get your hopes up, but at the very least, it's giving us a reasonable justification to comb a wider radius with a search team. That's all," Detective Foster shrugged, his voice soft, now obviously up to speed on Sioux's imagined paranormal connection to her sister, aware that the girl was sitting just a few feet away. "I am so sorry. Honestly, I am. I've never seen anything like it in my career, and I'm not just saying it. There is usually something— some kind of physical trace, some crumbs you can follow. But short of strange little blips and behaviors, it's truly like she vanished… I'm sorry, I should not be this frank."

The last time Evelyn's braid was this tight was when she was a preschooler in Soviet Union. She could feel it in her temples, her eyes seemed to begin to slant. Her stomach turned and she wondered if it was related to the migraine she was giving herself.

"I appreciate it," she mouthed, barely audibly, before unspooling her hair, feeling vertigo begin to set it. Her pain in the ass daughter could not just disappear. There had to be a logical explanation. She couldn't "vanish." She wanted to yell that at the cop in front of her, but the man's forehead had such deep crevices in it, she felt both sympathy for him and the desire to feel and trace their lines. After brief consideration, she did nothing, her hearing diminishing by the second, a whoosh so powerful in her ears, she was afraid she'd never hear again. Instead, she peered over the man's shoulder at Sioux and Gael. The two sat intertwined, the boy's eyes on Evelyn, Sioux's head on his shoulder. He was an exotic looking boy but what a fucking dweeb, she lamented.

"You mentioned a favor?" Detective Foster brought her back.

"Right!" she almost exclaimed, her ears popping. She saw Sioux jerk in her direction and waved a dismissive hand her way.

The man in front of her nodded expectantly, gulping more water from the bottle that she could see now had seen better days. She wasn't sure what he was doing there. She understood what he explained about needing to remain visible at this particular address, but he didn't need to stay here as long as he did without anything of value to report or any snide remarks to make. This felt like a date. Evelyn hadn't been on one of those in ages.

"Look, I know it's not a lot to go on, but you know this kid at the store where you found Peta's car? He's in his young twenties, long dreadlocks…"

"Yeah, that's John. Peta saw him before she headed to the train station."

"What? Him specifically?" Evelyn heard her voice quiver. "Why did I not know about this?"

"This is hardly classified information. Peter knows all about it. We questioned the guy, even—sounds like Peta may have wanted to set him up with Sioux over there. She wanted him to come down to Seattle with her."

"And then what happened?" Evelyn couldn't be sure, but she felt as if her lungs suddenly grew paper-thin.

"Nothing. She left, he stayed. You really didn't know any of this? Shit, you were right to come by then. Sorry."

Evelyn was afraid that her eyes' rapid movement gave away her trying to align all the characters in her mind's eye.

"Question—do you know who his parents are?"

Detective Foster shrugged. He scratched the top of his head, a gesture Evelyn found repulsive but restrained her facial muscles from betraying her.

"Well, his mother is Lena Burgos—Peta's shrink. She thought your daughter had a crush on her son. Imagine that!"

"My God, please tell me you checked that out!"

The detective laughed. With every gesture, with every phrase, this meeting felt less and less official. If they had a meal between them on the granite surface underneath their elbows, the optics he spoke of so recently would be entirely suspect. Also, if the topic of conversation did not involve her missing daughter. That, too.

"Evelyn, you underestimate us. Just because all you see is us likely driving your son-in-law to a nervous breakdown, believe it or not, we are decent fucking cops," he laughed. "Of course, we did! Don't tell Peter, but as soon as we realized that relation, he moved to number two on our list of suspects. And then we see that Lena Burgos was also at the store at the same time as Peta—oh man, we thought we were done right there. She's all incognito there—sunglasses and all. But turns out the lady stomped out of the store, got into her truck and drove away—"

"She could have followed her!" Evelyn hissed through her teeth so as not to alert Sioux. The girl was lying down now, her head in Gael's lap. The boy remained alert, however—his back as straight as a tree trunk.

"Oh my, Evelyn, thank God for you, because we totally did not think of that," the cop gushed mockingly as he rolled his eyes. Catching himself with a scoff, he continued, "We followed the same CCTV track. It looks like the doctor didn't have the patience for Peta to figure out her car issues. She drove out of the lot long before Peta walked away. She has a drinking problem, rumor has it."

"Peta?"

"No! Dr. Burgos. We checked with her neighbors, tracked her phone—she went straight home and called her ex-husband, eventually. Long story short, it wasn't her. I wish it were that easy."

Evelyn felt her eyes fill. She was on the verge of something; she could feel it.

"Do you happen to know who that boy's father is?"

"Her ex-husband—Andrew Burgos."

"Could it be him, then?"

"Why would it be him? He lives in Alaska."

"They used to date."

"Who?"

"Peta and Andrew Burgos."

"Okay…"

"And then he and I did."

Gael

It was common knowledge that Evelyn was to be revered by those who knew her, and even more so by those who did not. She was second to none in just about everything. There was nothing she didn't excel at: she was a great artist, a gifted cook, an inspired musician, an enviable beauty. She was disciplined, she gave the best advice. She was smarter than average, and even her immigrant grammar was better than that of a native speaker's. She probably fancied herself the best whisperer, but Gael could hear everything the woman thought she was asking the detective in a highly proficient act of covertness. He had doubts as to her other unquestioned talents, but that, like much of what he had to do around his girlfriend's family, he had to so mutely.

Proud of himself as he was, Gael wasn't sure how to process what he was incidentally learning without alarming Sioux. He'd already figured out that the grocery store guy must've been related to Sioux's father—he saw that in the photo they'd found. Sioux may not have seen it, her vision obviously distorted now, but Evelyn too must've seen the similarity. But at least now he had his full name to go on. Once Sioux was fed, he would gently share it with her before taking it over to Google. The kid's mom was, he had to admit, a revelation. That would explain who the lady in that picture was. Sure, this added color, but the cop preempted any theories his mind could've been busy weaving right now. By far the most interesting piece of information was not that Sioux's father and Peta used to date but that Evelyn did too. Presumably, this was before Sioux. Gael's heart was racing. This would make her world implode. How could Sioux, enamored with her sister like a hostage suffering from Stockholm Syndrome, ever come to terms with the fact that her mother dated her sister's boyfriend and the relationship resulted in her? No, that was out of the question. He wasn't telling her that. He was happy the girl was weak enough to appear to be napping in lap now. It bought him time. Maybe he'd Google Andrew without her. Somebody had to put Sioux first.

<u>Sioux</u>

I feigned sleep until the detective left. My head remained down until I was able to confirm his departure by waiting to hear the sound of a couple of camera shutters outside and the click of the lock. Listening to mom's mock whispers and low-key flirtation with the tall man who is supposed to be looking for my sister, not putting in billable hours with my mother, were difficult to sit through, to lie through, but, just like most other things in my life—I did just what was expected of me. Namely—I played dead in my boyfriend's lap, the helpless, sick, skinny bird of a girl destroyed by her sister's disappearance.

I perk up like a sunflower sensing the sun on the horizon at the sound of the door thudding closed, part my lids, and stretch my neck to steal a peek at mommy. She is pinker than usual. Surely even Gael can see that. Her skin is fairly alabaster, and her face and neck only get blotchy in those crescendo peaks of arguments. The same has happened countless times in arguments with roommates, in deliberations with landlords. She is flustered now, but who isn't. That alone is not strictly evidence of anything. The fact that the woman managed to meet my eye for a split second I couldn't possibly measure before turning her attention to the sink, however, shoots a blast of something cold and unfamiliar up through my limbs and to my chest. My mind suddenly at one and a half speed, it plays Peta's voice; it rings in my ears as I try to shake off Gael's concern. Her voice is clearer now, somehow, though I haven't heard it since I played her message up in her bathroom.

I got some hardcore intel for you... you'll see mommy-dearest in a whole new light.

I plant my feet as hard as I can into one of Peta's many area rugs. My toes flex, straining and hurting against the fabric, I will mommy to turn back and look at me, but she's busy with the sink, scrubbing something away from my field of vision. I squint, I flare my nostrils, but I cannot command her attention. My mind buzzes and blurs, tears sting the corners of my eyes. I have so many questions.

Peta dated the father of the guy from the store? The one with the butterfly tattoo? The only other black person I'd seen all week being here? And so did mommy?

"What did you do, mommy?" I hear myself scream before I take to the stairs, Gael too slow to catch up to me before I slam the door to Peta's bedroom in his face, his legs capable of making strides much shorter than my own. Just as the doors shuts, I see the look of pure amazement on his face. Or is it fear? He hasn't quite had the experience with this pep in my step, this sudden burst of energy. Neither am I. I wonder what mommy is thinking, likely having levitated from her spot in the kitchen where the detective had left her, drawn by the unfamiliar volume of my voice.

...you'll see mommy-dearest in a whole new light.

Peter

Peter liked driving. He didn't get to learn to drive until college, and didn't get to drive a car that was his own and not his roommate's until his third year, but ever since he could place his hands on the wheel, his right foot alternating between pedals, he did it with valor and pride. He particularly liked broad expanses, with as few traffic signs or lights as possible. The longer he could drive as slow as his Jeep would allow, the clearer his eyes saw. He'd savor the slow roll of the tires, the mild vibration of the shell, whenever the opportunity would present itself.

There were no opportunities now. One had to be realistic because unrealistic expectations only brought more pain along with them; he learned that the hard way, many times over. No, it was better to prepare for no more leisurely drives. Alone at the wheel, Peter took the long way home from Dr. Burgos' office.

He wasn't sure what he was expecting to get out of his meeting with Dr. Burgos'. In less than an hour he saw what a sharp woman this psychiatrist was. Sparring with her was a privilege. She divulged nothing, citing her professional code of responsibility, but the occasional twitch of her ankle, a refolding of her palms, a lengthy blink allowed Peter to confirm for himself what he was able to piece together on the floor of his daughter's bedroom. Of course, Peta confronted the doctor before she went missing, of course she asked her questions she did not answer. The woman was an enviable mausoleum, no words of confirmation or denial could be pried out of her now and Peter imagined it must've been the same with Peta. The woman grew nervous, sure, that much was obvious, but no one could accuse her of divulging confidential information. Confidential to her patient or to herself was a separate question. Armed with little else but his own silent confirmation as to his mother-in-law's despicable nature and the doctor's heartfelt offerings of free and discounted sessions for Peta's mother and sister, Peter sailed down the road as slowly as he could without coming to a grinding halt. Once he saw the news vans that marked the final approach to his own house on the horizon, he considered slowing down further. He was tired of those same faces, both outside the house and in.

It was then that he noticed them—the lights. More lights that he'd seen on his front lawn in the recent days, he noted. In fact, he corrected himself as he squinted, leaning over the wheel, his face closer to the windshield, there were never flashing police lights at his door step. Reluctantly, his foot found its way over to the right pedal, jolting the truck along with his heart.

Peta, he thought he heard his temples thud as he pushed the car into "park," blocking his own driveway. His knees soft, his ankles doing most of the work, he stumbled his way to the front door, past the flashes, past the mics.

Peta, he heard again as the door clicked shut behind him.

Sioux

I fume. That's all I do in Peta's room. I have all these kernels of thoughts popping in my head, but they are too fast, too hot to make sense. My pouty lip out, my arms across my chest, I realize I look like a toddler mid-tantrum, but I can't seem to do anything else. I need answers, but how do I get them? Tears stinging my eyes, it's not until I hear Peter exclaim *Peta* downstairs that anything other than my own seething half-thoughts enters my muted universe. I am airborne. I am at the door. I am flying down the stairs.

"Peta?!" I hear myself scream.

My vision a tunnel, I see the detective is back and question for a moment if he'd ever left to begin with. When I ran away to contemplate all things mom may be guilty of, was he there? No, he'd left. I'm sure of it. But now, he is back and his partner is here too. For the first time, I crack myself up for noticing, she is not wearing lipstick. In fact, she's even plainer than usual. What a useless thing to notice. Who gives a flying fuck if Detective Clark has makeup on? My sister is back.

"Is she here? Peta! *Peta!*" I trip on the last step. Gael catches me as I feel my ankle roll. Like dominos, each person congregating around the landing lets out a gasp.

"Honey," I hear mommy start but hiccup before any kind of follow-up. Her eyes are glistening. So are Peter's, to her right, but his are always moist and I refuse to take it as any kind of indication. "Honey, have you eaten? Honey…" mommy tries again, her voice breaking around the second "honey." I try to wrestle out of Gael's arms, but his grasp is too strong.

Gael

Gael tried to control the involuntary curl of his lip but he was pretty sure he was unsuccessful. He felt his brows draw together, his nose crinkle. It was too late. To his left, Peter folded into a squat that lasted long enough to make him wonder if it hurt. The man's elbows were pressed against the insides of his knees, pushing them out. His face rolled into the palms of his hands and stayed there. He wondered in vain if Peter's wet eyes flushed themselves the exact moment Detective Clark finally informed the entire family gathered around the two officers that the body was indeed finally found. They were in a rush here, apparently; the news broke and they didn't want the family to find out about the discovery from the press outside. Good call, Gael agreed. With the words "rotated body," Evelyn, to Gael's right, exhaled with a wail he was sure Sioux would admonish her for on account of potentially waking up Gwenny, but instead, his beloved girlfriend thrashed out of his arms to confront her mom by grabbing ahold of the lapels of her cardigan, losing grip, and trying over and over again, all to no avail. It was a painful scene to witness. Gael was convinced he saw Peter peek out from behind his laced fingers.

"What did you do?" his girlfriend shrieked, her throat sounding raw as early as word number two. She wasn't made for this. She didn't have the frame necessary to withstand such a growl. Before she could do any further damage to her vocal cords, the cops interfered, prying the mother and daughter apart, Sioux too flabbergasted at the number of hands on her body to protest vocally, only her skinny limbs flaying all about, and Evelyn stoic like a monument to a woman-warrior, her self-composure due to shock or theatrics, Gael could not be sure. Mute himself, he followed the detectives who carried Sioux away to the furthest couch in her sister's living room, and knelt in front of her, presumably to extract some kind of un-enforceable assurances that she will not try any more funny business. He lowered himself next to her and wrapped a tentative arm around her shoulders, the tips of his fingers cold. Taking in the scene around him, he wondered how the news made him feel. He'd been able to gather very little from the tidbits the cops told the family before Sioux became undone. A sliver of red—that's all it was, her red jacket giving her away. Somebody spotted that sliver of red in the bushes. That's what that other detective was attending to when that tall one was having a leisurely chat with Evelyn. All the dog searches, all the CCTV camera searches, and it was a jogger who found the body. The credit card bit was apparently Detective Foster's ad lib for Evelyn's benefit. It was allegedly decided that it was better to go with that than to tell this poor mother that her daughter's lifeless remains had been found until they were reasonably sure. In fact, she still had her wallet on her. This shit's straight out of the *Law & Order*, Gael nodded to himself as he listened. It was when they mentioned the fact that Peta's body may have been moved by some living creature, if one examined her skin and the soil around or some such, that Evelyn had heaved. Understandable, Gael considered. He couldn't remember at exactly which part of the narrative did Peter's collapse into a quasi-fetal position. Pathologists had their work cut out for them, but circumstantially, she had to have been lying there since Sunday. Gael knew for certain he would not have wanted to be that jogger, but that was about all he could surmount when trying to figure out what he felt about the fact that his girlfriend's missing sister was now found

227

dead. He squeezed Sioux's shoulder tighter and when no tears came he nuzzled his head into his vibrating girlfriend's neck and squeezed his eyes shut.

Evelyn

She was right. Or, at the very least, she wasn't wrong. The fact that her daughter walked over an hour in one direction, and then attempted another trek that too was over an hour spoke volumes as to her state of mind. She could, and would, debate anyone who would attempt to argue that she was responsible for it all. Sioux, however, was not wrong demanding to know her part in it. Her entire frame buzzing, Evelyn crossed the living room to follow her restrained child and knelt in front of her.

"You're right."

The way her little girl gulped for air made Evelyn want to go find Marsha and wrestle Gwenny out of her grip and nuzzle her to her own chest.

"Which part?" Sioux hiccupped.

"To ask me what I did." Evelyn felt her braid loosen as she nodded her head in rhythm of her rapidly stacking thoughts. As if stacked by an expert bricklayer, her memories grew, tangible around her. Leningrad, Topeka, Portland. "Do you know how Peta came into this world?"

Visibly aware of the detective's hands ready to pounce and restrain her once again, Sioux settled for a scoff.

"No offense, mom, but maybe now is not the time to go on yet another reverie about how much you hated having to be a mother so young, and how Peta takes after her ugly father, how much you hate her. If she is dead, I know for a fucking fact it's because of you—"

"Actually, preliminary examinations indicate that it was an accidental death. Peta was walking through Fairhaven Park, that area of the trail that is not terribly populated, in the direction of home, presumably. Her ankle is broken, her head is… Well, presumably, she must've tripped and knocked herself out. This is off the record, so don't ask the pathologist about it when we head over there soon, but there was a packet of a pharmaceutical sample found on her person. We would have to wait for further exams to rule on the cause of death. It's too early to say. Did she routinely put in such lengthy distances on foot, Mr. Knudsen?" Detective Clark, at the foot of the couch, turned her gaze from Sioux to Peter, still crouched by the stairs. When he didn't answer, let alone move, the detective continued. Even to Evelyn, who ordinarily would've made a point of not hiding the dramatic roll of her eyes at this theatrical display of mourning by her son-in-law felt the sting of shame on behalf of the detective. "Well, from what we've been able to gather over the last few days, Peta Knudsen hasn't been in the best frame of mind recently—"

"I don't hate my daughter," Evelyn heard her own voice leave the confines of her mouth, happy it interrupted the detective before she went into an unnecessary recitation of facts of all the one reason why Peta Knudsen hasn't indeed been in the best frame of mind recently. "I never did. I'm sorry that's what you thought of me all these years." Her hair now loose but she suddenly felt too tired to re-braid it.

Her daughter didn't seem convinced. She wriggled out of her useless sack of bones of a boyfriend's embrace and leaned in closer to her mother, her elbows on her knees.

"I'm supposed to believe that? I don't remember a single day of my life when you didn't say something derisive about her!"

"Honey, you know the story of how I conceived you, right? How I conceived of you?"

"Yes, everyone knows, mom. You tell everyone who wants to listen and everyone who doesn't."

"Yes, you're right there," Evelyn tried to smile but her lips didn't cooperate. Instead, the corners quivered. She did not remember such a thing happening ever before. "Well, Peta was different. I— Sweetheart, let me ask you a question—has anyone ever put anything unwanted inside you? I sure hope not. But I was not much older than you when I was raped. And not only that—that rape resulted in a child. I was violated, pregnant, and I understood only about every tenth word of the language being spoken all around me. However, none of that means I hate my daughter, Sioux. How dare you!"

She could not confirm this, not having the energy to turn around, but she was somehow sure that, at this, Peter finally peeked from behind his fingers. She could never refuse an audience. Gael, next to Sioux, appeared to sit up in full attention, for one.

This wasn't how she wanted to tell Sioux any of this. She wasn't ever sure that she should do it at all. She'd told Peta all wrong too, but then again many things she'd ever said to Peta was wrong. She was around seventeen and they'd been fighting. She couldn't remember what about that particular time, there'd been so many. The short attempt at quantifying them made Evelyn let out a blubbering sort of noise, something akin to mid-sob or a gulp. Why were there so many? She was a loud, dramatic teenager. Not like the meek, compliant Sioux. She must've screamed out something along the lines of "Why did you even have me?" and Evelyn told her. She didn't mean to, she was raped, she was stuck with her, she made it easier to stay, made her case more sympathetic, she didn't know how to get rid of her. It'd all flown out in one long, breathless utterance. Before she knew it, it was done. It was out there, between them, and there was no way to swallow them back down.

Watching Sioux try to compute this new information and reconcile it with her view of her odd little family, Evelyn tried to remember how Peta had reacted to this information in the past. From what she could remember now, her reaction was underwhelming. It was almost like none of it surprised her. It was almost like hearing it out loud confirmed what she'd known all her life. It was chilling. The girl simply slung her back bag on her shoulder and went to work. Evelyn couldn't remember where the child was working at the time—the library or some tutoring service or other. Evelyn wasn't the type of mother who kept close tabs on her child back then. She'd learn a lot in time for Sioux, but back then, if the girl was out of her hair, she was out of her daughter's hair. That day too—the day she told her daughter she was a product of rape, she let her walk off without much of a second thought. She remembered her hands shaking with the adrenaline of the conversation for a while, not letting her continue with her sketches, but even that had subsided soon enough. Everything seemed fine.

Sioux sat unmoving, haltingly still now. Her posture was once again implacable. She had resisted ballet growing up, but Evelyn was glad the girl had this rigid backbone to fall back on. Somewhere, lost in her reverie, Evelyn didn't notice as the girl calmed down. The officers who were ready to pounce minutes prior too sat mesmerized by the tale. The room was so quiet, she could hear Peter breathe rapidly behind her back, the cathedral ceilings working their magic on the acoustics. It was a powerful story. She could've used it to the same effect throughout his life, it suddenly occurred to her, her eyes filling. Its only flaw was that it was real.

"Mommy—," Sioux's voice broke like that of a boy going through puberty. "That's really awful, mommy. I'm so sorry. I wish I knew this before," the girl smiled, not unkindly, holding her mother's gaze unwavering. "However, I genuinely wish you had told me this literally any other day other than the one I had to find out that my missing sister was found dead on some abandoned trail." Her voice broke again, along with her perfect posture. "Now, if you don't mind, we can resume making this all about you later, but since it appears you're on a truth-telling kick, answer this: who is my dad?"

Her cheeks stung, prickling with invisible needles. Refusing to blink, Evelyn waited for her body to reabsorb the moisture that pooled behind her eyes as she briefly wondered if this was what life was like for Peter. It took Sioux this long to challenge her mother; she couldn't fuck this up.

"I never lied to you about that—a model."

"Was this model your daughter's ex-boyfriend, by any chance?" Peter interrupted; his voice now closer than where Evelyn imagined him to still be sitting.

Peter

Peter wasn't sure why they were all still having circle time with Sioux at the head. Light outside was beginning to change. Surely there were things that needed to be done. Wasn't anyone going to ask him to identify the woman in the red leather jacket the cops have so quickly presumed to be Peta? Wasn't there press to address outside? Any moment now there was going to be a leak. No, instead, they were learning about a rape case four decades old and discussing paternity issues.

"Cat got your tongue, Evelyn? It's a straight forward question." His voice, his words—they were easy. The only reason Peter had to stop was to examine if this was something he was imagining. He had to try again to be sure. "I found that journal you mentioned, Detectives. I don't think you would find it of any interest or consequence, so I hope you do forgive my failure to hand it over. I mean, honestly, besides her little detective work about Sioux's father, there wasn't much in there that you didn't already know." It was true—his words flowed without any speed tables slowing them down. It'd been years since they'd gone to print straight from inception, no extra breaths gulped in order to emit them. He wondered if it was for the best. He wanted to ask Peta. "Speak, Evelyn!" he screamed when he felt hot tears hit his face. "Speak, for fuck's sake! This little family drama of yours seemed to really revitalize Peta, distract her from Harry. In fact, it revitalized her so much, she fucking died trying to solve the useless riddle."

The tears lined his face length-wise. It was a strange sensation—foreign, or at the very least, long-forgotten. When has he cried before, he tried to remember as he studied his mother-in-law's face, which remained stoic but for the corners of her eyes, which danced, unable to commit to either smiling or crying.

"I don't owe you any explanation, Peter," she declared evenly, looking to the two detectives for approval. None came, although neither did disapproval—the female detective was now typing away on her phone and the man was raising from his seat on the floor to take a call. They were likely satisfied that Sioux was tranquil enough to no longer present any physical danger; it was nice to watch them be busy with something they were paid to do. Clearly the journal was of no interest to them, after all, as the question of paternity. They made it known that they fully believed the cause of death to be accidental, but, his voice now back in its full velocity and vigor, Peter would make it his mission to make sure they definitively rule out foul play. His daughter wasn't going to grow up like he did, wondering how the many people in his life died. No, Gwenny would have answers: her brother died on anaphylactic shock and her mother, sunk deep in a depression so profound, walked aimless miles until she tripped and fatally hit her head, to be found almost a week later.

"But you owe one to me, mommy. He is right. Peter was coming to tell me something that involved you, and then Gael and I found a photo of what is very clearly my dad. This is what was on Peta's mind when—" Sioux was interrupted by mucous rushing out of her nose and Evelyn could not stand the sight. It was only made worse when Gael reached over and wiped her nose with the back of his palm.

"I don't understand why this is such a big deal," Evelyn began but Peter, his heart feeling too solid inside and his tongue impatient, interrupted her.

"Oh, you mean you see no moral implications in making your older daughter's boyfriend the father of your younger daughter?"

"My Goodness, you make it sound so seedy!"

"It's not?" he scoffed as he squatted down to meet Evelyn's icy glare. This could very well be their last conversation.

"Look," Evelyn began with a swallow. "You don't understand. I don't understand…"

"Well, let's see if we can work it out together," Peter prodded, landing his body next to his now former mother-in-law at Sioux's feet. Her boyfriend gripped the girl tighter when he saw Peter approach. He too must've sensed whatever it was that was now in charge of Peter. Whatever it was, it was dizzying and familiar. He could practically hear his voice pronounce every morning a good one.

Good Morning, Bellingham!

The light was changing. He wasn't sure what time it was and didn't want to check, but either the fog was rolling in again or evening was here. The static was loud. One *if only* on top of another, if Peter did not continue interrogating Evelyn, he was sure his stutter would jump into his throat as suddenly as it had years ago. If only there was no great big mystery, if only noticing her doctor's family photo was no big deal, if only she could've talked to him and not storm out with an empty gas tank.

Sioux was looking paler than usual. What was she thinking about? Did she have midterms? She was probably going to miss them now on account of her sister's funeral. She missed her SATs because of Harry's funeral and made sure everyone knew about it. What a grand sacrifice. Much like her mother, Sioux rarely made do with the feelings of others' taking precedence to her own. If Sioux was hungry, she was fed; if she was sad, she was coddled, and if Sioux had schoolwork—well, then why not bitch about it at a toddler's funeral.

"Peta—she'd taken everything from me. My freedom, my innocence..."

Peter had to give credit where credit was due—Evelyn was trying.

"Pardon the interruption," he nodded, approvingly, the two of them sitting cross-legged across from one another, as if engaged in partner yoga. "Any chance you could be specific? What exactly did she take from you?"

Before Evelyn could answer, Sioux crawled down to sit at her mother's feet, Gael following. For a second, Peter wanted to abandon the quest and go nuzzle his baby girl.

"Are you fucking stupid?" Evelyn erupted before he could make up his mind. "Her father raped me! Do you understand what that means? And not only that—once he pulled out, *she* remained! I was Sioux's age! No family, no language I could understand—"

"You could've gone home."

"No," she sighed. "I wanted to stay."

"Did being pregnant help you stay legally?"

She nodded. This wasn't satisfying.

"You have kids—"

"Kid," he corrected.

"Whatever—you know what I mean. They take over everything. I couldn't sleep, I couldn't eat, I couldn't do anything. I was young, I was suffocating. And she was stubborn and headstrong." Come to think of it, Peter had never seen Evelyn actually cry. Not genuinely. There were probably tears at Harry's funeral, but he couldn't recall now. Now, here was this unbecoming mess, her perennial kohl liner running down her face, and Peter found himself missing the stoic, bitch of a mother-in-law he feared and hated his entire married life.

"You became a renowned sculptor! Whatever can you possibly mean?" he hissed just to interrupt her, the four of them comprising a semi-circle, as if in a séance. Wouldn't it be wonderful if they could summon the spirit of Peta, he wondered.

"Honey, you have to understand—she wasn't like you. It doesn't mean... Look, I can't lie to you—I truly have spent a great deal of my life resenting your sister. I'm not proud of it. And I'm prepared to do better now that I'm conscious of it," Evelyn, changing her approach, ignoring Peter's passive-aggressive question, faced Sioux and attempted to stroke her face, her own features contorted unnaturally, with peaked eyebrows and a crinkled nose. Sioux, in turn, jerked away, as if flames were threatening to caress her law line. "Well, I suppose you don't need to understand. It wasn't your life. It *isn't*. But, imagine—all those sacrifices and then, poof, she just can't wait to get away from you and go away to college. As if I'm some sort of an abusive mother she's sought to escape all her life. I understood it, too—she wanted to get out from under my shadow, be the prettier one, the smarter one. I appreciate that it was hard for her in my company. But it still hurt. So...so, I had to take something of hers. And create a new life—one that was more pliable, more in my control. You understand, right, darling? Do you forgive me?"

Sunday, October 7th

Peter

Peter would've preferred to be alone. Even in death, there were onlookers to share his wife with, Peter sneered mutely as that starched sheet was thrown off Peta's waxen face. The shriek Sioux managed to produce from her partial view of his shoulder gutted him. How much of her sister's deformed forehead did she even see? He had the full view and he wasn't even crying. What was there to meltdown about from her point of view? Her mother's daughter this one was. Was this Andrew of theirs like this too? Surely two defects of the narcissistic gene would do that. He hated himself for thinking this as he screwed his eyes shut away from this last image of his wife, but now that it was over, would Sioux and Evelyn finally leave? Now that this was over, could they just go?

This was yesterday. He'd thought all of this yesterday. Between Sioux's shrieks and Evelyn's intentionally audible gulps. Between the pathologists inquiring whether or not he knew if his wife was taking any kind of medication that could cause drowsiness, he felt waves of violence undulate deep inside his belly. When the expletives he wanted to hurl at the doctor stuck in his mouth, Detective Foster provided context—they were simply trying to explain what could've caused Peta to act so irrationally as to attempt a walk that wasn't characteristic of her, to see if the actual act of tripping itself could perhaps be pharmaceutically explained. This was all yesterday. Yesterday, the three of them, with Gael at their heels, as he'd grown accustomed to, were escorted out of his house, through brushing shoulders of producers he folded inside the black unmarked vehicles, only to repeat the process in reverse when the car parked at the curb, adjacent to a building that lacked color as much as it lacked character. Yesterday, they were told it'd be a couple of days until they could pick up the body but they were now free to make arrangements. Yesterday, when the fellow members of the press, now fully caught up, were waiting for them right outside, shouting questions over each other. Walking in an impromptu diamond formation, with Evelyn to his left, Sioux to his right, and Gael directly behind. He did not have eyes in the back of his head but he imagined them all stoic, chins erect, eyes on the opened car doors held for them by men and women in uniform. That was yesterday. And then it was today. Today came too soon.

On impulse, once back home, having elbowed and shouldered his way through all the many rows of microphones and lights, he'd grabbed Gwenny with his hands slick with sweat and told Marsha not to come in in the morning. His stomach bouncing between his heels and his throat, he'd paid her an advance. He was the father. He'd had enough of other people handling his kids. Once he'd go back to work, yes, he'd need her back, but she had a solid week off. Gwenny had cried, not used to the type of a snatch that hurt her ribcage, but she was calm soon enough. Children are resilient—that was something his numerous social workers had said to him and it turned out right. Now, today, that came too early and with a weak announcement of an anemic sunrise that had still somehow managed to rouse Gwenny with it anyway, he wasn't as convinced he wanted the single father part, even on probationary basis. Plus, with Marsha out there in the wild, there was no controlling the many viral interviews she could be giving while Peter lay in bed, painfully awake, listening to his daughter cry.

<u>Sioux</u>

Another morning in Bellingham, or so says the light on my ceiling. This one is one too many. I'd thoughts so before, but I mean it now. There are no good mornings here.

I don't think I've blinked since the morgue. On the one hand, maybe blinking would erase the raging hematoma on Peta's face from my memory. On the other hand…it could erase it from my memory. Perhaps were Gael awake, I'd attempt this, but I don't want to wake him. Not out of the goodness of my own heart, I'm not sure I have one. No, I know better than that. I know I don't want to wake him because I'm not sure he's not making these awful Bellingham mornings worse.

It's Gwenny's voice that gets me out of bed, that gets my blood circulating. My feet naked and cold on the parquet floor, my body is at once invigorated. I should've gotten out of that sleepless bed hours ago. I am drawn to that wail like a siren's call. I approach like a charmed snake, my charmer in her crib, mouth stretched to a degree that seems improbable, libs akimbo. Her father is supine on the floor, his fingers a makeshift hammock for his head, his eyes as empty as my own had been prior to Gwenny losing her shit, zero to sixty. This is apparently customary for her; I've been here not a week and I know this. Still, Peter makes no effort to move, as if the sound isn't bothering him. It's impossible that it doesn't. How can it not? She is loud and relentless. Wet or hungry, occasionally her cry reaches a frequency I can barely hear. And yet Peter is unmoved. He needs his time, I understand. We all process differently. I get it. I'm already up.

"So, who killed your sister? What say you?"

His voice stops me in my tracks and somehow also quiets Gwenny.

It is my turn to stutter.

"What— What do you mean? She tripped and fell, they said."

"Right, but why in the world was she stomping through the town aimlessly? This looking for your father project of hers literally made Gwenny an orphan!" he is still lying down. I am not looking at him but I can feel he isn't looking at me either.

"She has you, she's not an orphan!"

"Not into dramatics all of a sudden, are we?" I can hear him scramble up to his feet, his unexpected burst of laugher high pitched. "Pardon me if I don't buy into that after all the fainting and the shrieking." When I don't take bait and turn my attention to the now quiet Gwenny, he continues. "To answer my own question—I'm going to say you or mommy-dearest. Maybe that fucking shrink, too."

Feeling his words hit between my shoulder blades, I scoop up Gwenny from her crib. She smells sour, her diet still primarily dairy. She nuzzles my neck and I nuzzle hers. We make it over to her changing table, Peter a step behind, before I bring myself to mutter, "And you?"

"I beg your pardon." It's impressive how quickly his voice regained that enviable TV presenter's confidence, that Standard American familiarizing itself with the contours of his mouth once again. The churn in my stomach proved that two conflicting sentiments are having a hard time fitting within its confines. I am happy for him, sure. I'd heard, I'd seen the toll the losses took on him. But I resent the implication. My eyes sting and my throat feels as if I swallowed a filleting knife. I try to swallow it all down but the pain makes my throat constrict and I cough instead.

"Well, good for you and all that, but you did not know any of this, either—none of her thoughts, none of her 'projects,' what have you. This somehow makes you escape all culpability?" I focus on Gwenny—on her organic diaper cream, on the organic wipes as my heart beats against my temples. She hates the feel of both of these things, squirming, wiggling, but she is quiet now.

Somewhere between throwing out the old diaper and getting out the new one, I manage to bring up my eyes to meet his. They are watery, as usual, but their color is somehow more translucent now, as if all that moisture finally washed some of the color away. His lids are red, but I think that's something we all have in common in this house. This grief is shared, not much makes him special under the circumstances. We all lost a loved one in a clumsy way. But I lost a sister but potentially found a father, I have to admit to myself. I swallow down the blades in my throat, deciding to give him a break. He needs this more than I do.

I swing Gwenny onto my hip and head for the door. Peter, on the other hand, remains stoic, his eyes glistening but not quite watering. His posture is familiar—rigid with just a hint of a shoulder droop. But it's that ghost of a stare that sends a chill from the base of my skull down to my tailbone. It's almost like he forgot something important but can't quite remember what it is now that he finds himself barefoot in the middle of a nursery. A sob bobbles in my throat but I catch it, corners of my eyes prickling.

"Are you going to meet him?" I hear him ask when my hand is on the handle and Gwenny remembers that unhappiness is her favorite emotion.

"Who?" I choke out.

"Your father."

Evelyn

Evelyn wasn't sure if she'd moved all night. She hated her daughter's living room with its cathedral ceilings, exposed beams, and windows so excessive in size they seemed indecent. Still, she found herself straight backed in the armchair of questionable function stuffed in the furthest corner of the living room when the sun rose and she heard Sioux's feet on approach, Gwenny's gargles a soundtrack. She couldn't remember when she'd first sat down there. Logic would dictate that it must've been after they'd gotten home from identifying what was termed "the body," "the remains." It hurt Evelyn's ear to hear them use a term so biological in nature when describing her daughter. She wasn't "the body," her bruised and bitten flesh wasn't "remains"; she had a name and it was Peta. Why *Peta?* She never did have an answer good enough to share publicly. Or privately, for that matter—she hadn't even told Peta herself. She'd considered manufacturing a story about looking for a way to honor her late father named Peter, but the truth was that her father was alive when she'd left and his name was Fyodor. No, that wasn't why. The real inspiration was the English word for a domesticated animal—*pet*. The role of genders in her native tongue delivered the "a" at the end. She thought it was cute, it was as simple as that. She thought it sounded strong and unique. It sounded different than anything she'd ever heard before and different was everything she was here to seek and find. And, if anything, it was an ode to the English language: it fascinated Evelyn that the term for a domestic animal wasn't simply "house animal," like it was in Russian, but a whole new word was crafted just to deliver the difference. But Resident Alien or not, she realized the second she neatly printed *Peta Morozova* that this was not something she should be volunteering. She wasn't even pronouncing it correctly in her head until a pudgy, red-nosed nurse read her neat little form aloud. It wasn't a statement of any sort, but much like fairly everything that left her lips since the day she petitioned to stay in the country, this too would be parceled out by syllables and weighed. This word she made up had only two syllables—it wouldn't be that hard.

Light crept inside timidly. Though only tentative streams of it appeared on the floor at Evelyn's feet, she still felt the urge to screw her eyes shut against it. It was too early for light. Or too late. She wasn't sure what time it was. All she knew was that that "body" was now engraved on her brain, its features memorable, prominent—the bruise of improbable size above her overgrown eyebrows, the upsetting color under her tired eyes, the concave shape of her empty cheeks. She would've enjoyed telling that middle aged cop he was wrong. Even more so—she would've loved telling that snide little girl one that she was shit at her job, that this wasn't her daughter, wasn't her Peta. But the stubborn nature of the image in her mind's eye begged to differ—it was exactly her. Even in death she was winning, her willfulness outliving her.

"Do you know why I called you Sioux?" Evelyn felt her voice box come to life, her eyes now shut against that shy light of the Pacific Northwest October morning. It had to be past seven, but how much past? She must've sat motionless for roughly ten hours, give or take, she attempted to calculate in the time she estimated would be required for her daughter to cross the floor to join her. When she didn't hear a reply, she peeked, lifting an eyelid. The act only gave her fright as it appeared that her daughter was indeed in front of her, silently bouncing her granddaughter on her hip. As the girl continued to stay silent, her coffee eyes solid on her mother's now open icy ones, her jaw clenched so tightly she wanted to offer a warm washcloth compress, Evelyn continued, "I liked the name 'Susan.'"

The girl, so solemn and serious just a moment ago, couldn't control the chuckle this explanation prompted. Evelyn counted on this. This one she knew like the back of her hand.

"Seriously!"

Even Gwenny let out something that could be willfully mistaken for a giggle.

"That's not my name," Sioux eventually asked, patting Gwenny between the shoulder blades in a way that looked entirely too possessive for a stand-in, Evelyn thought to herself. She considered rising but she felt it was important to keep their heights this uneven somehow. Just for this conversation.

"I know! I liked 'Sue,' not 'Susan,' per se, I guess. But the conventional spelling was just that—too conventional. Boring. You were more special than a regular 'Sue.' So I figured I'd throw in a few letters. I should've anticipated all the questions I'd get. And I did, to be fair. 'Sioux Morozova' hardly rolls off anyone's tongue, I suppose," Evelyn shrugged with a tentative chuckle of her own.

"Why don't I have his last name?" The tightness in her jaw was back, the muscle protruding painfully. Gwenny, the observer, had stuck a thumb in her mouth, sucking ferociously, as if figuring this was not the time for her shenanigans.

"It wasn't part of the deal."

"Was there a contract?"

"Goodness gracious, of course not." Evelyn's limbs were waking, begging to be stretched now that the rest of her was awake, but she stayed folded in the chair for her daughter's sake. Surely it was important for the child to look down at her mother, if only for the moment. "Look, there is nothing I can say now. I can only say I'm sorry so many different ways. It was stupid and petty—all these things, I admit it now, from the position of my tender age of…well, you know how old I am. To think—I wanted to punish my daughter for changing the course of my life by seducing her ex-boyfriend. How shameful, how idiotic, my gosh! Of course I sound like a lunatic when it's recited like that—out loud. And maybe I am! Maybe your mom is crazy. But you…I did want you, don't doubt that. That part of it was genuine and I don't regret it. I had never had interest in a life-partner, you know that, but I needed *someone* to father you. And in all honesty, your sister aside, he genuinely was a good candidate." Keeping her voice even was no easy feat, but Evelyn felt she succeeded. However, when she heard her frail little girl's high-pitched laughter, she began to doubt herself, her extremities at once numb, bracing.

"Do you even understand how insane you sound right now?"

"I do." She saw no other way but to accept this. Gwenny was alert now, listening. She considered snapping a photo of the two girls for that little project idea for her but her phone wasn't on her. She'd have to take a mental picture. "I do, baby. But there is nothing I can do, nothing I can say. It's done—over two decades ago it was done."

"It's not done, mom!" The girl wanted to scream this; that much was audible. Still, raised right by her mother, she controlled her volume for the sake of her baby niece. Little

Gwenny had plenty of responsibility to shoulder. "Mommy…Peter is right—*this* is what ultimately killed her. You understand that, right, mommy? You killed her!" She was climbing in octaves now, growing hysterical. What Gwenny needed to do now was start to fuss. Otherwise this pitch was about to hit all the wrong nerves for Evelyn.

"Don't be stupid, baby. Her son's death, untreated post-partum, plain ol' grief and depression—that's what killed her," she barked involuntarily, maybe a beat too quickly, on second thought. "And we're yet to see the toxicology—who knows what kind of revenge there could've been exerted by that doctor of hers given our delicate connection." Her bones hurt, her eyes stung. Her head wasn't clear.

"You see! You see it too! It was this…*quest* of hers that sent her spiraling! So by extension, it was you…"

She had to be stopped.

"Do you want to meet him? I won't be mad, sweetheart."

Sweet Sioux paused, breathed, and considered the offer. This was effective. Even in grief, Evelyn was not losing her touch.

"I don't," the girl shrugged, magnanimously.

Gael

"You don't want to meet your father?"

Gael had woken up alone. He was used to this. It wasn't lost on him that his relationship was not reciprocal. He was never under the illusion that it had ever been or would eventually become anything otherwise. It suited him fine. It was good to be needed, if not necessarily wanted. A breathtaking girl with more need than he'd ever encountered in his life. It was exhilarating—he'd be there with an iced latte after an all-nighter and she'd beam as if it wasn't caffeinated drink richly diluted by milk but some life balancing serum, that little crinkle on the bridge of her nose making an appearance for a moment so brief, he was sure only he was privy to it. And it'd be intoxicating to be the one to be able to bring it about. Satisfying, gratifying. It didn't matter that she'd never asked him how he was doing. It didn't matter that no matter what he would do, she never seemed to want to get any better at life.

"After all this, you still don't want to meet your father?" Gael bellowed.

He didn't know why this angered him. Still sleepy after the night of superficial sleep filled with Sioux's sobs and gulps, he made his way downstairs in search of his girlfriend. He'd looked in Gwenny's room first but found only Peter inside. The man looked like Peter, anyway, but his features were harder than what Gael had gotten used to, the rims of his moist eyes tighter. They exchanged nods but neither had enough energy inside to feign interest in small talk. Gael knew better than to look in Evelyn's room and headed downstairs with eyelids as heavy as his gut.

"Why in the world not? Wouldn't this at least make some of this worth it?"

Evelyn, folded neatly in an armchair by the draped window, raised a curious eyebrow. Gwenny erupted into a wail. He must've been yelling again. She was a helpful barometer against which one could check himself. An infant of many trades, this one.

Too eternally lethargic to whip around to face Gael, Sioux shuffled more than turned. Never having heard her boyfriend raise his voice in her direction, it was not surprising to see alarm in her dry eyes. She patted little Gwenny's back protectively, only angering Gael further, the implication of the gesture rousing him irrevocably.

"How does this concern you?"

Breaking character of a mother in mourning, Evelyn all but applauded, her lips forgetting their place and erupting into a smile.

"How this concerns me? You have the physical audacity to ask me this? After all the shit you've put me through? I'm like your personal servant boy. I don't enjoy putting my life on hold for your insane fucking joke of a family to then be told I have no right to an opinion. Fuck you!"

Ceremoniously, her feet soundless on the floor, Sioux hugged Gwenny to her and strolled over to where Peter had wordlessly descended. It was as if this entire clan shared an invisibility cloak and the ability to materialize out of thin air anywhere they chose. Peter stood just as vacant as the last time Gael saw him. Could it be that now that the man finally had his syllables back he lost all muscle tone in his limbs, lost all actual words? Gael wondered. He watched as Sioux handed over Gwenny to her father and finally faced him head on. She stood taller than ever and Gael never wanted to be further away from her gaze.

"Gael, you've been helpful. I appreciate you, I do. But my sending more people's lives into upheaval won't bring my sister back—"

"Your sister gave her life for this!"

"Oh don't be so dramatic, Gael," Sioux quipped back. If he closed his eyes, he could swear it wasn't the meek, little Sioux he'd been nurturing for almost two years now. This was Evelyn. The woman herself rose out of her seat, obviously celebrating the same. "Peta was upset for many reasons. She wasn't walking with her head clear. She tripped. And don't forget—we won't get the toxicology for a while, but who knows what that shrink may have given her. She obviously had an axe to grind."

Lightheaded, Gael turned to Peter. Certainly he must've heard this uncanny resemblance of daughter to mother. But no support was forthcoming. The man held his child awkwardly. How many more deaths should this man be reasonably expected to process?

"But— but aren't you proving the very reason why you should meet him? That's what Peta wanted!"

The smile was slow to upturn the corners of her mouth. She was sad, she was disappointed. She was her mother.

"No, Gael. Peta wanted me to know the truth. And I know it now. Mommy told me what Peta wanted me to know. The rest is irrelevant. The man never wanted to be a father to me—he was earning money for his son. Mommy is my only parent. And now I'm the only child she has. You won't come between us. Not now." Before he could attempt to make another fruitless argument, Sioux strode over to the front door and swung it open, welcoming immediate flashes of dozens of cameras, shouts from twice as many reporters. "You may go home now. I'm needed here now."

Andrew

Andrew would be lying if he said he recognized his daughter right away. Sure, there were similarities—the shape of the mouth, the height of the cheekbones, but were he to pass her on the street, he wouldn't stop and wonder if there's an outstanding order of child support against him. It did, however, amaze him how much his two children looked alike. Again, no one would wonder if they are twins, but if one was familiar with one kid, they'd see the similarity in the other, that was for certain. It was in the skin tone, the jaw line, even the choice of hairstyle. Was that, too, genetic? He couldn't be sure.

On TV, the woman walking a step ahead of the girl he now understood was his daughter was indeed the artist who paid him to pose for her sculpture. Peta's mother. He wondered now, inconsequentially, if the finished product existed anywhere. Was it on display somewhere in the world—his naked form?

She looked older, sure, Andrew admitted, but the twenty plus years had not been cruel to her, Andrew assessed as best he could in the few seconds the family was shown on its procession from the government building to the government car. Her hair wasn't as shiny as he remembered, and the skin on her face looked looser, but the posture, the presence remained intact, untouched. Would he recognize her on the street? He wasn't sure. But in context, it was clear as day, and clear as day he could see her hand, wielding a stack of cash with a coy smile as she thanked him for his services. He presumed it was etched with many more wrinkles now.

Did John see it? His son was sitting at his side on the couch, he could've just turned slightly to confirm, but chose not to. The clinical setting of his wife's living room didn't lend itself well to warmth, the bare white walls all around providing little by way of comfort.

"No fucking way," Andrew heard the boy mutter under his breath, his mom, seated on his other side, having sucked in her breath at the sound of the same news.

Good morning, Bellingham. We're sorry to start your morning with such a tragic turn of events in the statewide search for Peta Knudsen, but we have to report that the body of our very own, very much beloved meteorologist has been found in….

The sky still had hints of red behind the peppy field reporter—an eager, bright-eyed young woman named Lucia, who stood proudly in front of the entrance to the Fairhaven Park, yellow police tape just a distant dot behind her one could barely make out in the twilight. Sleepy, the branches around the reporter twitched lazily, not ready for this much pep. It felt heartless to wake them up this early and with such sad news. Surely no harm would be done if the press descended on this place a couple of hours further into the day. The way it all stood now, everyone was up. The coffee machine in his ex-wife's kitchen could be heard yawning itself awake—a groan, a whistle; it didn't let him hear Lucia's last name. Before he could wonder about it, the screen switched back to the footage of the family being shuffled around between the government building and a government car.

The footage was from yesterday. Who knew how they were all doing now. The body unlikely released from the authorities this quickly, when would they be able to plan a funeral? Would members of the general public be welcome, Peta being who she was. Was this when he was supposed to make his introductions? He was supposed to make those, right? It was too early to think. And nobody slept all night— not Andrew, not John, not Lena. As the news gave the spirit of Peta Knudsen a break and switched to the weather update, likely seeing no irony in any sense of the word, Andrew looked over at his family. Lena's hand clasped over mouth was all the emotion he saw demonstrated.

It had been Lena who broke the news to him. Muttering under her breath, and shrieking over it at times, Lena stumbled into her house all but twelve hours ago, her heeled shoes flying off her feet as if they weren't just being actively kicked off but were hurling themselves off Lena's feet of their own volition. She'd met Peter Knudsen, apparently— Peta's husband. She was wondering out loud if she could get the rest of the family to come in now—Sioux, in particular. Get to the bottom of the "things," as she put it. Andrew and John were still huddled around the kitchen island. The well of questions was bottomless; whenever Andrew thought he was done, there'd be another. Another face, another remark that must've sounded way cleverer inside that young head of his than once it was uttered in real life. They simply were not be done. Coffee had turned into Chinese takeout, and variations of the same story were told over and over, dizzying as the process was.

Somewhere between the change in the light outside, John had asked why Andrew and his mother had broken up before she found out she was pregnant. Andrew had to admit, this was a good question. He was surprised that he wasn't asked this sooner—surely he'd raised a critical thinker. But late was better than never, as his students liked to tell him when they were late turning in their term papers. For the life of him, however, he could not come up with an answer worthy of his son's query. Having been asked this, he recalled Peta asking the very same question. What did he tell her then? Honestly, there wasn't anything dramatic he could point to, then or now. It hadn't been a long relationship. They met at a party, they hung out mainly in groups. A few times, after drinks, they'd gotten intimate. There wasn't even a breakup, as such, to speak of; they'd simply stopped hanging out once summer came and jobs and internships took over whatever leisure time students had. No hard feelings and absolutely no drama. This was how he'd imagined his college and law school life. And thus far, it'd worked out. If she had reappeared two months later with a positive pregnancy test, he would not have spent a single night awake trying to recall her features.

Whether he wondered as to his paternity was another question of Andrew's. It wasn't an unreasonable thing to ask, given the rest of the fact pattern. But before he could answer, John must've caught a sight of his own reflection in the toaster sitting just a few feet away, because he laughed. It was precisely then, when the mother of his son had returned home and tossed her shoes aside; when she turned to check her phone for any new e-mails in order to pretend that the fact that he'd spent the day doing nothing but talk to their son didn't bother her in the slightest, that that muted *Oh* had escaped her lips.

"What?" John was rarely able to contain contempt for his mother. Andrew knew he failed as a father in that regard. He should've done better. Should've at least tried, given it the requisite shot. But there'd never been any time. There was work to do, money to earn, a program to set up, students to teach, errands to run. Stopping to pause and correct the way his son addressed his mother was not much of a priority. Or at all. Not all children got along with both parents. It wasn't unnatural. He was hoping he'd simply outgrow that snarky phase of his. Or maybe she would. She was the one with a degree in subject matter much more relevant; this should've been her project. This was her failure, he'd decided before his ex-wife could explain her exclamation. He was innocent.

"She's dead."

"Who?"

"Your ex-girlfriend."

"Peta?"

He wasn't sure why the news pulled on his guts the way it did, but it felt as if he was being turned inside out. He'd hugged himself, delicately, as if afraid that his skin would rupture at contact strong than a classic arm fold.

"How do you know?" he heard John's voice pipe up, breaking midsentence. "You don't know!"

"John, I know that you think your mom is an idiot, but I know how to read!" Lena barked in response, sounding almost sober. "I don't know if you heard anything of what I said, so deeply engrossed in your own conversations, but her husband came to see me today. Trying to follow his wife's breadcrumbs, I guess. Adorable. But it's irrelevant now, of course—check your phone! They found a body. No confirmation yet but it's female, red jacket—it's Peta!"

Her feet free, Lena was giddy. News of any kind is exciting, Andrew supposed. It wasn't unusual. People often reacted to a death of a loved one with inappropriate laugher, questionable jokes. He understood this. And yet something irked him in a way he could not swallow down.

"I'm sorry, but what exactly makes you think that this woman's death makes the fact that her sister is my daughter irrelevant now?"

John

If those headshots and old storm reports seemed posthumous before, the pretense can finally be dropped now. Silver lining? Closure? There is a death date now. Well, a year, at least. According to all the talking heads mom, dad, and I have been watching all morning (me sandwiched between them like a kindergartner), it'll be a little bit until they pin down the actual date, but I'm not confident. It's over now. Another day of the hype and it's sure to die down. Sorry, folks, nothing to see here, move right along. A woman forgets to breathe between actions and *poof*, now she is known as "remains," a "body." Surely these things happen every day, with or without the backdrop of the soap opera worthy life. A tremor imperceptible to my parents makes its way through my shoulders, down into my belly, and out of my heels. And now my eyes begin to tear, but I'm not sure if it's from the strain of having them open for so long or from actual sadness. And if it's sadness, I'm going to need some help from mom to pinpoint the source.

Dr. Burgos

It was as if the three of them were up to watch the royal wedding. There was no good reason for the three of them to be up at this hour, lined up pristinely on the couch, attention undivided. Granted, they were not dressed for a wedding of any kind. She, for one, was dressed in her work clothes from the day before, and her men still in yesterday's pajamas.

This wasn't the death of Michael Jackson or Kim Kardashian's latest outfit. There was no actual, reason to stay up through the night, glued to the television set in hopes of more information. It barely qualified as news, anymore. Even given the current media climate, new details weren't exactly coming in on hourly basis. They could've easily had gone to bed and not missed anything. She would've, but if the boys were staying up, that meant so was she.

The hiss of the coffee machine was a welcome distraction from the sight of the mouths hanging agape to her right. She could taste its bitterness long before she made herself get up and get a mug she already knew she would fill to the brim. Still, she lingered on the couch. What were they waiting for? CNN knew less than NBC, and NBC knew less than Bellingham's own. There was no new information. All they had in their rotation is the constant reiteration of the timeline, a few stock images of the park, and the thirty-second video of her family being walked from the station to the car that most likely took them back to that glorified lodge that Peta and Peter Knudsen used to call home.

She'd met him just that many hours ago. She had plans for him. She had plans for all of them. She wasn't supposed to be sitting on a couch that belonged to her only so long as she didn't miss more than x-many payments; she wasn't supposed to be pretending not to want a drink. She was supposed to be working out what sequence made more sense. Peter was clever. She hadn't expected that much from the composite sketched by Peta's various references. He was more graceful than expected, not as clumsy with words. Sure, he tripped on them here and there, stumbled over them, but his word choice was meticulous. Elegant, she would even say. He was a man on a mission, he knew his purpose there, a step ahead of her in his own deliberate preparations. Everyone always seemed to be. Still, she was proud of herself. She did not say anything she didn't mean to, and her voice did not quaver. These were wins in her book. She would swear they would be wins in anyone else's. That's what she would say to a patient. So, what was this feeling masquerading as a flutter behind her ribcage? She couldn't term it any other way other than call it for what her vibrating gut told her: resentment, disappointment, even. She had a plan and now that plan was useless.

And what was that plan, exactly, she asked herself as Peta's mom, John's half-sister's mother, folded her long body into a police car. She was old, much older than Lena, but even in grief she was enviably lively, her step confident, her hair in a braid. She wasn't jealous per se; Andrew didn't leave her to have a secret family with a woman twice her age. She was a gig, the progeny was a contracted product. And yet, she couldn't help but curl her lip at her image, her heart rushing to her ears as she forced herself not to turn to her right to check on Andrew's reaction at the sight of the woman. She breathed through it like the most compliant of her patients.

So what *was* her mighty plan? Did she really offer coupons for free sessions to members of Peta's family, figuratively speaking? And then what? Was she going to interrogate Sioux to be sure enough of the fact that she did not, in fact, know her father? To what end? And why did any of this even hurt her? It's been ages since Andrew had been hers, if ever. What did the existence of a daughter he never met have to do with her life now? Why couldn't she simply tell her hysterical patient all that she knew—that yes, her Andrew was in fact, *her own* Andrew and help her piece it all together? Surely the woman would've walked out of her office that day in a much calmer state, unlikely to have stomped into her son's place of employ, and unlikely to proceed, on foot, to march through the town like a maddened warrior, clad in her red leather jacket and sneakers ill-equipped for hiking. She saw her when she followed her to the store, where she hid by some mass-produced bagels to try to read what was said between her maddened patient and her son. So why did she need to stomp her foot when the lady insisted that she wasn't being truthful? Why did she kick her out of her of her office, informing her on the spot that she was firing her as a patient? And, God almighty, why did she give Peta Knudsen a sample of a sleeping aid she'd been begging for all along as a parting gift? Was she in the right state of mind at the time to accept it? And did she care? It made sense in the moment—anything to get the screaming woman waving photos in her face out of her sight before she herself could dissolve into sobs that would eventually destroy a few of the paperweights she had lying around her office, the pieces she'd carefully selected in Pier 1 Imports to look as if she'd spent decades traveling. No, that was dumb. She should've followed her past the store, she knew now, but instead, tears blurring her vision, rage stirring up her blood, she'd sped home and began drinking earlier than usual. There was no professional code of ethics for this. This was all her—haze and impulse and all. Most importantly, still, Dr. Burgos wondered why all of this came rushing at her now that she was clad in stale and wrinkled clothes, with an off kilter bun on top of her head? A rational, educated woman, she should've been able to make all these connections without hearing the overeager TV reporter recite such a basic end of the town's darling.

To rest her eyes from the looping coverage on TV, Dr. Burgos closed them and immediately feared not being able to open them again, heavy with sleep. When was the last time she slept? The night before Peta's last session—that was it. Alcohol-aided, yes, but she'd always before been able to get some solid eight hours a night. How could she let the woman's family drama turn her life upside down? She wanted to laugh at the absurdity of her state but was afraid such would be misconstrued given the fierce concentration on the faces of the men next to her. How silly she has been. How immature. How else could any of this have ended?

About the Author

Marina Raydun's published works of fiction include a compilation of novellas *One Year in Berlin/Foreign Bride,* a suspense novel entitled *Joe After Maya,* and a two-part series, *Effortless.* Born in the former Soviet Union, Marina grew up in Brooklyn, NY. She holds a J.D. from New York Law School and a B.A. in history from Pace University. She is an avid music fan, a cat lover, and an enthusiastic learner of American Sign Language. Whenever she is not writing, Marina enjoys spending time with her family, catching up on Netflix, and baking.